Revenge
at Kings
Mountain
Crisis in Conscience

Revenge at Kings Mountain

Crisis in Conscience

To God Be the Glory

Ed DeVos

Ed DeVos

DEEDS PUBLISHING | ATLANTA

Published by Deeds Publishing in Athens, GA
www.deedspublishing.com

Printed in The United States of America

Library of Congress Cataloging-in-Publications Data is available upon request.

ISBN 978-1-941165-93-5

Books are available in quantity for promotional or premium use. For information, email info@deedspublishing.com.

Cover design and text layout by Mark Babcock, maps by Mark Babcock and Matt King

First Edition, 2015

10 9 8 7 6 5 4 3 2 1

Contents

To Daughters of the American Revolution (DAR) and to the Sons of the American Revolution (SAR) for their selfless service in reminding us of our American heritage.

Acknowledgements

THE SEEDS FOR WRITING THIS BOOK WERE PLANTED WHEN I VISITED Kings Mountain five years ago, spending two days there, walking the trails, trying to picture what happened in those peaceful woods in October 1780. After that visit, I could not put the story of the spirit and resolve of these men who fought there out of my mind. The picture I wanted to write about crystallized when I later spent time at Cowpens, Sycamore Shoals, Musgrove's Mill, Waxhaw, and Camden.

My research on the battle was greatly aided by a number of books that address our nation's struggle for independence. Scheer and Rankin's *Rebels and Redcoats*; *The Spirit of Seventy-Six*, edited by Commager and Morris; Daniel Barefoot's *Touring South Carolina's Revolutionary War Sites* and *Touring North Carolina's Revolutionary War Sites*; Bobby Gilmer Moss' *The Patriots at Kings Mountain* and *The Loyalists at Kings Mountain*; John Buchanan's *The Road To Guilford Courthouse*; Robert M. Dunkerly's *The Battle of Kings Mountain Eyewitness Accounts*; and Pat Alderman's *The OverMountain Men* were all of great assistance. While each of the wonderful authors/historians used a number of other sources in their writings, almost all of them make reference to Lyman C. Draper's *Kings Mountain and Its Heroes: History of the Battle of Kings' Mountain, October 7th 1780*, which I read as well. It was published in 1881 and is still available today.

Once the story began to come together, I enlisted the help of others to provide suggestions and improvements. I am indebted to Dr. Tom Thompson; Dr. John Brinsfield, Chaplain (Colonel) USA (Ret); Dr. Bruce Johnston; Jane Fairburn; Charles Parnell; Bucky Jones, Col, USAF (Ret); Joan Prince; and Marcia McManus and Tim Taylor of the US Army's Chaplain Museum for their time and interest in this project. Special thanks must go to the Daughters of the American Revolution (DAR) whose faithful support and encouragement helped keep me focused. Likewise the project could not be completed without the efforts of Deeds Publishing in Athens, Georgia and the patience of my wife, Susan, who is always a constant help in keeping me grounded.

Finally, with all this information available, I took into account that with any battlefield, two men, standing only steps away from each other, will have different remembrances of the same event, particularly when they recall their impressions years later. Therefore, what you are about to read is my interpretation, and mine alone, of what might have occurred in 1780.

Introduction

COME SIT WITH ME FOR A WHILE ON ONE OF THE BENCHES ALONG
the well-maintained path that circles this hill, a hill that hardly qual-
ifies to be called a mountain by anyone's definition. Study the monu-
ments to our left and right. Read about what happened here. Memorize the names of the men who fought here. And as the peaceful
surroundings of the tall hard-woods wrap their arms around us, let the
uneven ground and the rocks and boulders close to us testify to the
sacrifice these men made here on our behalf. Close your eyes and smell
the heavy dense smoke that obscured the hilltop that rainy afternoon
so long ago. Sense the hot lead zip past the men who fought here as
the riflemen above tried to bury a lead ball into their chests. Hear the
cries of Patriot leaders as they lead the charge toward the crest of the
high ground above. Can you see it? Can you smell it? Can you picture
it? Can you sense it? We are at a place of hallowed ground.

We are at Kings Mountain National Military Park, four thousand
acres of history and beauty, road signs pointing to its existence barely
noticed by most travelers as they speed along Interstate 85, between
Spartanburg, South Carolina and Charlotte, North Carolina. Despite
its relative obscurity, this battlefield holds an important place in our
nation's history. President Herbert Hoover, our thirty-first President,
once described Kings Mountain as a place where "History has done
scant justice to (its) significance, which rightly should place it beside
Lexington, Bunker Hill, Trenton, and Yorktown."

More than two hundred and thirty years ago two thousand Americans fought here on a Saturday afternoon in early October 1780. Elev-
en hundred men defended the top of the mountain while the other

nine hundred attacked up the rock-strewn, steep slopes we see before us. In one hour over two hundred men died here. Most importantly to our nation's history, this is where the momentum of British-led forces during the American Revolution took a turn, the first of many that halted what seemed to be an unstoppable march by the Redcoats to victory.

Kings Mountain was a battle of brother against brother, of neighbor against neighbor. It was a battle fought for pride and honor. It was a battle for the desire to be free from tyranny on one side and loyalty to a king on the other. And for many who fought here, Kings Mountain was a place to seek revenge for a loved one murdered or to avenge the destruction of property. It was a civil war -American versus American—before that title was given to another conflict eighty years later.

So sit with me for a spell and let the men and women who lived in those days tell you a story about courage and valor, about integrity and honor. And yes, they will tell you about the revenge they felt in their hearts. Our tale begins four months before the Kings Mountain battle on another battlefield where the spark was lit that led us to where we now sit.

—Ed DeVos

the
**SOUTHERN
CAMPAIGN AREA**

1. Slaughter

South of Waxhaw, South Carolina
Late morning, Monday, 29 May 1780

THE BRITISH CAVALRY COMMANDER KNEW HE WAS GETTING CLOSE. His men and their horses alike were lathered up with sweat, evidence of his pushing them hard, covering one hundred miles in the last fifty-four hours in pursuit of his enemy. Some of his best horses now lay dead along the road behind, but to him, the sacrifice was worth it. Through questioning several Loyalists he had passed along the road, he knew the Rebels could not be too far ahead, maybe fifteen miles at the most, so close he thought he could almost smell them. If he could catch the insurgents before dark, he intended to attack them straight from the march. Otherwise, his men would give out from utter exhaustion. Even his hard-charging, battle-toughened soldiers could do only so much. After a few moments of deliberation, a thought came to him. Reaching into his pack for his writing materials and after making a few quick strokes with his quill, the twenty-six-year-old colonel called out, "Captain Kinlock."

Captain David Kinlock, robust and sturdy, the Commander of the Headquarters element of the British Legion, had been with his colonel for several years. He had received special mention a few weeks earlier, during the attack at Moncks Corner, west of Charles Town, as he led his men to cutoff the last escape routes of the enemy they had bottled up in that small village. Upon hearing his name, he immediately broke away from his lieutenants, leaving the hungry officers to tear into the flanks of the roasted wild pig they had shot some miles back.

At six feet tall, Kinlock towered over his shorter, stocky commander who was garbed like the majority of his men, wearing a white summer uniform instead of the more traditional short green coat with narrow gold lace signifying their cavalry unit.

"Sir?"

"The Rebels can't be too far up this road. To make sure we catch them today, we're going to employ some deception. I want you to ride ahead under a white flag and find their commander. If our Loyalist friends I spoke with are correct, that will be Colonel Abraham Buford."

Handing Kinlock the folded parchment, the colonel continued, "Present him this letter which gives him two choices. He can either surrender to us immediately or be destroyed when we attack. My letter tells him we have seven hundred men with us and Lord Cornwallis is right behind us with an even larger number. Tell him we are an hour away. I am suggesting to him that he should surrender and that I will not repeat my offer. And if he chooses to oppose us, any blood spilled will be his responsibility. Wait for his reply."

Kinlock smiled as he nodded his head in understanding.

"I expect Buford will discuss my proposal with his officers, and as he does, we will continue to close the distance between our forces. Obviously, do not reveal our actual strength. It is my intent that this message will slow down their retreat so we can attack today. Questions?"

"No questions, sir, but I have one request. Before we attack, give me time to rejoin my unit. I don't want to miss this fight."

Banastre Tarleton grinned. "Of course. You know me better than that. I would never deny you that honor."

After a quick salute, the captain mounted his horse, spurred his animal into action, and kicked up some dust as he rode northeast on the well-worn rutted wagon trail.

Tarleton smiled to himself as he took off his distinctive helmet made of bearskin with the fox-tail plume. He was a man of supreme confidence, which helped him achieve a meteoric rise in the ranks.

The son of a wealthy merchant, he had purchased his commission as a cornet, the lowest officer rank in the British Army, only five years ago. But through a combination of luck and good fortune, he distinguished himself first at White's Tavern in December 1776 and then in January 1778, when he was part of a cavalry force that battled the famous rebel cavalry leader, Henry Lee. By August that year, he became the Commander of the British Legion, a regiment of cavalry and infantry recruited largely from the New York area. *What more could I ask for? Four years from cornet to lieutenant colonel, one promotion skipping over the rank of major entirely. Commander of one of the most legendary units of this war. What more could I ask for indeed?*

Considered ruthless by some, extremely aggressive by others who used a more polite phrase, Tarleton's methods of combat, terrorizing both the enemy and the population at large, found favor with Lord Cornwallis. Success after success, victory after victory, his modus operandi for conducting warfare mirrored that of Cornwallis. Attack! Attack!

Although Buford's force consisted of more than three hundred and fifty men, Tarleton believed his two hundred and seventy men would be victorious. With his message now on its way, he gave the command to resume the march. Watching his men mount their weary steeds, Tarleton nearly burst with pride. Even though almost all of his men had grown up in America, their allegiance to King George III was not in doubt, unlike those they now hunted.

NEAR LANCASTER, SOUTH CAROLINA
EARLY AFTERNOON, MONDAY, 29 MAY 1780

The two officers sat under the limbs of a large live oak, their blue tunics unbuttoned to let in some of the breeze flowing in their direction. Like their men around them, the two officers searched for relief from the sun's penetrating rays. "Think we got a little breathing room, Major?" asked the younger of the two men.

"Wouldn't bet on it, John," the major said as he swatted at a big black fly which buzzed around his head, the bug looking for some exposed skin to attack. "Yesterday's march took a lot out of all of us. The rain felt good for a little while, but now today, this humidity wears on a man downright quick."

Pausing to evaluate the men around him, the major continued, "I appreciate the colonel giving the boys some rest since we've been marching hard now for what, eight or nine days? While I'd like to think we've got some distance between us and the Redcoats, if Tarleton is on our trail, we can't rest too long. Hillsborough is still a long ways away. A good thing Governor Rutledge decided to go on ahead. We don't need to worry about escorting him anymore."

"You're right about that. This way the colonel can concentrate on these men instead of securing the hide of the governor of the great colony of South Carolina."

Gazing to the northwest, Major Robert Crawford let his mind wander from the war, thinking of more pleasant times. "Did you know my farm is only few miles over those trees there? I'm looking forward to the day when I'll be able to sit on my front porch and watch the tobacco fields and fruit trees grow, and watch my children laugh and play, all this marching and shooting and killing a thing of the past. Yes sir, one of these days."

He looked at his companion. "How 'bout you? You gonna get back to lawyering again once this is over?"

"Yeah, that's my plan. Folks will always need someone to help 'em figure out the law. Way too complicated to try and do it on your own most of the time."

Twenty-four-year-old Captain John Stokes leaned back against his knapsack, reflecting on events of the past few weeks. "Still wish we'd been able to help General Lincoln at Charles Town. We were so close, what thirty-five or forty miles away? Close enough to hear the cannon fire going back and forth. Looked and sounded like a big thunderstorm all night, all those flashes and deep rumbles. And now all those men are in British hands. Good men, some maybe now on prison ships, the rest God only knows where. Heard they even got Thomas Heyward. Since he was one of the signers of the Declaration in '76, I suspect things will not go well for him."

Crawford nodded his agreement as he looked once more at the soldiers around them, many of them making fire-cakes, the mixture of flour and water that was heated on either rocks near their fires or in the small iron skillets some carried. It took only a minute or so to make the cake, heating it on one side before flipping it over for a short time to cook on the other side. The men then devoured the bland food with either their wooden spoons or quick fingers. While not too tasty, it was a staple the men depended upon. These soldiers knew their priorities: eat, rest, and get ready to move. To a retreating force nothing else mattered.

"Guess I'll always wonder if we could've done any good if we'd met up with Colonel White and his men at Lenud's Ferry. We were so close and now we're running for our lives, like dogs with our tails between our legs. I don't like it even if we were outnumbered. Orders are orders I guess."

The two sat still, absorbed in their own thoughts. They knew what had happened. Less than a month ago, their unit, the Virginia Continentals under the command of Colonel Buford, was dispatched to reinforce Charles Town. After coordination took place between Buford and Colonel William White regarding the Virginians' support of White's attack of the British along the Santee River northwest of Charles Town, confusion or misinterpretation of their agreement affected Buford's ability to assist White, resulting in the loss of the last escape or reinforcement route for General Lincoln's army trapped in Charles Town.

With few options available, General Lincoln, under enormous pressure from Charles Town's civilian leaders to save the city from further destruction, surrendered. Five thousand men were now in British hands. To add further insult, Sir Henry Clinton, the overall British

Commander, did not accord Lincoln and his men any of the normal military honors when the surrender took place. When word reached the Virginians about the city's fate, Buford received new orders to retreat to Hillsborough, North Carolina to join with other units to form a new army. Their march northward, over the same steps they had marched earlier with such optimism and hope, was now a march filled with questions and doubt.

****

The sudden appearance of a rider on his fast-moving horse kicked up a cloud of brown earth as he approached from the south drew the attention of the entire Patriot force, the white flag the man carried visible to all. It could mean only one thing: the pursuing British soldiers were close.

Crawford and Stokes watched as guards confronted the rider, forcing him to dismount. After a few heated words, the guards accompanied the intruder to Colonel Buford's location on a small incline in the center of their formation. No one thought to blindfold the intruder.

After eyeing the man with suspicion, Colonel Buford hollered to Crawford, "Major, gather our officers over by your tree. I suspect we'll have a few things to discuss shortly."

Staring at the man in front of him, Abraham Buford took his time putting on his blue uniform coat before he returned the British officer's salute.

"Sir, my name is Captain David Kinlock of Colonel Tarleton's Legion. I have a letter from my commander. Do I have the pleasure of addressing Colonel Buford?" he asked, his mouth turned up in a twist of superiority.

Ignoring the man's arrogance, Buford replied, "Yes, you do. May I see the letter?"

After reading its contents to himself, the thirty-two-year-old officer turned, walking over to where his officers assembled. Besides Crawford and Stokes, Captains Wallace, Catlett, and Carter, commander of the cannons, Lieutenant Henry Bowyer, Buford's adjutant, and Doctor Robert Brownfield, the regimental surgeon, gathered under the stately tree.

After reading the letter to his officers, Buford gazed at them. "It seems we have several options. First, we could comply with Tarleton's demands and surrender. Or we could abandon our baggage and our wagons filled with our supplies and try and out run him. Or third, we could defend ourselves here or on some ground nearby. Gentlemen, your thoughts?"

The officers looked at each other around the circle before acquiescing to Major Crawford who spoke for them all. "Sir, we started this march to meet the enemy weeks ago. When word came about Lincoln's surrender, we got orders to retreat, to turn tail and run. While we have some veterans from some fights at other places like Saratoga and Monmouth, most of our men have not been tested. But that doesn't mean that they don't want to fight."

He looked about at the soldiers nearest them, all of whom were watching the officers' deliberations with great interest. Some showed fear in their eyes; others showed anticipation.

"Look at 'em. They're proud men. They left their homes and families and volunteered to fight for our cause. They don't want to run any more. They're tired of showing their backsides to the likes of Tarleton and that condescending captain over there. There's no honor in that. I say we fight. I for one want to see if Tarleton is as good as they say."

With his dark piercing eyes boring into the colonel's, Captain Stokes nodded, "Sir, I agree. Our men are spoiling for a fight. Let's give 'em a chance to preserve their dignity. This is what they signed up for. Not to have the shoe leather rot off their feet marching backward. Let's give these men a chance to be men."

Buford studied the others, each nodding in agreement. With the decision made, he signaled the guards to bring the British officer to him. When Kinlock stood in front of him and his officers, Buford drew himself up to a posture straight and tall. "I have considered your colonel's proposal and I reject his offer."

Without another word or the customary salute, the cavalry officer sneered at the rebels as he turned, mounted his horse, and immediately broke into a gallop as he sped south.

As the dust from the horse mushroomed over them, Buford's orders came out crisply. "Wagons filled with supplies and the cannons under the command of Captain Carter are to continue north. We'll keep moving north up this trail behind them looking for some defensible ground. Once we find a small rise or hill, we'll make our stand there. This terrain has many large trees, but with large gaps between them and little underbrush. Not much to slow down a cavalry charge. If Tarleton reacts as he has in other battles, he will charge our lines directly from the march with a combination of foot infantry and cavalry in a frontal assault. When we deploy, I want the two companies of the 2nd Regiment on the left side of our defense and the 7th Regiment on the right. When Tarleton charges, no one is to fire until I give the order. I want to let 'em get close before we cut loose with everything we've got. Major Crawford, have Lieutenant Pearson command the rear guard to put a buffer between our main body and Tarleton's men. Move quickly now, boys. I don't think we have much time."

Crawford spoke up. "What about the forty prisoners we got?"

Buford looked up and thought for a moment before responding. "Keep 'em tied up and on the wagons just like they are. Can't do much else with 'em right now."

Without having the luxury of time to discuss the merits of Buford's plan, the officers saluted, passing out their orders as they scrambled to mount their horses. No one asked about a reserve or about using Carter's cannons to disrupt Tarleton's charge. Neither did anyone ask why the twenty-six wagons could not be turned over to serve as barricades. Although each man longed for the opportunity to show his individual bravery, none of the officers had enough experience or time to question Buford's orders.

WAXHAW, SOUTH CAROLINA
MID-AFTERNOON, MONDAY, 29 MAY 1780

Using his time wisely to close the gap between his men and the enemy, Tarleton showed no surprise to Buford's answer, meeting it only with a grunt of satisfaction. With the distance now only a few miles between the two opposing forces, the Legion Commander pressed his men to move faster.

Racing ahead with his officers, Tarleton watched as Buford's men began to form in a line near a lightly wooded area at a crossroad less than five hundred yards away. After studying his enemy's dispositions from his observation post from another hill south of the Rebels, the Legion Commander thought to himself, *Buford has found the place he wishes to make his stand. God be with him.*

As he watched the Rebel line begin to spread out, their units seemed to be in one long line with no reserve. It didn't matter much to him because his tactics rarely changed; he would use speed and mass to attack and overwhelm them. Gathering his officers, Tarleton issued his orders.

"Major Cochrane, you will attack the enemy's right flank with one-third of our infantry and sixty of our cavalry. Captains Kinlock and Corbet, you will strike the rebel center with forty men of the 17th Dragoons and sixty of the Legion cavalry. I will attack their left flank with thirty horsemen and the remaining infantry. It is my intent for my element to loop around their main body and get at the rear of their formation. We will leave our one cannon in reserve. I doubt we will need it and it will just slow us down."

As his officers began to return to their units to issue their orders, Tarleton observed about twenty of the enemy moving toward him, acting as an outer shield for Buford's main body. It was a simple tactic designed to break up the momentum of his formation during the assault, but their numbers appeared to be too small to stand in his way. Looking about, he pointed toward the enemy. "Major Cochrane, do you see the Rebel rear guard to our front?"

"Yes sir."

"Your thoughts?"

"I think we should sweep them away as one would use a broom to brush away a bit of filth and grime. I'll see to it immediately."

****

Within minutes Lieutenant Thomas Pearson watched as an element of British cavalry began to move directly toward him through the thin woods, the enemy approaching him with their horses at a canter.

"Get ready to fire, men," he ordered as the horsemen changed their pace to a full gallop as the distance narrowed to less than one hundred yards. "Fire!" he shouted.

When the smoke cleared from their volley, Pearson realized his fire had little effect on the attackers as they barreled toward him. Even though several of his soldiers got off another round, Pearson and his men were quickly overrun, cut to pieces.

From his observation post four hundred yards away, Colonel Buford watched a British officer's sword slash Pearson's face, tearing apart the young man's nose, tongue, jaw, and lips. With the British cavalry now in the midst of where his men made their stand, he could not detect any movement from Pearson's men.

****

With the Rebel rear guard now shredded, and the weariness of his soldiers' long march now forgotten as the object of their sacrifice was so near, Tarleton thought only of those in front of him. *These Rebels, this treasonous lot, can't stop me.*

Ordered to advance, his men and animals stepped forward. As his main body closed to within two hundred yards of Buford's lines, Tarleton quickened the pace, going from a trot to a canter before he ordered his bugler to sound the charge. With the heavy hooves of the horses shaking the ground and with screams of terror on the lips of their infantryman, the men of the Legion rapidly closed the distance between the two opposing forces as there were few natural folds in the ground to slow their momentum.

The soldiers of the Virginia Regiments watched with grim determination as the mix of white, red, and green uniforms came flying at them, growing larger by the second. But they knew Buford's orders—Hold fire. Hold fire.

Even as the British masses closed to one hundred yards of his lines, Buford still waited. "Steady men. Steady! Let 'em get closer!" His soldiers looked at each other, uncertain of the outcome. One veteran from the 1778 battle at Monmouth muttered to no one in particular, "If we don't watch it, that man is gonna get us all killed. We need to fire now. Otherwise we've got no time to reload."

Another soldier answered, "You're right. I've got a bead on one of their officers. I could take him down now but...."

Finally as the Legion came within fifty yards, the order came. "Present your weapons! Aim!" With the distance now reduced to less than thirty yards, the command finally came. Fire!"

Lead bullets belched from the Patriot rifles. Some of the attackers and their horses felt the effects of the well-aimed volley, but the energy of so many eight-hundred-pound beasts moving at thirty miles an hour carried the Legion into the Virginia lines in seconds, ripping through their formation, entangling men of both sides in a death grip where cold steel of the bayonet and the curved swords of the Legion's cavalry ruled. With no time to reload their weapons, Buford's men could only swing their unloaded rifles against the seventeen-inch bayonets affixed to the British rifles and the slashing steel blades of the cavalrymen.

Even though the thick smoke hampered his view of the battlefield, Colonel Buford saw enough as the two forces intermingled, and the cries of men tangled in a duel to the death filled his ears. It was clear that Tarleton's men had gained the upper hand. The British Loyalists were too quick, too well-trained and too audacious in the use of their weapons. Any hope of an American victory evaporated in the first minute of the engagement. To resist further was useless, the shedding of more blood was unnecessary and without purpose.

Turning to Ensign Cruit, the officer standing nearest him, Buford shouted above the noise, "Go toward those British horsemen with a flag of truce. We're not ready to stand up to such an attack."

Hailing Major Crawford, he shouted, "Pass the word for our men to lay down their arms."

But to the shock of Buford and his officers, the flag of white, universally understood by all armies as a sign to surrender, had little effect on Tarleton's men as they cut down Cruit with rifle fire and bayonets. Across the battlefield British officers and sergeants ignored any attempts to halt the slaughter as their soldiers shot, clubbed, and stabbed anyone in their path.

"What are they doing?" Why aren't they honoring our flag?" screamed Buford as he watched his men become isolated, fighting as individuals or in groups of two or three or kneeling with their hands raised in surrender. It became a massacre, men murdered even as they pleaded for mercy, shot and then stabbed over and over by Tarleton's men. Attempts to capitulate met with ruthlessness and vicious brutality.

In twenty minutes Buford's unit ceased to exist.

****

When the noise from the slaughter finally ended, some hardy souls, mostly women and children from the nearby countryside, came to lend aid to the wounded and dying. One mother brought her two sons with her to care for those in need. As Andrew, the younger of the two boys, helped one of the men into the Waxhaw Presbyterian Church, he asked the man what had happened.

The young man, perhaps in his early twenties, could only mutter, "Murder...murder."

Young Andrew Jackson, just thirteen, no stranger to the ravages of war as his oldest brother had been killed at Stono a year before, looked at the man with questioning eyes.

With tears flowing down his cheeks, the wounded soldier told his story. "I was near Captain Stokes' position when the British burst through our lines. After a few minutes I found myself on the ground wounded. When I looked around, I saw my captain lying near me, sword and bayonet wounds to his left arm and head. At least one finger was hacked off. Because he was an officer, he got special treatment as one British soldier stood over him, asking him, "Do you expect quarter?"

With young Jackson's help, the wounded soldier sat up a bit, his eyes now fixed straight ahead staring at nothing. "I heard my captain say, 'I will not ask for quarter. Finish me.' So without another word, the Legionnaire bayoneted this brave man again and again. Seconds later another soldier came by and he too thrust his cold steel into Stokes' body."

The man started to cry. "I think he's dead. Murdered right next to me. Not sure but...."

****

Within a day the countryside was abuzz about the battle. Neighbors made up mostly of Scot-Irish background assembled in both small and large groups, some calling the engagement "The Battle of Waxhaw" because Waxhaw was the nearest town. A woman who had bandaged the soldiers at the church called it "Buford's Defeat."

The men who worked their small farms were inclined to refer to the battle as "Buford's Massacre" or "Tarleton's Quarter" because these phrases captured the savagery and brutality of Tarleton's men.

Regardless of who told the story, it was spread to all points of the compass throughout the North and South Carolina colonies. It was some time before the full impact of the slaughter was known but as one farmer noted after putting all the rumors and facts together, "Tarleton murdered more than one hundred officers and soldiers and severely wounded a like number."

"How about Buford? Someone asked. "What happened to him? And what about Tarleton's losses?"

The wise old farmer smoked his pipe slowly before he answered the questions. "First, Buford and several others escaped on horseback during the melee. As for Tarleton, he had five killed and twelve wounded. That about says it all."

2. Boiling Pot

*Clinton's Headquarters, 27 King Street in Charles Town,
the home of Rebecca Motte
Early evening, Monday, 5 June 1780*

SIR HENRY CLINTON TWIRLED THE GLASS IN HIS HAND, ENJOYING THE red claret he favored, this one shipped in especially for him from a winery near Walthamstow, England, whose vineyard was noted for producing a superb flowery bouquet. He closed his eyes, and a satisfied smile came across his face as the early evening breeze carried the smell of the nearby salty sea air through the open windows, the warm Charles Town day now beginning to cool.

I always enjoy hearing reports from Tarleton. Oh how that man can fight. His aggressiveness is hard to stop. He gazed around at the elegantly furnished room filled with the highest quality furniture of the day, the color of the fabrics a pale blue, a sure sign of the owner's wealth. Thinking of a different time and a different place, he spoke more to himself than to the other officer in the room. *We are the world's premier power. It is folly to oppose us. If they continue to resist, Tarleton and his men will crush them until they are either dead or wishing that were the case.*

Lord Charles Cornwallis glanced at his fifty-year-old commander, a man, who like him, had invested six years of his life fighting on this continent. *How the years of conflict have aged him. He used to be such a vigorous man, but now look at him. His face and body show signs of too much stress, too much physical inactivity, and too much excellent food and wine, maladies so common to many high-level commanders. I can only hope I will not fall victim to those same trappings.*

15

"While what you say about our Legion commander is true, we still face challenges with the back-country of this colony being as large as it is. We control the lands around the more populated towns like Camden, Cheraw, Georgetown, Ninety Six, and now this jewel of a city, and more are flocking to our side because they want to be on the winning side. Still, there remain a number of the rebellious persuasion that may not agree with the ultimatum we have just given them, to say nothing of those who would just like to be left alone. From their perspective, our ultimatum gives them only two choices. Either they sign an oath of loyalty to the King or they will be considered our enemies. It leaves no room for those who wish to take no part in this conflict whatsoever."

Clinton shook his head as he studied Cornwallis. "Ah, Charles, while what you say is true, you worry too much. With Tarleton's resounding triumph at Waxhaw even the most fervent of these Patriots, as they like to be called, must see that to continue to oppose us is futile. The power of our forces must be obvious even to the most die-hard of their breed. And as for those who wish to straddle the fence, the purpose of our challenge is to push them to our side now. Otherwise, they might make the wrong decision and we cannot have that, can we?"

Standing up, he moved to nearest window to catch more of the breeze. "Surely these dissidents understand what we have accomplished in the last nine months. We are squeezing them as a python squeezes its prey. First we took Savannah. And now Charles Town is in our hands with its harbor and prosperous plantations. And imagine, we defeated their army of five thousand, a staggering number by anyone's measurements. It is safe to say we are now firmly in control of this colony. And as you know, most of their key generals are now our prisoners. With Tarleton's thrashing of Buford's Virginians, they have no organized force to oppose us, save for a few small bands led by men of questionable abilities."

Clinton paused as he gazed in the direction of Sullivan's Island which lay northeast across the harbor, the site of his first attempt to seize Charles Town four years before. That attempt had cost him not only his pride, but over two hundred and twenty men and five of his nine ships. *At last I have my revenge. Finally this city is mine. And many of those who caused me such angst four years ago like Moultrie are now feeling the pain of defeat that has burned in my soul. And what are my naysayers thinking now? Those who thought I should have not been given command of all British Forces? I have prevailed. Charles Town is mine. The colony of South Carolina is mine. Yes, I have succeeded in spite of those who wished failure upon me.*

Both men stood and bowed as Mrs. Rebecca Motte entered the room carrying a large crystal decanter filled with wine on a most-refined, elegant silver tray. As the lady of the house served these men, her critical glance spoke volumes of her discontent that the first floor of her two-story Georgian mansion, known by most in the city as the Miles Brewton House in honor of her late brother, was now the British headquarters. She prayed every day that a time would come when she would be treated to the sight of their British backsides in full flight as they fled the city she loved.

"Ah, Mrs. Motte, you must have read our thoughts. More wine, please."

Rebecca remained silent as she filled the two glasses before quietly leaving the room, thinking about what Miles and her late husband Jacob would be thinking if they were alive. *Even though Jacob has been gone for ten years, he never wanted to live under the shackles of the King. And now his son-in-law, General William Moultrie, is a prisoner of war. Maybe it is best that Jacob's other son-in-law, Thomas Lynch, a signer of the Declaration, died at sea. Thank goodness, my own son-in-law, Thomas Pinckney, keeps on fighting. We are blessed to have men of steel and courage. With men like them on our side, we will prevail. And when that day comes, I will throw my best wine in the faces of these two animals instead of pouring it politely into their glasses. What a glorious day that will be!*

Clinton glanced at Cornwallis, his subordinate a man of medium height and heavy build, several months shy of his forty-second birthday. The two men were dressed alike, their coats a brilliant crimson with gold-and-white piping on the shoulders and arms signaling their rank. Each wore white leggings which matched their woolen powdered white wigs; their highly polished boots showed no signs of the tough campaign recently concluded. "Charles, I have every confidence that you will gain control of this entire colony in short order. And while you are subduing these remaining radicals, I'll focus on the northern colonies again starting with New York."

Cornwallis sat still as he sipped his wine. *While I am now the Commander of the British Southern forces, this land is too big, the people too independent-minded to be bent easily to the will of any British soldier. Yes, my command will be successful, of that I am certain, but the challenges will demand much, occasionally taking unexpected turns in direction, much like the wind which seems to have a will of its own. No doubt it will take an iron fist to keep what is left of this rabble in check. My will must be unyielding and firm to the core.*

"I understand your wish to subjugate all those in this territory, but I must say, to make your desire a reality, we must vigorously deal with them with a firm and unrelenting hand, showing no mercy if our demands are not met. These Scots-Irish are a contentious lot who understand only toughness, so we must be tougher than them."

Searching for the conclusion Clinton had in mind, Cornwallis queried, "Am I to assume that once we have this southern expanse totally bending to our will, you have a grand strategy in mind? We've talked before about eventually moving this army north, bringing all of our power to the Mid-Atlantic region and further north. Is that still your vision?"

"That is exactly what I have in mind. While the specifics of such an operation will be determined in time, that remains my long-range goal so that we can bring this rebellion to a close. But first, as you have suggested, I believe we must show these treasonous malcontents what happens to those who resist the King. They must be taught a harsh lesson. Bear in mind that it is essential that when you move north, you make sure your base of operations here in this city and the surrounding lands remains secure."

After acknowledging Clinton's warning with a "Yes, sir, I understand," Lord Cornwallis sat back in his chair digesting both his thoughts and Clinton's remarks. After more reflection, he got up from his chair and looked out over the harbor as the light faded quickly. "As I think about these backwoods people more and more, one must admire their tenacity, their stoutness in dealing with difficult circumstances. They have endured years of living off the land, of struggling against whatever came their way: Indians on the warpath, threats from marauding bears and coyotes, violent storms that seem to appear with little warning. They understand life and death. They ask for no quarter and expect none in return. However, in their minds, extreme, unmerciful violence without reason may not be so easily forgotten. While Tarleton's victory over Buford was significant, I wonder if there will be a price to pay for the slaughter that came after the victory was well in hand."

Clinton stared at Cornwallis, uttering only a quiet, "Go on."

"Because of the stubbornness of these people in the backcountry in some incidents which we've already heard about, I suspect we will see more clashes of neighbor against neighbor, father against son. I recall one of our spies telling me once about the thoughts of that infamous Rebel, John Adams. It seems Adams believes that one-third of this country wishes to remain loyal to the King, another third wants to live in an independent country, and the last third simply wishes to be left alone. My major concern is that if we push this last third too harshly, we may stir them up and cause them to join those who oppose us. I offer this opinion because while I favor your uncompromising approach, we must be prepared to face some backlash from time to time."

Clinton smiled, but not before he raised his glass. "A wonderful speech, Charles. Truly a wonderful speech. But since today is the day when you officially become the Commander of the Southern Forces, I leave both those challenges and our four thousand soldiers in your capable hands. Congratulations and Godspeed."

NEWBERRY COUNTY, SOUTH CAROLINA
LATE JUNE 1780

"You Elijah Teague?"

The fifty-four-year-old farmer looked around at the eight men who slowly encircled him. "What a dumb question. Most of you already know that. What's it to you?"

The man nearest him sneered, "Word is that you're a Rebel officer."

Teague chose to stand still, saying nothing.

"Well, is it true? You a Rebel officer?"

Teague, a man of pride and integrity who had lived in these lands for many years after he moved from Maryland, drew himself up to his full height before he answered with a resounding, "Yes. Yes, I am. You know that I am and I'm proud of it."

With those words ringing through the air, the eight Loyalists, grabbed Teague and hanged him from the nearest tree, showing little remorse in the process. Within a week of Teague's death, his three sons hunted down seven of the eight men and killed them. Like those who murdered their father, the sons felt no guilt or sorrow. In the backcountry, the English translation of the Latin *Lex Talionis* was played out once more. *An eye for an eye.*

CORNWALLIS' HEADQUARTERS IN CHARLES TOWN
EARLY EVENING, FRIDAY, 30 JUNE 1780

Lord Cornwallis glanced up at his aide-de-camp, Captain Alexander Ross, as he finished reading what Ross had penned. A gentle breeze blew through the open windows, rustling the papers before him, this late afternoon zephyr giving him some relief from the uncomfortable humid temperatures that had plagued the city for the last week.

"You've done a good job drafting my thoughts, Alex. This is exactly what I want to convey."

"Thank you, sir. I tried to find a good blend of optimism and reality in this letter based on your guidance and the reports you've received. I trust Sir Clinton will be pleased."

"Yes, I think he should. I especially like these two phrases, '...We have put an end to all major resistance in South Carolina,' and the one that tells him we will leave South Carolina secure when we begin to head into North Carolina around the first of September. That colony has been a cauldron of rebellion for too long. Do you have a quill for me to sign this?"

"Yes sir. Right here. I also have some other short messages you asked me to draft up, telling our various commanders to prepare for our advance north, and instructing them to store up the provisions we'll need in a few months. I also directed them to remain quiet regarding our future operations."

"Excellent. Let me sign all these now so they can be dispatched immediately."

As Captain Ross stood by his leader's side, he considered another dispatch he had recently drafted, this one to the commander at Camden, Lord Rawdon, a letter in which Cornwallis expressed some concern that the Rebels would not give in without a fight and that unrest was certain to break out somewhere. "Sir, if I may, I have one concern."

Cornwallis put the quill down as he stared at his aide. "And what would that be?"

Ross hesitated. He wanted to be truthful and at the same time supportive of his commander. To do otherwise would be unprofessional. Yet it would also be considered unprofessional if he did not state his opinions, even if they had not been asked for.

"Sir...Sir, I'm wondering whether we should include some information in the letter to Sir Clinton about what our men have encountered these past few weeks. The engagement at Ramsour's Mill in North Carolina clearly favored the opposition, and as you know, we seem to be getting more reports of their increased activity throughout the backcountry."

Noting that Cornwallis was paying attention, Ross pressed on. "In my opinion, these actions indicate that they have some ability and willingness to confront us. They do not seem to be submissive to our desires. Your recent letter to Lord Rawdon expressed some of these same concerns. Individually each of these actions is a small pin-prick to our overall mission, but if they are taken together and if the trend continues, they may mean something of significance. I was just thinking that it might be prudent to perhaps include a line or two in the letter to Sir Clinton that expresses at least some uneasiness toward these recent activities."

Cornwallis stood and walked over to the window. Staring at the large two- and three-mast ships of the British Navy swaying peacefully at anchor in the harbor, he remained fixed for several minutes.

"Alex, what you say bears some consideration, but in war, a commander must pick and choose from the options available to him. There will always be risks in any course of action. What you say is true. There is still some unrest in the frontier, and given these sentiments, I suspect our concerns about the more troublesome ones will be with us for some time to come. While I would like to hang everyone who opposes us, I am afraid that is just not possible. The question, then, is how long can we wait before we move north to bring this rebellion to a close? Another year? Two years perhaps? Three years? How long can we afford to be held captive by our fears that some rebellious few in our rear may make it uncomfortable for us as we press for victory?"

He turned to face his aide. "And how long will our political leaders across the sea continue to support this venture both financially and materially? If we do not seize this opportunity to end this conflict, who can say when we will have another chance?"

He rubbed his mouth for a moment as he stared back out the window. "Part of me wants to write what you suggest, but if I do, Clinton might become timid, and if he chooses to hold me back from moving north, well...I do not want to take that risk."

He walked over and put his arm around the captain. "You are a loyal servant, Alex. While I appreciate your willingness to speak your mind, we must put caution aside and move north as soon as possible even though there may be a Rebel dog or two nipping at our heels."

Ross came to attention. "Yes sir. I understand."

Cornwallis nodded. "I depend upon men like you to share your thoughts with me. Do not let this decision I am making today hinder you from continuing to give me your council. Leaders at all levels need to consider what those around them are thinking. That is one of the signs of good leadership. Remember that as you progress through the ranks."

Deep in his soul, Ross knew Cornwallis was right, but he remained concerned. *There is too much unrest, too much uncertainty, too many hard feelings that each side harbors against the other to call the issue settled. It is a civil war by anyone's definition. Every incident against one side brings a similar reaction from the other. Lex Talionis.*

FARMER'S CABIN WEST OF WAXHAW
EARLY EVENING, TUESDAY, 10 JULY 1780

The young couple watched the low flames in their fireplace dance, the crackle of their small fire giving off its melodic tune, their busy day of toiling over their land now drawing to a close. The sun had been down for an hour and their two small children, ages four and six, were now settled in their small beds in the undersized loft of their log cabin.

"Josiah, so much has been going on these past few months, it's hard to tell fact from fiction. I can't help but wonder if I'm hearing rumors or the truth. All the women are talking about it: Loyalists murdering people, Patriots fighting back, children being abused for no reason. When will this end? I know we've tried to stay away from taking sides so we could focus on raising our children and farming our land, but I fear it's time to take a stand in one direction or the other."

The woman was quiet for another moment before she put down her sewing, one of her endless tasks required to keep her children in proper clothes. "I wonder if the Loyalist soldiers really murdered an innocent child a few weeks back. The women up the way are saying a boy was simply walking down the road with a Bible in his hand when a gang of scoundrels commanded by a man named Huck just ran him down and shot him. I can't imagine why they'd do that." The woman shook her head. "It just doesn't make sense. No sense at all."

Her husband closed his eyes for a while before he slowly got up from his wooden rocker, the chair one he made a few years ago when they settled on this land after moving from Lancaster, Pennsylvania. Climbing the ladder to the loft, he looked at his two children as tears came to his eyes. He, too, had heard the same story as his wife, except that the farmer who told him about it added that the boy was a simple-minded youth, not one gifted with much common sense. "Can't explain it, Martha," he said. "There's no way to justify or explain it... As you say, it's hard to tell facts from rumors, but that's what folks are saying."

When Josiah sat back down, he stared again into the fire, his eyes looking right through the flames. "Over the last few years we've both seen and heard about folks getting tarred and feathered by those with opposite views on the rebellion. And while things like that caused a ruckus for a time, nobody got killed. But things are changing. Resentment for grievances in times past is building. Hearts are hardening in one direction or the other. As you've said, trying to stay on the fence any longer may not be an option."

He turned to his wife. "Tarleton's men murdering Buford's men at Waxhaw won't soon be forgotten. And when Huck's men burned the churches and libraries of those two Presbyterian preachers east of here, they used the pages of some of those men's own Bibles to help start the fire. Can you imagine that? Our Bible over there on that table in the corner is not just a Bible. It's our only book. It's how we teach our children to read. I figure our preachers only want the best for us, so when British troops abuse them, it makes my blood boil. The British say they want our loyalty, but when they abuse our clergy, burn our Bibles which were published in England, and then plunder the countryside all in the name of King George, it doesn't make sense. Not one bit of sense."

He took a moment to light his pipe, savoring the tobacco smell. "They do all this looting and killing and burning, thinking we'll be motivated to think like them. To join their cause. Their side. Trying to govern by fear and intimidation. Trying to scare us to their side. In my mind, it's doing the opposite. It's making me want to join those who are standing up against them."

Martha sat still for a long time as she stared into the fire in front of them. Although not given to violence, her words and her thoughts mirrored those of many of her neighbors. Grasping her husband's hand, she looked into his eyes. "I can't see us ever siding with the British. I wish men like Huck were dead."

YORK COUNTY, SOUTH CAROLINA
EARLY AFTERNOON, TUESDAY, 11 JULY 1780

The two men had been working for almost three hours, carefully melting chunks of lead in a small pot over the open fire and then ladling the hot shimmering silver liquid into molds to make bullets. It was a slow, tedious process. Three hours of work had yielded one hundred good bullets. "We got enough yet?" the younger man asked.

"Getting there, James. We got enough lead to work for maybe another hour or so. Just keep at it. We've got a good feel for the work, so let's keep going 'til we run out of lead."

Glancing up, Edward Martin looked at the younger man's mother and his wife, Mary, who was James McClure's sister. The two women were busily preparing a meal of corn meal and venison. Martin smiled. "I think you women should be proud of James. These bullets he's making are as good as I've ever seen. And we appreciate you letting us do this work here at the outside fire instead of using the one inside the cabin. Would have been way too hot to do this kind of work in there."

"Making bullets is important, so just keep at it," said Mary. "Does my heart good to see my husband and my brother work so hard for a good cause."

Martin grunted as he stopped again to inspect their work. These lead balls are round and tight. No scratches on the edges to cause them to go sideways. *Could've melted down some pewter plates but that mixture of tin, lead, brass, and copper is not as good as pure lead. Heard some have tried that, but this is the right way. Need good hard round lead balls to go after what we're aiming to shoot at.*

But before he could resume his work, a band of men, most of them wearing the green uniform coat of Tarleton's Legion, came out of the woods, encircling the four. The leader, a man with medium dark hair and a beard to match, laughed, "Looks like we've got ourselves some more terrorists, men."

A second man piped up, "You're right, Captain. Looks like we got us some who need a good lesson in the King's justice. What do you want to do with 'em?

Before the Loyalist officer could respond, Martin stared at the man, the one addressed as Captain. "You wouldn't be that murderer, Captain Huck, would ya?"

"Now why would you say something so un-neighborly like that? We're just simple men doing the King's bidding. Based on your tone, I'm thinking you're Edward Martin. And I'm betting this youngster next to you is James McClure. Folks around here who are loyal to the King told us about you."

Showing great courage in front of so many men, McClure's mother looked at the captain. "You didn't answer the first question. You Huck? Heard you and your kind shot a boy who was walking down a road a few weeks ago for no reason. Why'd you do that? Because he was reading a Bible or just because you didn't like his looks? Heard you were at Waxhaw, too. You murder some men there too?"

Captain Christian Huck's face flushed with anger. "Woman, I don't owe you any explanation. What I can tell you is that because we caught these two dead-to-rights, making bullets to shoot at the King's men, they're getting hung at dawn and left out to dry so that others around here will get the message that it's best to be loyal to the King."

Huck, a man who earned his living before the war as a Philadelphia lawyer, who had his property confiscated by some Patriots after the British evacuated Philadelphia in 1778, and who now sought revenge against any who opposed the King, said to one of his men, "Tie 'em up good and tight. They'll get their due in the morning. For now, search this cabin and that barn over there. Take whatever you want—food, bullets, blankets, anything."

Before he could take a step back, McClure's mother grabbed Huck by the arm, pleading, "Don't hang my boy. He's too young."

"Get away from me, woman," Huck shouted as he struck her with the flat of his sword. "If he's old enough to make bullets to shoot at me and my men, he's old enough to hang."

Speaking in a tone that could have cut a stone in half, he said, "Leave these women with nothing. Take everything." Stomping away, he signaled for the bulk of his men to follow him into a small clearing near McClure's barn.

With his thirty-five British Legion Dragoons, twenty New York Volunteers, and sixty Loyalist Militia around him, Huck smiled. "Gentlemen, we've done it again. This is exactly why we're here. To rid this land of vermin like these.

"Our mission is to make every one of 'em who opposes the King pay for their lawlessness. The people around here need to understand that anyone who sides against His Majesty brings death and destruction upon themselves. You men should be proud of what we've done in the past two weeks, torching the homes and the libraries of those two seditious Presbyterian preachers who were stirring up the people with all their hate and vitriol against us, and then destroying all those tools and equipment at Hill's Ironworks. We tore it apart good and proper. They won't be making any cannons again there for a long time."

Huck paused, looking around at his men. "And now, right here, we've captured two more of these scoundrels. This is why we ride men:

to quiet the backcountry, to put the fear of God in these enemies of the King! What do we do with these who make war against us? Against His Majesty?"

With the shouts of "Hang 'em. Hang 'em," ringing in his ears, Christian Huck gave the order to mount up so they could pursue another man who opposed the King who lived a few miles away.

****

It was several hours before dusk when Huck's formation arrived at the home of Colonel William Bratton, another man on Huck's list to find and eliminate.

After terrorizing three older men he found outside, he strode into Bratton's home, a substantial two-story farmhouse, confronting the man's wife, Martha, demanding, "Looking for your man. Where is he?"

"Can't rightly say," Martha said, her tone reflecting that she would not be easily convinced to tell this Loyalist commander anything.

"Woman, I'll ask you again. Where is your husband?"

"Don't know. Even if I did, I wouldn't tell you."

With that, one of Huck's men standing behind him, grabbed a reaping hook fastened to the wooden wall nearby, and raised it over his head, ready to bring it down on the woman. But before he could complete his swing another Loyalist, Captain John Adamson, grabbed the man's arm. With his eyes glaring, Adamson's words came out firm and steady. "I'll not have you cut this woman. She is only doing her duty to her husband."

After a moment of silence on both sides, Huck nodded at Adamson, "All right, John. We'll do this a different way. We'll just surround this place and wait for the good colonel to make his appearance. And then when he shows up, we'll hang him."

Turning to Mrs. Bratton, he smiled, "Madam, because this good officer just saved your life, we'd be obliged if you'd fix us a meal worthy of his kindness."

****

As Martha Bratton and several servants prepared the meal Huck demanded, the Loyalist chieftain moved his formation a half mile down the road to Williamson's plantation where he put all his prisoners; McClure, Martin, and the three older men, into a corn crib to await their fate.

Unbeknownst to Huck, while preparing the meal, Martha Bratton dispatched one of her trusted servants to find her husband. During the night, this servant found his owner who, upon hearing about his wife's situation and Huck's intentions, assembled ninety men. Using the cover of darkness, Bratton and his men approached Williamson's plantation.

Just before first light Bratton's scouts reported, "We didn't see any pickets or any patrols except for a few sentries near Williamson's house. Huck's probably there. All the rest of these Loyalist fools are sleeping, even heard a few of 'em snoring. Appears we got 'em with their pants down, Colonel."

Armed with that knowledge, Bratton ordered his men to wiggle their way to within seventy-five yards of the dozing enemy. At dawn Bratton's men opened fire, splitting the calm still air, taking Huck's men completely by surprise. The battle lasted only fifteen minutes.

****

Later that morning, Colonel Bratton gathered his leaders together. "Gentlemen, we killed thirty-five and captured a good number of 'em. Only a handful got away. Huck is dead. All the men he intended to hang are safe. And after talking with Martha, it seems one Loyalist we captured who's gravely wounded, a man by the name of Adamson, saved her life yesterday. I want him treated with the utmost respect."

3. Victory in Sight

Lord Cornwallis' Headquarters, Camden, South Carolina
Late afternoon, Sunday, 20 August 1780

LIEUTENANT COLONEL JAMES WEBSTER, THE BRIGADE COMMANDER of both the 23rd and 33rd British Foot Light Regiments in the recent battle, stopped under a huge oak tree in front of the substantial two-story building that served as Lord Cornwallis' headquarters. He recognized the horses of his fellow commanders tied to the two hitching rails near the entrance to the home knowing that, they too, had been invited here to celebrate their victory over General Horatio Gates' American Army. As in all his other previous engagements, Webster distinguished himself four days ago in the Battle of Camden. Rock steady and courageous under fire, he was humble in victory. A professional soldier by any standard.

Webster had been a member of the 33rd Foot for the last twenty years, progressing upward through the officer ranks, participating in many of its battles to include the first attempt to seize Charles Town in 1776. Later he played critical roles at Long Island, Harlem Heights, Brandywine, Germantown, Monmouth, and most recently in the successful second campaign to seize Charles Town. And because of his long relationship with the 33rd, the colonel took great pride in the Regiment's nickname, 'Pattern,' because it symbolized that this unit set the standard in all matters of military excellence that all other regiments sought to emulate.

The colonel stared at the white mansion in front of him. He knew that the owner, Joseph Kershaw, amassed a great fortune from his mercantile business, becoming the patriarch of this town, the major inland trading location in South Carolina. But from the British perspective, Kershaw had one great failing: he was a staunch Patriot, one of those men Webster and his command intended to eliminate. As punishment for Kershaw's leanings, when the British command established its headquarters in the man's home, they exiled him to Bermuda.

As Webster walked up the steps leading to the first floor, the magnificence of the home, over two thousand square feet of living space on each floor, struck him once again. The design and structure rivaled the ornate Charles Town homes, with edifices that set the standard for Southern style and architecture. Entering the large room to the right of the spiral staircase that led to Cornwallis' private suite upstairs, he joined the other officers who had been invited to this small gathering.

The senior officer present was the twenty-five-year-old Marques of Hastings, known by most as Lord Frances Rawdon, Commander of the Volunteers of Ireland. Next to him were Lieutenant Colonel John Hamilton, Commander of the Royal North Carolina Regiment; Lieutenant Colonel Samuel Bryan, Commander of the North Carolina Volunteers; and Lieutenant Colonel Alexander McDonald, Commander of the two battalions of the 71st Highland Regiment. The only man who appeared to be missing was Tarleton. Each officer present had seen to it that his uniform was now clean, the smell of highly polished leather replacing the unmistakable stench of sweat and blood and gun-powder from a few days ago. Servants moved about silently filling the soldiers' wine glasses as necessary.

Each of these men had played a significant role in the victory that had taken place in the wooded area eight miles north of their present location. While they expected to provide details to Lord Cornwallis concerning the status of their units, their priorities over the past few days had been replenishing their supplies and caring for their men. Invitations to come to the headquarters had not been unexpected as it was time to celebrate their triumph and look to the future. These men also looked forward to bantering with one another, the good-natured revelry that always seemed to accompany any well-earned victory. They were a self-assured, professional group who enjoyed sharing time with their commander.

Suddenly, the man of the hour came down the staircase. As the senior officer of the group, Lord Rawdon called the others to attention. "My Lord, may I have the honor of proposing the first toast?"

A poised smile came across Charles Cornwallis' face as he stepped to the center of the room. "Yes, Lord Rawdon. By all means, the honor is yours."

Rawdon, thought by many to be the ugliest man in the Army, bowed to Cornwallis before he gazed at the others before him. He then raised his glass and in a most solemn voice proclaimed, "To King George III, our Ruler, our Sovereign, our Majesty."

"To the King," echoed the officers as they raised their glasses, nodding their approval of the toast as they drank heartily from Joseph Kershaw's finest crystal glasses, these particular ones purchased by Kershaw and imported from Holland before the hostilities began.

Then it was Webster's turn. The short, stocky officer, only two years younger than Cornwallis, spoke. "I wish to propose the second toast."

As Webster began speaking, the servants stationed in each corner of the room moved forward to refill the now empty glasses. "At the risk of being labeled a sycophant, I propose a toast to our leader. As we know, just four days ago, although outnumbered by a force nearly double our size, he led us and our fine soldiers, the cream of the British motherland and Loyalists to the Crown, to a convincing victory over the insolent Rebels. Their commander, General Horatio Gates, was last seen galloping north on his horse, fleeing from the steel of our bayonets."

Looking about at the heads bobbing and smiling faces around him, his voice rose. "We, on the other hand, are led by a man of experience and courage; a man who has fought in these lands for over five years; a man who is steadfast and brave; a man who is determined to lead us to victory for the glory of Britain. Gentlemen, please raise your glasses with me. To Lord Charles Cornwallis, our commander!"

Without hesitation, those around the room gave a hearty, "Here, Here," toasting their leader. "To Lord Cornwallis," they cheered the man in the center of the room as they downed their wine with considerable gusto.

After emptying his glass and watching the servants once again perform their duty, Cornwallis gazed upon each man before him. "Gentlemen, I thank you for your kind words, but it is I who should be toasting you. Seeing you here reminds me of your valor under fire both here and in our earlier conquests. It was you and your men who carried our colors forward at Savannah, at Stono, and at Charles Town before the battle here. In light of all you have accomplished, I wish to propose a toast to the future, to what I hope will be the final campaign. For it is the final campaign that will allow us to return home—home to the land we love, home to our families."

He paused. "To Victory!"

****

The room quieted down as the servants cleared the table of the last of the plates purchased by Kershaw from Germany's finest china markers, the bellies of the officers now full of the succulent fresh venison, turkey, and wild boar topped with mounds of sweet potatoes and fresh carrots. The good-natured conversation during the meal centered on old soldiers they had known and the stories of good natured rivalries as well as tales of a fair damsel or two some had become acquainted with during their short time in Charles Town.

The door to the dining room, which had been closed to ensure their privacy, suddenly sprang open as another officer, this one wearing a dirty green uniform coat and leather leggings burst into the room. His boots showed a modest attempt had been made to clean off the first layer of dirt, but from the sweat on the man's uniform, it was obvious he had ridden hard and fast to make his appearance.

Saluting Lord Cornwallis, Tarleton stood at attention. "I apologize for my tardiness, sir, but I have just returned from the mission you assigned me several days ago."

Cornwallis raised his glass in the officer's direction. "And were you successful?"

Tarleton smiled, "Yes sir, of course. We caught up with Sumter and his eight hundred men two days ago at a place called Fishing Creek. Our attack late in the day caught them by surprise as many of his men were in various states of relaxation, sleeping or bathing. Their confidence so great, they had posted no security to speak of."

The Legion commander looked about at his contemporaries as he continued. "Needless to say, they suffered greatly; at least one hundred and fifty of them are dead and another three hundred captured, and we liberated one hundred British prisoners from their possession. We lost sixteen men dead or wounded. Regretfully, Sumter eluded capture by jumping on a horse and galloping away just in front of my men."

With laughter in his voice, Tarleton concluded, "I've been told he barely had any clothes on, but I can't vouch for that."

Sitting back in his chair, Cornwallis nodded his approval. "Excellent. We will talk later so you can give me more details."

Turning to the others in the room, he said, "Gentlemen, I am certain you will allow our young friend who just joined us a chance to fill his plate as we reflect for a moment on the past few days. After that, I want to focus on the future. Mr. Ross, would you please get our maps?"

The aide nodded, disappearing without a word before returning a few moments later, spreading out a large map of North and South Carolina and Virginia over the fine oak table now cleared of dishes.

"Based on your reports and information we have gleaned from our prisoners and from our loyal sympathizers, we know we dealt the Rebels a noteworthy blow. If George Washington expected Gates, their hero at Saratoga, to stop us, he must be quite disappointed. From what we have learned in the past few days, Gates' army consisted of almost four thousand men, one thousand of which were regulars. The remainder of his force consisted of ill-prepared, ill-trained militia. As best we can determine, we killed or wounded nearly one thousand and captured another thousand. Eight of their artillery pieces and a substantial number of wagons filled with baggage and provisions, along with a large supply of their ammunition, now belong to us. Those who fled the battle early in the fight, which included Gates and the bulk of their militia units from Virginia and North and South Carolina, were last seen in full flight heading north."

He paused briefly as he considered the other side of the coin. "We badly mauled their best unit, the Maryland Continentals, as they did their duty and stood their ground. To their credit, those men under the command of Baron de Kalb, and a few other brave commanders, fought and died like soldiers. I'm sure your casualty figures bear evidence to their courage and valor. If you have not already heard, despite the efforts of our best physicians, including my own, de Kalb died yesterday succumbing to his numerous wounds. We also hold two other generals prisoners. One of them, Griffith Rutherford, is being treated for his wounds. Like many of the other senior leaders we have captured over the past several months, he will be taken at some future date to Fort Saint Mark, or as the Spanish called it, Castillo de San Marcos, in Saint Augustine for the duration of this rebellion."

After a hardy gulp from his wine glass, Cornwallis continued, "While the men we killed or captured, and the equipment seized or destroyed are significant, more importantly, we now hold this colony firmly in our grasp. Opportunity beckons us to take the next step. But before we talk more of that, I want to hear from you and the status of your units. Lord Rawdon, how did the Volunteers of Ireland fare?"

"Sir, because we were in the thick of it, we started the battle with three hundred and three men. Seventeen were killed and seventy others wounded; the majority of those men will be returned to duty within a few weeks."

"Colonel Webster, same question? By the way James, is your wound healing properly?"

"Thank you for asking, sir. My arm is healing nicely. I anticipate no long-term effects. Regarding the 23rd Regiment, we began the battle with two hundred and ninety-two soldiers. Six were killed, eighteen wounded. The 33rd Regiment bore the brunt of the action against the Maryland Continentals. We started with two hundred and thirty-eight men. Eighteen were killed, eighty-one wounded. One man remains missing. Over forty percent casualties. Like Lord Rawdon's unit, most of our wounded will be fit for duty in several weeks."

Cornwallis looked at Webster for a long time. They had served together for many years and knew each other well. If there was one man Cornwallis could always count on, it was Webster. Turning to the others he asked, "Hamilton, Bryan, McDonald, what about you?"

Hamilton answered first. Three killed and fourteen wounded out of two hundred and sixty-seven for the Royal North Carolina Regiment. Bryan, whose unit had played an irrelevant role in the fight, related that his North Carolina militia had only two wounded and three missing out of three hundred and twenty-two men. Lastly, McDonald reported that ten were killed and thirty-four wounded in the two battalions of the 71st Regiment's two hundred and forty-four men.

"And you Tarleton, what were the Legion's casualties during the fight?"

"Sir, I am pleased to report that of the three hundred and eight men of the Legion, counting both my cavalry and infantry, we had only five killed, and sixteen wounded."

Pointing toward Tarleton, Cornwallis said, "I am pleased Colonel Tarleton gave his brief report earlier about his clash with Sumter because it illustrates how we will continue our campaign."

Looking about, he continued. "I want to keep the pressure on our opposition every chance we get. We will show them no mercy. While you use the next few weeks to care for your wounded and reconfigure your units, I want you also to replenish your supplies in preparation for our advance north."

Cornwallis then drew their attention to the map spread before them. "Sometime between the fifth and the tenth of September, we will move a significant part of our army into North Carolina. The village of Charlotte will be our first objective as it is where a number of roads meet. Hillsborough north of there, Rebel headquarters for both their military and government, will be our second objective. I am ordering Major Ferguson here from his western location to discuss our plans for the upcoming campaign. His mission will be to protect our left flank, skirting the edge of the taller mountains to our west as we move northward through the less strenuous terrain. You can anticipate more specific orders within a week.

"In the meantime, get some rest, resupply your men, and see that your wounded are cared for. Continue to encourage the loyal followers you meet to recruit their neighbors to our side and impress upon them in the strongest possible terms, how we will deal with those who choose to oppose us. Congratulate your men and officers for me on a job well done. I am sending Captain Ross back to England in the morning with dispatches about our victory here. The information you gave me today will be part of that report. In the meantime, Colonel Tarleton, come with me and tell me more about your encounter with Sumter. For the rest of you gentlemen, thank you again and goodnight."

SIXTY MILES NORTH OF MUSGROVE'S MILL, SOUTH CAROLINA DAWN, MONDAY, 21 AUGUST 1780

The oldest of the three men looked at the other two as he tried to refresh himself with a tea-like brew of a mixture of raspberry and blackberry leaves, heating up this concoction over the open flames of their small fire. While it was not to the standard of tea one would find in Boston, it was a fair substitute from the bounty from the mountains of the Appalachian chain. The first sign of dawn, the dim-light to the east, slowly interrupted the deep dark sky. The man closest to him was the first to sit up.

"Prewitt, you stink bad. Your eyes are almost black. You didn't look too good before, but now, after no sleep for the last few days, you look worse than ever."

Laughing quietly to himself, Josiah Culbertson shifted his glance to the third man, who was now starting to move about. In his distinctive tone of Pennsylvania words mixed with dialect of the Carolina backwoods, Culbertson spoke again to Prewitt. "Despite how bad you look, you still look better 'an Ebenezer over there."

A farmer all his life, the twenty-eight-year-old Prewitt had joined the militia only six months earlier as a substitute for his father, Thomas. Despite his age, he was the least experienced warrior of the three men. Having survived his first taste of being shot at and returning fire three days ago, his adrenaline still ran high. "From everything I could tell, we stopped 'em cold. Couldn't see it all because of all that smoke, but I sure saw them Redcoats running at the end."

Culbertson nodded in Prewitt's direction. "Yeah, you're right 'bout that. We got 'em good; trapped 'em in a vice and they couldn't get out until they ran back the way they came," said the tall, rangy man, his physique fine-tuned from an abundance of farm work and living on the frontier. He was not a man to be taken lightly as he proved in many battles over the past five years, first against the Indians and most recently against the British at Savannah, Stono, and Charles Town. A deadly marksman with a determined fighting spirit, he was a man everyone wanted by their side.

"Seems to me that considering the whippin' we gave 'em and after a couple of hard days and nights riding away from God only knows what, I'm ready for a good meal and a little sleep. After that, I'll be ready to go after 'em again. A man can get by on a few bites of corn, some way-too-young apples, and a little water for only so long."

Ebenezer Fain, six days shy of his eighteenth birthday, now sat fully awake, silently replaying the fierce battle and their timely retreat over and over again in his mind. As a youngster, he moved with his family as they traveled southwestward on the Great Wagon Road, a journey that began in Pennsylvania and ended in the Virginia farm country. When the War for Independence broke out, Ebenezer enlisted at the age of fourteen but saw little action. Then he wandered around for a time before he enlisted again, this time in Isaac Shelby's militia. From everything he could tell, he killed his first man three days ago at Musgrove's Mill, the Redcoat falling down in a heap forty yards away with a bullet fired from Fain's gun buried in his head.

Shaking his head in an effort to think about something else, Fain glanced over at another small fire thirty yards away where three older men sat. "Look at those three. They got to be as tired as us. They may be older but they sure can fight. Got guts. You see Colonel Clarke during the fight? Buried his hatchet into one of them Redcoats and then he fought another one right after that. The other two, Shelby and Williams, were right in the thick of it, too."

****

Elijah Clarke, the leader of the Georgia militiamen who fought at Musgrove's Mill, wrapped his hands around his legs, trying to ease some of the cramping he felt deep in his body. Though he was still wiry and strong at thirty-eight, the stiffness in his limbs reminded him of his earlier exploits against the Creeks and Cherokees, the wounds he had received, and his earlier bouts with smallpox and the mumps. Though he was a man of little formal education, he knew instinctively what they accomplished a few days ago. While they had lost several good men, they had given out far more than they had received, causing the British forces to retreat to lick their wounds.

"Been in many a fight and I tell ya, that was one of the better ones. We gave 'em the what-for, didn't we? Yes sir, we gave 'em the what-for. Our two hundred against their five hundred and we still took it to 'em. Ole Shadrach sucked 'em right in to our little trap and they never knew what hit 'em till it was too late." He paused to stretch out his legs. "Boys did themselves right proud." He sighed for a moment before he finished. "Got to tell ya, I'm missing Shadrach already. He was a good man."

Isaac Shelby, a big thick man six months shy of his thirtieth birthday, looked over at the Georgian and nodded his agreement. Like Clarke, he had learned much about fighting from his experiences of keeping his land safe from marauding Indians, all of which led to his appointment by the North Carolina governor to lead the Sullivan County militia.

He smiled at Clarke. "You're right about Shadrach Inman. He went out in front and the Redcoats couldn't resist chasing him. They followed him neat and pretty as he pretended he was falling back, drawing 'em into our killin' zone like sheep being led to the slaughterhouse."

He looked around at the small clusters of men all around them. "We're blessed to ride with so many good men. Did you see William Smith shoot their colonel, Innes I think his name was, right outta his saddle? When that man hit the ground, his men took notice. They still fought pretty good after that, but you could tell their hearts weren't in it. And then when Josiah Culbertson and his boys hit 'em from the flank, it was all over. Got to say for an old man, Elijah, you did some pretty good fighting."

Before Clarke could reply, the third man piped up. He was the oldest of three men at age forty. "I'd say we all did right well, but like you said, if they hadn't taken the bait like they did, I don't know if we'd be talking so much about how we got the better of 'em." James Williams was orphaned before he was twelve. He was raised by his brother, who saw to it that James received a good education, which he used wisely to establish a thriving farm and a mill. With the outbreak of the war, Williams recruited and trained a militia unit in the Spartanburg area which he led at Savannah and Stono.

Shelby leaned back against his saddle to help relieve some of the pressure on his back. "You're right, James," he said as he stared out at the steep hills not far away, the early morning fog and dew making the air cooler.

Williams' tired eyes watched the flames of the fire dance in front of them. "Regardless of how good we beat 'em, we made a smart move to head north when we did. Good thing we got that message when we did or else we might have found ourselves in something we couldn't get out of. To stay near the battlefield without knowing where the Loyalists might be was just too risky."

The three men stayed quiet for a few minutes, remembering what brought about their long three-day ride. It started when a lone rider found them just as the last of the gunshots faded away from the battle. The rider, recognizing Shelby, thrust the message into his hands. "Got a message here from General McDowell for you. Been trying to find you for two days."

Shelby had taken the letter and read it to Clarke and Williams. "McDowell says here that General Gates lost nearly his whole army fighting Cornwallis at Camden a few days ago. Because he's got really no good idea where the enemy units might be, particularly those around Ninety Six like Ferguson's, he strongly suggests we look out for our safety."

Shelby closed his eyes, remembering those moments. "Yeah, you're right. It was a good thing we left when we did. Still feels good to know we killed sixty or seventy of 'em and we've got another seventy with us as prisoners." He stopped to take a bite out of a raw corncob he had picked up yesterday by the side of the road. "You're right, James. It was a good thing that messenger got to us when he did. Otherwise, we might be finding ourselves in a real pickle if we had headed for Ninety Six. It's just too strong of a fort for us to attack without having everything working in our favor."

He played with the fire with a large stick, watching the flames spring up in the middle of the wood. "But now we got to make some decisions. Part of me wants to rest up for a few days, get some good food in my belly, send some scouts out to find out where the Recoats might be, and then maybe head for Ninety Six. But if Ferguson is close, we might find ourselves in a bad way real quick. And we've got to decide about all these prisoners. Can't let 'em go and we can't shoot 'em."

Clarke stared at his friend. "Isaac, your rambling on 'bout Ninety Six makes no sense. Ferguson and his men could be on that next ridge looking down on us right now." He stretched his legs out before finishing his thoughts. "I'd like to go there more than you. It's closer to where I live and that makes it a bigger threat to me than it does to you. But first I want to know what we're up against. Getting scouts out searching ahead of us and behind us is what we need to do no matter what. Don't need to be stumbling into something we can't handle."

The debate went back and forth for another fifteen minutes before Williams made a proposal. "Since we all know we have to do something and since I've got the shortest distance to travel, how 'bout I take the prisoners to Hillsborough and put them in the governor's hands. That way I can fill Rutledge in about what we did at Musgrove's Mill. Maybe that'll take some of the sting off Gates' defeat. Meanwhile, you two can head for home and rest up for the next time we do some more fighting."

Shelby was the first to respond. "Makes sense to me. Considering how long my boys have been away from their kin, they won't mind going home. Got crops to harvest, firewood to cut before the cold sets in, and you never know what the Indians might be up to. In the meantime, let's keep in touch by sending riders back and forth to each other so if we need to come together again, we can do it quickly."

****

As the soldiers watched their commanders issue orders to prepare for the move, young Fain asked Prewitt, "William, you think we'll ever be seeing another big group of men like this again or will everyone just stay home and mind their own business?"

Prewitt put a big hunk of tobacco he had been saving in his mouth, chewing it for a time before he spoke. "My guess is that we'll see each other again real soon. We're not done with all this yet. Too many Redcoats and Loyalists around for us to ignore, and some of our boys got a lot to settle with 'em. Barns burned. Livestock stolen. Crops burned down to the ground. Womenfolk mistreated. And no one's forgetting what they did at Waxhaw. Like I said, the way I see it, we got a lot to settle with 'em before this is over."

He spat on the ground. "And there're a goodly number of men like us who oppose their kind just on general principles. Sooner or later somebody's got to win this thing. From what I know 'bout those leaders over there, none of 'em is one who will let things go unsettled. So, yeah, I expect we'll be getting together again real soon. Don't know when or where, but someday soon."

4. Decisions

South Carolina backcountry
Early afternoon, Wednesday, 23 August 1780

MAJOR FERGUSON'S FACE SHOWED HIS FRUSTRATION. DESPITE GOING back and forth, fording one creek and river after another, and investigating each rumor given to him by the Loyalists he had talked with, it seemed that Clarke, Shelby, and Williams had vanished, disappearing like ghosts even though he sensed their nearness. And now from the informants he spoke with and the tracks his scouts found, it appeared these traitors had split into three groups and were a day or two ahead of him. So here he sat. Even though he had parts of seven militia battalions with him, the North Carolina battalion and six South Carolina battalions, he had nothing to show for his efforts. And now he had to leave the search. What was so important that Cornwallis ordered him to come to Camden?

Captain De Peyster was a capable officer but …. "Abraham, you're in charge even though these militia colonels think they know what to do. I've told them that so they won't be confused. While I don't want to leave you, an order from Cornwallis cannot be ignored."

"Yes sir. I understand."

"The message gives no hint as to why he wants to see me, and as you know, I'd much rather be here instead of playing martinet to the likes of Rawdon and the others but....Don't have much to tell you except keep looking for Clarke and Shelby, and if you find 'em, don't wait for me. Do what you think is best."

The twenty-seven-year-old captain, nine years younger than Ferguson, came from a staunch Loyalist family. Two of his brothers were now serving in Loyalist forces far to the north. De Peyster was an experienced officer having served with the New York Loyalist Regiment for over four years. While some called him the "Dog's Pup" for his role as Ferguson's deputy, the man was known to be tough and brave in battle, not easily panicked. Ferguson knew that if an opportunity presented itself, this man would not back away from a fight.

"I know you want revenge after what happened to you and your men at Musgrove's Mill, but be careful. Clarke and the others are crafty. If they can draw a man like Innes into a trap, they might try the same thing on you. Remember, if something doesn't look right or feel right, back off. If the situation looks too good to be true, go slow. And for God's sake, keep scouts out in all directions."

The younger man nodded. "I understand. With all their years of fighting Indians, these backwoodsmen know how to use the woods to their advantage, but as we know, many of our men have learned these same lessons from fighting those same Indians. Our men are just as seasoned. But I hear what you're saying. We'll be careful."

Ferguson eyed his subordinate. "You do that. Like I said, sometimes we see what we want to see. And because of that, we sometimes miss what's really in front of us."

The major sighed as he examined the soldiers nearest them, these men he had spent so much time training. "Meanwhile, I'll see what Cornwallis has in mind. Even though these backcountry dissidents have caused us to lose some good men and some of our pride, it seems to me that from the larger perspective, we have got them dancing to our tune. The men we're after must know they're outnumbered, and since they've split up, they'll be able to move faster. Considering that all of the larger fights of the past few months, except for Musgrove's Mill, have gone our way, I don't see how they can rally much of a force against us. If I were a wagering man, I'd say Cornwallis is thinking we should head into North Carolina, but that's only a guess on my part. We've got South Carolina pretty well tamed except for those we're chasing and a few other small bands near the coast. Makes sense Cornwallis will want to head north. No other direction to go."

De Peyster grunted. "I've been thinking along those lines myself."

Ferguson studied the tops of tall pines and hardwoods above as the wind pushed the limbs eastward. "Yeah. It seems that way to me. I'll catch up with you soon as I can. Hopefully, before anything big takes place." Smiling, he added, "After all, I can't let you have all the glory."

Mounting his favorite horse, the big white charger, he shouted, "Can't see that we'll be gone more than a week at most." With that, Major Patrick Ferguson wheeled his horse about, heading east southeast with Elias Powell, the man who served as his aide, riding at his side.

LORD CORNWALLIS' HEADQUARTERS
AT CAMDEN, SOUTH CAROLINA
LATE AFTERNOON, THURSDAY, 24 AUGUST 1780

"Captain Brown, please show Major Ferguson in."

Stepping forward to greet the man walking behind his new aide, Captain William Brown, Cornwallis held out his enormous hand, forgetting momentarily about Major Ferguson's well-known injury to his right arm. Quickly recognizing his *faux pas,* Cornwallis grabbed the man's left arm. "Major Ferguson, it is good to see you again. I heard you arrived several hours ago. I trust you have had an opportunity to shake some of the dust off your uniform since your arrival."

"Yes sir, we have. We have been treated very well, thanks to Captain Brown."

"Good, I am pleased to hear that. He is my new aide and I believe him to be a most efficient officer. Now, have a seat and enjoy some of our excellent wine before we feast on some of the bounty of this land. Since we have some time before the dinner is served, tell me about your pursuit of these insurgents you have been chasing. Are you closing in on them?"

"Not as close as I would like. Indications are that they number around two hundred. Several hours before I left my men, we found some fresh tracks that suggest they have split into three groups. Based on these signs, I believe that Clarke and his Georgia renegades are headed west back into Georgia, toward their base north of Augusta. Since Shelby and his men live northwest across the mountains, we assume the tracks that lead in that direction belong to him. And the third set of tracks is most likely Williams. He appears to be heading toward Hillsborough. It is this third group that most likely has our men who are their prisoners since these tracks show their few wagons are quite heavy."

"Why would they split up?" Cornwallis asked as he took a big sip from his wine glass.

"These men are experienced Indian fighters. They know that if strength or surprise is not on their side, it's best to keep moving until the odds shift in their favor. To us, that seems a bit ungentlemanly, but to them, it's a smart way to fight. I must give them credit. From their perspective, it makes them dangerous because their movements are more unpredictable, and of course, smaller groups can move faster than larger ones."

Cornwallis stared at the major. "It sounds as if these men have earned your respect."

"Respect, yes, but I don't fear them. If we understand their way of thinking and their tendencies, we have a better chance to prepare for their way of fighting."

"So aren't our Loyalists who have the same experiences prepared to deal with them?"

"Yes sir, they are. They're cut from the same cloth. They have the same skills as the men Clarke and Shelby lead. They understand Indian fighting just like the Rebels. And we outnumber them and we are on the side of right. In the past few months as we trained these new recruits, it is clear theses men have willing spirits and look forward to convincing their neighbors that our cause is just. My men and I are looking forward to putting these radicals in their place much as you did a few days ago here at Camden with their hero, General Gates."

Cornwallis smiled as he quickly polished off his wine, reviewing in his mind what he knew about the man before him. Commissioned at fifteen, this Scotsman seated across from him had twenty-one years of service, his initial fame coming from his skill as a marksman and as the inventor of an improved rifle. As Cornwallis watched Ferguson lift his wine glass to his lips with his left hand, the commander remembered that the major's right elbow had been shattered by a rifle shot at Brandywine three years ago. "Is there any improvement in your arm these days?"

"No sir. It is something I will be dealing with for the rest of my life. I've adjusted to the inconveniences."

Cornwallis considered that response. *While I still have questions about this man, Clinton holds him in high regard for all his work leading our militia units in the hinterlands. While I can see why some of my more conventional-thinking officers oppose this man's patient style of leadership, his methods toward recruiting and training are yielding satisfactory results. Perhaps Ferguson's nickname, "Bulldog," speaks more of this man's capabilities than I had previously considered.*

"I appreciate your comment about putting the Rebels in their place. Since we have a few moments before dinner is served, let me show you our future plans." After filling his glass and Ferguson's again with the fruit of the vine, Cornwallis stepped over to a large table upon which lay a map of North and South Carolina.

"What I am about to show you is to be held in strict confidence. When you return to your unit, you may brief only your officers on what I'm going to tell you. Is that clear?"

"Yes sir, I understand."

"Good." Cornwallis then pointed out the various locations on the map as he unveiled his plan. "Right now, we hold all the major towns in South Carolina—Charles Town, Camden, Ninety Six, and George-town. And with our victory here last week, I anticipate we will have almost complete dominance over the rest of this colony soon, although I anticipate some resistance from some of their smaller bands in the eastern sector closer to Georgetown, the most troublesome of which is commanded by a man named Marion. Another one is led by Sumter. We are dealing with these men now in the sternest way possible. Two days ago I dispatched Major Wemyss and a large detail from the 63rd Regiment with specific orders to disarm all untrustworthy men and hang, without trial, anyone he determines to be disloyal to our cause."

Ferguson glanced up. "Sir, if I may say so, I received similar orders several days ago. In my experience, I have seen how instructions such as these can result in a negative effect on some parts of the population, particularly those who previously declared their neutrality in this war."

Cornwallis gave a short snort. "I considered that possibility before I issued those orders, but if I have learned nothing else in my years in this land, it is that these people will respond to fear and intimidation. I believe most will cower before us. Oh, I recognize a few may become hardened against us, but I do not envision their numbers to be significant."

The man smiled more to himself than to Ferguson. "To demonstrate how serious I am about this, I recently ordered several Rebels hanged with only the briefest testimony against them but that is not why I summoned you here. You and your men are about to embark on a far more important mission."

While Ferguson turned his attention to the map in front of him, something made the hairs on the back of his head stand up. *Could he be right? Yes, he's older and more experienced, but my knowledge of these people, particularly those in the backcountry, tells me these Scots-Irish have a spine and a will to fight back. They will not sit idly-by as we threaten their lives and their property. I want to believe this man but....*With little time to dwell on the subject, he perked up immediately at the words, "far more important mission."

"While Weymss and his men deal with the likes of Marion and Sumter, we'll be moving the bulk of our forces north, first to Charlotte, and then eventually toward Hillsborough." After looking at the map for a time, Cornwallis shifted his glance toward Ferguson. "You and your men will play a key role in the accomplishment of this mission."

"Pattie" Ferguson looked down at the map in front of him, studying the places Cornwallis' fingers touched and pointed to, the words "key role" ringing through his ears. Quickly recalling memories of his twenty years of sacrifice—the cold and miserable days and nights of rain and snow, the whine of bullets whistling so close to his head, the ever-present pain in his right elbow—it seemed now that all his years of faithful service were about to be rewarded: a key role. His chest swelled with pride. What will historians write about me?

"Not later than Friday, 8 September, we will begin our move north. As I mentioned, our first objective will be to secure Charlotte and the road network in that area. Once we establish a base there, we will continue north as soon as the situation allows. While I would like to start that movement now, it is important for us to wait for a few more weeks to build up supplies and to heal our sick and injured from our battle with Gates. This will also give Weymss more time to deal with Marion and those like him to better secure the country to our rear and right flank, keeping our lines of communication and supply open to the coast."

"And my mission, sir? You haven't said what I am to do."

Cornwallis smiled, "Patience, Major. Patience. You and your men will protect our left flank as the main body moves north. You will parallel our movement of the main body, maintaining a distance of sixty to eighty miles west of our location. This will put you in the rougher terrain, closer to the taller mountains of North Carolina."

"I understand, sir."

"During your movement, you have two missions. First, your primary task is to keep any opposition from those who live in those mountainous regions from interfering with the movement of the main army. From what you indicated earlier, I specifically mean Shelby and the others like him. If you have an opportunity to deal a death blow to them, do so, but not at the peril of your primary mission. Second, continue to recruit more faithful men to our cause, particularly in the Tryon County area and around Gilbert Town, North Carolina as well as north of there. This will help accomplish your first mission and it will give us a base for further operations. Throughout your movements, you must keep me informed of your progress as I cannot move too far north unless you are protecting my flank. Is that clear?"

Ferguson's career flashed before him again. Key role. Opportunity. History. Controlling his excitement as best he could, he looked at his commander. "You can depend on me, sir." All thoughts in his conscience of how the people would react to Cornwallis' stern measures vanished. They would not be recalled for many days.

ISAAC SHELBY'S CABIN IN WESTERN NORTH CAROLINA
EARLY AFTERNOON, MONDAY, 28 AUGUST 1780

Isaac Shelby let the rocking chair relax his weary body as he swayed back and forth on the front porch of his simple wooden-frame home, admiring the beauty and serenity of the mountains all around him. It had taken almost a week for him to get his unit home after parting with Williams and Clarke. With the sights and sounds of battle behind him for now, it was time to enjoy the sound of bees buzzing around the wild flowers and the sight of his cattle grazing in the nearby pasture.

As he rubbed the ears of his companion, Duke, an old brown and white coon dog, he thought about the last six weeks. *The days went by fast. I'm glad we answered General McDowell's call to help stop the British. Those Redcoats have been having their way for far too long. The men did everything I asked of them. Fought three times: Thicketty Fort, Cedar Springs, and Musgrove's Mill. Two clear victories and one draw. Thankfully, casualties were light. And now I'm home on the land I love. One day... One day there'll be a large stone house sitting right by those big oaks over there. It'll have two stories in the main house, a single story wing on each side. It'll have a big barn. Plenty of cows and horses. Just need some money and time. Money and time.*

He was about to nod off when Duke raised his head and then stood up. It was then that Shelby spotted some dust being kicked up by an approaching rider, the man galloping on the path next to Shelby's eastern-most field. When the horseman slowed down to a walk as he neared Shelby's cabin, he tipped his hat. "Colonel, didn't wake you, did I? Hope you don't mind if I sit for a bit?"

"I'd be delighted, Josiah. Have a seat. Been what, two days since I saw you last? Figured your wife would have enough chores to keep you busy for at least a week. You need a break from all that work already?" Shelby smiled at the man as he spoke because Culbertson was one of his favorites amongst his men.

Culbertson laughed softly. "She does have a long list of things for me to do, that's for sure, but like I figured, Anne kept things running real smooth while we were gone. No surprise there. Been doing that for the last six years. Like most of these women around here, she is a tough Scots-Irish lass right down to her toes." With a smile on his face, he added, "And like most of 'em, she's a mite stubborn and independent, too. Wants things done yesterday. Today she wants the fields plowed, but I told her I had to see you on some important 'military' business. Hope you don't mind."

Shelby smiled his response as his visitor gazed at him, studying his ruddy face that encased those determined, honest eyes. Although only thirty, Shelby appeared much older because of the responsibility of leading men first against the Indians, and now the British. Culbertson thought, *Shelby is a tough old bird. A man you can trust. He's a man's man, just like my father and my brothers. I wonder how they're doing? They have been part of this fight for a long time. They're good honorable men, just like the man I'm sitting next to. Good men.*

Both remained quiet for a time, rejoicing in their surroundings, feeling the land wrap its calmness around them. Breaking the silence,

Culbertson asked as he petted Duke's head, "Colonel, never heard you mention much 'bout how you ended up in these mountains."

"Not much to tell. Born in Maryland Province. Folks moved there from Wales. My father was a farmer so I grew up workin' at that before I took up surveying. Was a deputy sheriff for a time, all before I was eighteen. Came here with my family ten years ago. My father helped build the fort and a trading post then herded some cattle."

"It true you spent some time with the Virginia higher-ups?"

"Yeah. A few years back when I was surveying land in Kentucky and Virginia, I hobnobbed a bit with Patrick Henry and Thomas Jefferson. Nothing to speak of really." Shelby paused to relight his pipe. "Despite all my travels, I feel most at home right here. With men who love the land, who are tough and know right from wrong; with men who are passionate about their views and who won't give up at the first sign of trouble; men who are as good with an axe and a plow as they are with a rifle.

He looked at Culbertson as he took a puff from his pipe before finishing his thoughts. "Good to have my brothers Evan and Moses close by, too. I'm truly blessed."

The two sat quietly again, neither speaking a word until Shelby broke their silence. "How about you? Most of your family still living down by Ninety Six?"

The soldier rubbed his cheek before opening his mouth. "Last I knew my father and my brothers were still going up against the Loyalists down there. Surprised I didn't see 'em at Musgrove's Mill. I came here five years ago to fight Indians, liked the country, and decided to move up here with Anne."

"Still just one daughter?"

"Yeah, Jane. Just between you and me, I don't think we can have any more kids. Can't tell you why. Just ain't happening. I don't mind that we keep trying if you know what I mean, but, maybe one day, God willing."

After swatting a troublesome fly away from his face, he changed the subject. "I love these wide open spaces, havin' my own land, knowing it's up to me to make whatever I can with it and not havin' to answer to nobody but the wife. Guess that's why I hate these Redcoats and those like 'em. Seems all they want to do is interfere with what the good Lord has blessed us with." Pausing he asked, "You reckon there'll be more fights coming?"

"Yeah, I think so. Too much going on not to get called again soon. With most of South Carolina in his hands, Cornwallis has got to be feeling frisky, and maybe a bit proud. A man's got to be careful when that happens. Sometimes a man's pride can overload his backside, if you know what I mean."

"I know what you mean. Ain't there something 'bout that in the Good Book? Pride goeth before the fall, or something like that."

"Think so. If it ain't in the Bible, it ought to be."

"You're right there. Well anyway, when you're ready to ride again, just let me know." Smiling he added, "Got to keep the King outta my business."

"Stay ready, Josiah. Stay ready."

LORD CORNWALLIS' HEADQUARTERS IN CAMDEN
EARLY AFTERNOON, MONDAY, 28 AUGUST 1780

"Captain Brown."

"Sir?" the aide answered as he stepped into Cornwallis' office.

"Prepare letters for both Sir Clinton and Lord Germain outlining the details of our plan to move toward Charlotte. In these letters specifically mention that Major Ferguson and his men will be guarding our left flank. Make it clear that I am somewhat concerned about Ferguson's lack of experience, but the use of his men in this manner is necessary as an economy of force measure so that all of our regular units will be available for our advancement through North Carolina."

"Of course, sir. Are there any others areas of emphasis you wish covered?"

"Yes. Tell them we are confident of our ability to control the rest of this colony, although several small rebel bands may still cause us some modest concern now and then. The tenor of the letters must be cautious optimism. I want to dispatch these letters not later than tomorrow."

"Sir, you said 'cautious optimism.' Based on almost all of your letters and information concerning the actions over the past month or so, may I ask why that phrase?"

The senior soldier stepped away from his desk to look out over the peaceful rolling hills to the east. "William, you are new to this position of aide, but I have known about you for several years. You have an impeccable reputation and Webster thinks you have all the makings of becoming a senior officer some day. Therefore, I have complete trust in you. In your new position there will be times when I share things with you to which others will not be privy. Do you understand?"

"Yes sir. Thank you. I will not let you down."

"You would not be here if I thought otherwise." Cornwallis paused. "The mission I have given Major Ferguson will be a test for him. If he accomplishes his mission, we will be able to advance northward without difficulty arising from his area of responsibility, and then we will forgo the use of the word 'cautious.'"

5. March North

MAJOR FERGUSON STARED DOWN ON GILBERT TOWN. IT HAD BEEN A long, difficult six-day march. His men had crossed six or seven rivers, he'd lost count, and like most of his men, he still had soaking wet feet from the last crossing several miles back. As they traveled further north, the elevation changes became steadily more severe. And with each piece of high ground they climbed, much larger mountains stood out to the north and west, their peaks in the distance signifying that these were true mountains. While they met no resistance to divert them from their goal, Ferguson sensed that unfriendly eyes knew every move he made.

The county seat of Rutherford County was not much to look at: fifteen to twenty small log cabins spread out around two large wooden structures with thick woods surrounding the village in all directions. The roads in and out of the town's center were nothing more than rutted paths, wide enough for two horses or one wagon at best, but it was the coming together of these trails going east and west, as well as north and south that made this town militarily significant. After one more glance at the woods around the town, Ferguson gently nudged his horse's side, signaling the three hundred men with him to follow, entering the town from the south on the Broad River/Cleghorn's Creek Road. Knowing Captain De Peyster was a day behind him with another eight hundred men, he smiled to himself. *Nothing can stand in my way. Accomplishing this mission is my destiny.*

As he and his men walked their horses into the center of the town, several dogs yelped a greeting as the major noted the courthouse and the tavern, their size and location within the town's layout making them obvious. While he observed only a few people milling about, Ferguson could feel eyes upon him from the windows of every building. Before he could even dismount, two men came out of the largest building—the courthouse, he assumed—and walked toward him. Both were of average height and build. They carried no weapons. The younger of the two, the one who carried a Bible, spoke first.

"Good afternoon, sir. My name is Reverend Morgan, Perminter Morgan, Pastor of the Mountain Creek Baptist Church here in Gilbert Town." Nodding to the man to his right, the reverend said, "This is John Earle, our justice of the peace. How can we be of service to you?"

The tone of Morgan's voice was neutral at best and his countenance displayed curiosity and a bit of defiance. Behind the first two questions, there were many more unasked. *Why is this large British force entering our town? Do you plan to stay long or are you just passing through? What do you want from us? How can we rid ourselves of you as soon as possible?*

Reverend Morgan and Judge Earle knew their town. Like so many of the population in these parts, there were some who tended to support Loyalist views while a like number favored breaking away from the British Crown. Despite the arguments that occurred at various times in the town tavern, there still remained another section of the population who voiced no opinion one way or the other as they were tired of the squabbling and just wanted to be left alone. This sometimes uneasy peace in Gilbert Town had never spilled over into open warfare but the venting of hard feelings was never far from the surface, the depth of which depended upon the vehemence expressed by those doing the arguing or the protesting. Over time, those on both sides learned to keep some distance from each other, although some of the more zealous advocates of the opposing sides kept stirring up trouble. It seemed to both Morgan and Earle that these fits of anger and rage served little purpose.

After dismounting, Major Ferguson shook hands with both men with his left hand. He wanted his first encounter with these town leaders to be friendly yet firm, reasonable yet productive, letting the obvious power behind his red coat do most of the talking.

"Gentlemen, I bring greetings from Lord Cornwallis and your Royal Governor of North Carolina, the Honorable Josiah Martin. My name is Major Patrick Ferguson of the 71st Foot. My men and I wish to establish a base of operations here so that we can secure your town from those who seek to rebel against our sovereign King George III." He smiled. "I trust my men and I will have your loyal support in this venture."

Noting that the two men glanced at each other when he used the words "base of operations," he continued.

"We will require some modest food supplies, water, and other necessary items for which we will gladly reimburse you. In addition, we will generously reward those who provide us information leading to the capture of those who stand in the way of the King's desire for peace in this area. I trust you and your fellow citizens will be grateful for the security we will provide you and be willing to assist the King's soldiers in any reasonable request we make."

Morgan and Earle could only look at one another. They knew Ferguson and his men had been moving in their direction for some time, but they assumed the Redcoats would only be passing through. The idea that Ferguson intended to establish his headquarters at Gilbert Town and stay for some undetermined period of time had not crossed their minds.

Before either man could utter another word, Ferguson asked, "Which house is William Gilbert's? Since he is your most prominent citizen, I would like to establish my headquarters there. And so we cause the least disruption as possible, can you recommend the best place for the remainder of my soldiers to encamp? I prefer them to be on some high ground close to a water source and near the roads leading west and north so we can move quickly as the situation dictates. When the rest of my men arrive here either later today or sometime tomorrow, we will have a substantial force available to protect you. Is the hill that I saw to the west of town suitable for our bivouac purposes?"

The two town leaders could only nod their heads as events were moving far too fast for them, and besides, they had no means to stand in the way of any demands Ferguson might make. After pointing out Gilbert's home to the major, they stood still and watched as the major walked straight to the front door of the man's home, entering it after a quick knock. Moments later, he came back out to the front steps signaling to a few of his men to set up his headquarters on the first floor of the two-story wooden-frame building. It was clear to Morgan and Earle how intentional this move was as everyone in the area knew about Gilbert's rebellious leanings, for even now he was at Hillsborough, representing Rutherford County there.

Reverend Morgan watched all the activity with his friend by his side. "John," he said quietly, "it seems to me our surly visitor has a very specific agenda. I wonder what it is."

Earle nodded but remained silent as the hustle and bustle went on about them. "Appears to me that with Ferguson now wanting to stay here for a time, it is possible the whole British Army might be heading north. When we can, we must pass this information on to those who might have more than a passing interest in this."

And with that agreement made between the two men, they spent the remainder of the day quietly observing the soldiers scurrying throughout town, knocking on doors to requisition supplies, and establishing guard posts on all the roads and trails leading into the town. All the while, the bulk of Ferguson's men marched up the hill to the west to establish their bivouac area, the land feature quickly becoming known to those in town as "Ferguson's Hill."

****

Near the end of the day, Ferguson penned a short letter to Lord Cornwallis stating that he had established his headquarters in Gilbert Town and that soon he and his men would begin to canvass the area for additional recruits. He also made a remark that he had met no resistance to date. From Ferguson's point of view, the first phase of Cornwallis' operation was proceeding according to plan.

CORNWALLIS' ARMY MARCHING TOWARD CHARLOTTE, NORTH CAROLINA EARLY MORNING, FRIDAY, 8 SEPTEMBER 1780

Cornwallis thought *Finally, we are moving. We can wait no longer. It is time to move even though some of my men are still healing from their wounds. The longer we wait, the more we lose the momentum.* He looked back at the columns behind him on the dusty road. *These men are like me. We have been at this task far too long. It is time at last to bring this rebellion to its rightful conclusion.*

At his side rode Captain Brown. "Sir, by the reports given to me early this morning, we have twenty-two-hundred men of whom fifteen hundred are regulars commanded by Lord Rawdon and Colonel Webster. The Legion is paralleling our march several miles to the west."

Cornwallis grunted. "I will feel more comfortable when Tarleton can conquer this illness that has him in its grasp. Major Hanger is a good officer, but as we both know, he is no Tarleton." *But who is? I cannot judge Hanger by measuring him against Tarleton. He is a different man and I must treat him as such.*

As his horse kept up a mesmerizing gait, Cornwallis once more replayed his plan in his head. *Ferguson is further to the west with specific instructions to keep any interference from over the western mountains at bay. We should be hearing from him soon. He must be kept on a short leash until he proves himself. To the east, near the coastline, our other formation is headed toward Wilmington, North Carolina to supply our needs as required. The major towns to our south are manned by sufficient troops to maintain order. And Major Weymss is pursuing the marauding Rebel bands north of Georgetown. It is a good plan, a reasonable plan, a plan with proper force and flexibility. Flexibility is the key to our success. With all these men under my command, we are like the biggest bear prowling through the woods. And as with that big bear, little can stand in my way.*

****

As the first hour passed, Cornwallis pulled his horse off to the side to wait for another rider to draw abreast. "Governor, I imagine you are anxious to reach Charlotte. How many years has it been since your government was forced to retreat from these lands? Four, maybe five years?"

The forty-three-year-old Josiah Martin took his time before replying. "Five years. And yes, nothing will give me greater pleasure than assuming my rightful place to lead this colony once again. Once your men tame those scoundrels in Charlotte, I anticipate the rest of the colony will fall quickly in line. Charlotte is the key."

Martin kept his eyes straight ahead as he recalled the major events that led to this day. *Fourteen-year military career in the British Army... Royal Governor of the colony of North Carolina in '71...I religiously followed the dictates of the Crown, maybe too religiously as I taxed the people as required. Looking back on it, perhaps our lifestyle in New Bern was too lavish for the people's liking. Then it all came apart. Rebellion. Elizabeth and the children had to seek refuge while I tried to govern from a ship in the harbor. Five years as a governor in name only. All because of these rebels. Now, at last, it is my time again.* He was so lost in his thoughts, he almost failed to hear Cornwallis' question.

"Why do you feel the support from the people around Charlotte is so critical?"

"That is the place where years ago some of my subjects wrote a document called the 'Mecklenburg Declaration of Independence' to express their deep feelings for freedom, its roots coming from the declaration conceived in Philadelphia by the so-called Patriots. So when you and your men bring these malcontents to their knees, I will once again govern this colony as the King intends."

"What exactly was in this declaration?"

Martin gazed at the countryside as his horse continued to plod along. "I can't remember all the words, but one phrase stuck out. They wrote, 'We do hereby dissolve the political bands which have connected us with the mother-country, and hereby absolve ourselves from all allegiance to the British crown.' Since five years have gone by since that pronouncement was made, I believe their fervor will die quickly when they see the power and authority you and your men will bring to them. They will cower before you, renouncing their old ways. I must say, sir, I have looked forward to this day for many years."

Cornwallis said nothing as he considered the situation from Martin's point of view. *I have known about this man's situation for some time, but today is the first time I listened closely to understand the heart of the matter. Will the people around Charlotte obey me like Martin thinks, or will this turn into a quagmire?*

GILBERT TOWN, NORTH CAROLINA
LATE AFTERNOON, FRIDAY, 8 SEPTEMBER 1780

Through silent agreement, three of the ten prisoners held captive by Ferguson decided to stay close to one another, particularly since several of the other captives talked in hushed tones about changing sides to the British cause knowing that they would then be freed from bondage. The three stalwarts viewed that option as abhorrent, wanting no part of being labeled as a traitor to the Patriot cause.

"What'd you think they've got planned for us?" the youngest of the three whispered as all the prisoners labored together to build their own place of confinement as the guards stood close by, monitoring their progress closely. The stockade, if one could label it as such, was not much to look at: just a barrier of heavy logs and limbs from the nearby trees spread over a large depression to confine the prisoners, giving each man just enough room to lie down. It had the prospects of becoming a miserable place as there was no shelter from the elements or any room to care for one's bodily necessities. Since the guards showed no signs of letting down their vigilance, escape from this hellhole appeared to be a slim possibility.

"Hard to say. My bet is they'll keep us cooped up here 'til Ferguson makes his next move and then they'll drag us along. No reason for 'em to do much else. We're cheap labor for them long as they can guard us good."

The one who asked the question studied the older man who had answered. "Your name is Sam, right?"

"Yeah."

"Me and my friend here only been prisoners for a few days. Ferguson's scouts picked us as they got close to Gilbert Town. They thought we were spying on them, which we were, but...How'd you get here? When did Ferguson's boys pick you up?"

The third man of three, this one sporting a large scar on his face chimed in, "Yeah, you don't sound like you're from around here. Where you from?"

Samuel Phillips gave the two men a hard look before he answered. "Own a small farm in Watauga County over the mountains west of here. Rode over the mountains a few months back with Shelby to fight the Redcoats. Got captured right as the battle of Musgrove's Mills was settling down. Dumb move on my part." Phillips looked around and spoke in hushed tones. "Soon as I can find a way, I'm out of this hole and headin' home."

The younger man looked about to make sure their talk was still just among the three of them. "Well in that case, you might get gone quick 'cause I heard they're taking us to Charles Town to put us on a Prisoner of War ship or maybe exile us on some Caribbean island crawling with insects and snakes."

"Don't see that happening. We're not that valuable to 'em. Besides we're going north in the opposite direction. Sometime, sooner or later, they'll slip up and I'll have my chance. Don't know when that time might come, but I'll be ready for it when it does. You can bet on that."

The two men considered Phillips' words carefully. He seemed to be a man of experience and common sense. They looked at each other. Phillips' words made good sense. Never know when that chance might come.

****

Dusk came rapidly over the western mountains as a cool breeze signaled the possibility of another heavy thunderstorm coming their way as the two Loyalist soldiers pushed the prisoner along toward Ferguson's headquarters. They shoved him into the large main room where the officer sat behind a small desk. The major continued to write for a few more minutes before glancing up, appraising the man before him.

"Phillips, it has come to my attention that you are related to Isaac Shelby. Are you his kin or not?"

Samuel Phillips stared at the major before nodding, "Yeah, that's right. He's my cousin twice removed. What's it to you?"

"It is not so much an issue for me. Rather it is more of what it means to you. Even though you have been our prisoner for almost a month, I have decided to parole you on one condition."

Phillips gazed at the major but said nothing.

"I want you to deliver a message to your cousin. If you give me your word that once you leave here, you will go straight to him and give him my message, you are a free man. It is that simple. Are you willing to accept my offer?"

Phillips stood still, thinking about Ferguson's words. *Shelby. Free man. What could Ferguson want from Isaac? All I have to do is deliver a message to him and I'm free? It sounds straightforward but there must be some kind of trap. Has to be. Only one way to find out.*

"All right, Major. What do you have in mind? And how do I know this ain't some kind a trap? That your men won't follow me?"

Ferguson studied Phillips closer. The frontiersman was of medium height with a strong build like so many who lived in these woods. His tattered leather and homespun clothes hung loosely on him, probably the result of the poor food and care he had received since his capture. Phillips' clear, blue eyes spoke of an intensity and intelligence that was hard to miss. *Yes, men like him could cause considerable problems to my mission. I must make every effort to keep them from interfering. I'm sure they'll heed my warning. We're too strong and they know that.*

The major looked to his left at Captain De Peyster, who had his eyes fixed on Phillips as though he were trying to see inside the man's thoughts. Ferguson thought again. *Yes, this is the right move, the right decision. Simple. Straightforward. Logical.*

Without any further hesitation, he gave the prisoner his proposal. "Phillips, I've decided to trust you and therefore, you have to decide whether to trust me. I want you to personally deliver my message to Isaac Shelby. I want you to tell him exactly what I tell you. Is that clear?"

"Yeah, Major, I understand that, but I'm still wondering if I can trust you."

"I understand. We will see to it that you have all the supplies you need for your journey. Our stable is filled with good horses and you can pick the one you want."

"And my rifle? I want my rifle back."

"Yes, your rifle will be returned to you."

Phillips looked at the wall behind Ferguson for a moment, staring at the British flag. He quickly made up his mind. "All right. What's the message?"

"First, make sure Shelby knows this message is coming from me."

"Easy enough."

Ferguson paused for emphasis. "If he and others across the mountains do not desist from their opposition to the British arms, I will march over the mountains, hang your leaders, and lay your country to waste with fire and sword. Do you think you have got it? Any questions?"

"No, I've got it. If Shelby and his men come after you, you'll come over the mountains and whip us on our land. I got that about right?"

The major nodded, "Not my exact words, but you understand the essence of what I want him to comprehend. Now as for your journey, you have my word that you will not be followed. You know the mountains better than we do, so there is no way any of my men could keep up. The fighting between your people over the mountains and the loyal subjects of the King has gone on long enough. I hope this will encourage Shelby and those like him to resume their normal lives and leave this war to those who live east of the mountains."

Phillips' eyes narrowed. The message burned into his brain. He had it all. It was a simple message. *Ferguson is challenging our manhood, our desire for freedom, our love of the land, and our way of life. Isaac will listen but...*

"Then, Mr. Phillips, if you agree to deliver my message, you are a free man under the conditions we have discussed. How long do you think it will take to get to Shelby?"

Samuel thought for a moment. A hundred miles or so as the crow flies. Up and down God only knows how many mountains, but he knew the way. The weather was good right now. Should not be any snow in the high country yet. With a good horse and no incidents with bears or Indians along the way..."I expect three to four days unless the weather causes me problems. Where's my rifle?"

"My men will return it to you as you get together whatever you need. You are now a free man, Phillips. I am counting on you." With the wave of his hand, the major dismissed the former prisoner.

But Phillips stood his ground. "Is there something else?" Ferguson asked.

"Just one more thing, Major. I heard what you said about no one following me. Just want you to know if you change your mind 'bout that and try and use me to find Shelby, I'll lead your men to Kingdom Come and they'll never come out of those mountains alive. We got a good understanding 'bout that?"

Ferguson leaned back in his chair. A slight smile came across his face. He liked the man's courage, his lack of fear in the face of adversity. "Mr. Phillips, as I said before, you have my word. No one will follow you. It is my sincere hope that Shelby will consider my message as a warning of such grave consequence that I will not see any of you men from the western mountains ever again. So, no, no one will follow you. You have my word on it."

Phillips nodded, turned and walked into the gathering darkness. There was much to do if he wanted to be gone soon. In less than an hour, he requisitioned the horse he had seen earlier tied up next to Ferguson's headquarters, gathered some corn, apples, some warm beef he smelled earlier, water, and retrieved his rifle. With his mind too charged up to think about sleep, he wanted to put as much distance as possible between him and Gilbert Town before the sun arose. *I'm heading home. Back to freedom. Back to my wife. If I ride hard and take only a few breaks to care for this horse, I should make it to Isaac's in two days, three at the most.*

CANE CREEK NORTHEAST OF GILBERT TOWN, NORTH CAROLINA EARLY AFTERNOON, TUESDAY, 12 SEPTEMBER 1780

"Look at them run, Allaire. I knew they couldn't stand and fight us. Once they see the power of our red coats, they melt away like snow on a warm spring day. There is no sense trying to follow them up in those hills; they're moving too fast."

Lieutenant Allaire watched the rebels scatter as he answered Ferguson. "You're right, sir. They're good shots, but there's just too many of us."

The two men paused for a moment to watch the last of the Rebels melt into the woods west of their location. "Have the men spread out and take anything we can use from these farms around here and then burn everything. I want to be heading back to Gilbert Town by early afternoon. You can find me under that tree over there if you need me."

Ferguson moved slowly to the large oak. He did not want to admit it to anyone, but his injured arm required considerable care and rest. After three years he was still learning to depend more on his left hand and arm, evidenced by the gradual improvement in his left-handed writing. It was a struggle, but all the practice was paying off. Sadly, he knew his marksmanship would never be like it was before. For now, he wanted rest.

The major and his formation of one hundred and forty men had started their march from Gilbert Town early this morning well before dawn to raid these farms twenty miles north of his base of operations, which, according to his Loyalist friends, was an area that harbored a number with rebellious leanings. While he expected to surprise his enemy, it was the Rebels who took the early initiative, ambushing his formation as he entered a narrow valley south of where he now sat. While his men reacted well to the initial fire and eventually gained the upper hand, the fight was sharp with both sides showing their mettle. Ferguson would not admit it to anyone except to himself, but the issue had been in doubt for a few tense moments.

Lieutenant Allaire walked toward him, interrupting his thoughts. "Sir, we're still looking around the area, but we've confirmed that the men we're up against belong to a local militia group commanded by Charles McDowell. We killed one of them and captured another seventeen including one captain, along with twenty pounds of powder and twelve horses. The prisoners say there were about three hundred of 'em in the area but that number seems high to me judging by the results of the fight. Our scouts confirmed that those who left are heading west into the mountains. I have some of our men securing all the approaches to our position while the rest are rounding up the beef and other food stuffs from the local farms. Got several wounded, including Major Dunlap. His wound appears to be severe."

Ferguson glanced up. Dunlap. The man had soldiered alongside him for almost three years. A man loyal to the core. The man with no mercy in his bones for any man who opposed the King and who, if given the chance, would tie a rope around every rebellious neck he found. "Keep pushing the men. I want to leave within the hour. It is unfortunate about Dunlap; I'll look in on him soon."

Leaning back against the tree, he considered his retreating foes. *With McDowell's men heading west, maybe they will pass on the word to the others living near Shelby that tangling with us is not in their best interests.* Thinking once again about Dunlap, rage played into the major's final instructions to Allaire. "Leave nothing these traitors might consider using later. Burn everything to the ground."

****

Less than a mile west of where Ferguson and Allaire talked, two survivors of the recent battle watched. They were well-hidden in some rocks and brush on a piece of high ground where they had an almost unobstructed view of the valley below them. "Look at those vermin down there. They're herding all the beef they can find. Bet they'll be butchered before nightfall."

"Things are gonna get tough for the folks left behind down there. You see that? Looks like them Loyalists are burning everything."

William Morrison grunted his reply. He was the older of the two at twenty-three. He had been in militia units for over a year, fighting at Bacon's Bridge, Monck's Corner, and at Ramsour's Mill. Having lived in this part of North Carolina his whole life, he could only watch as fire licked at the homes and barns of his friends down below. Sorrow and rage mingled together. He knew he couldn't do much about these atrocities now, but later, later there might come a chance.

"Sam, let's keep watch for a bit longer before we do what Captain Miller said; head west across the mountains to Sycamore Shoals. Never been there, but I'm sure we can find it."

Sam Mackie could not take his eyes off the activity down below. "You're right. We'll find it. Heard that Captain Vance is already there.

Right now, let's keep watch on these boys down below just to make sure they head back south."

They continued to maintain their vigil until the last of the Loyalist formation was out of sight heading back toward Gilbert Town. With two or three hours of daylight remaining, they started their trek west. Unless they could find some horses, they knew it would take them four or five days to get there. Morrison was comfortable being in the company of Sam Mackie. Like Morrison, Mackie fought at Monck's Corner. An Irishman by birth, like so many in these lands, he was tough, independent-minded, and an excellent marksman.

Mackie gave the scene one more look. "William, I'm looking to pay Ferguson back one of these days. He and that vermin, Tarleton, got a lot coming for what happened at Waxhaw and what they're doing to these good folks down there. Men like them don't deserve to live."

"You got a point there, Sam. A good point."

6. Challenge

Isaac Shelby's Cabin
Early morning, Wednesday, 13 September 1780

"WELL I'LL BE ..." SHELBY SAID ALOUD AS HE RECOGNIZED THE RIDER coming fast toward him as he came out of his barn. With Duke at his heels, Shelby walked up the road to greet the rider.

Slapping the man's back as Sam Phillips dismounted, Shelby said, "Sam, I thought you were a goner after Musgrove's Mill. Good to see you." Shelby studied the man for a long moment. "How'd you escape? Where are the other two boys who were with you? I see you got your rifle with you so that's good. Sit down and tell me everything."

Phillips knocked some dust off his clothes as the two walked toward Shelby's watering trough, both the horse and rider needing a cool drink. After several satisfying gulps, the man began his story.

"Good to see you too, Isaac. There were some days back a few weeks ago when I wasn't sure if I'd ever see these mountains again. Good to be back in this cool air again." Phillips took a deep breath, his head dropping down. "The other boys with me didn't make it. We got cut off near the end there. I was trying to stay with 'em to bring 'em home when I got myself surrounded. Since then, I've been the guest of Patrick Ferguson."

Shelby nodded. "Ferguson. Well it must be a good story since you got away from him with your rifle. His kind can be a nasty lot when they want to be. Anybody follow you?"

"No. I made real sure of that, doubling back every so often to check. For now, I'll make a long story real short. Three days ago Ferguson let me go. Even give me my rifle back. His only condition was that I bring you a message."

"What? From Ferguson? A message for me? What could he say to me that I'd be interested in? Is he ready to surrender?" Shelby asked with a wink.

"Not hardly. Actually he thinks his message is supposed to scare you off and everybody else around here."

JOHN SEVIER'S PROPERTY IN WESTERN NORTH CAROLINA
EARLY AFTERNOON, FRIDAY, 15 SEPTEMBER 1780

A number of small groups of men stood around the large open field inspecting the horses in the pastures, discussing the merits of what they saw in each of the steeds. At the two ends of the field were large flags made of white linen which marked the start and finish points of the contests of speed that were being held throughout the day, giving the prospective buyers a better indication of the investments they might be considering. Shelby slowly rode toward the largest gathering, knowing that the man he was looking for, the one who owned this field and who enjoyed hosting the horse racing and games of chance which drew such attention, would most likely be holding court in the center of that crowd.

The man did not see Shelby ride up as he was about to bring his latest yarn to a close, the story-teller holding everyone's interest to the last moment. Shelby and his brother, Moses, quietly sauntered up to the back of the crowd as John Sevier finished his latest tale, this one about a young Indian brave seeking to earn his manhood by fighting a huge grizzly. Without the privilege of hearing the narrative from the beginning, Shelby could only laugh politely when Sevier ended his story to the delighted applause of those assembled.

As the gathering slowly broke apart, Sevier spied his friend. "What a pleasant surprise. Isaac Shelby. You and Moses come to buy a horse or two? Or do you just want to lose a little of your money on a wager or two? We got some fast horses for you to look at if you've a mind to."

Sevier, a few inches shorter than the younger Shelby, smiled at his friend as he held out his hand. "Good to see you, Isaac. Heard you and your men put a whipping on some of those Redcoats." Looking into Shelby's eyes, Sevier said, "Glad to see you're still in one piece."

"Yeah, the men did themselves quite proud. We're blessed to have a lot of good men around here."

Glancing around at the knots of men around them, Sevier nodded, "You're right there."

Sevier paused to look around at the pastures. "Now I hope you've come to enjoy the fruits of your labor. I've already gotten into the pockets of my brothers and their friends and now I'm working to get some of David Vance's money. Since he was with you at Musgrove's Mill, he's the one who filled me in about your latest adventures. That man does know his horse flesh but..." He stopped. "Ah, Isaac, I know that look of yours. You got something more serious than betting on your mind."

"Can you and me take a little walk?"

"Don't see why not." Sevier smiled. "That'll give some of these other boys a chance to trade some of their money back and forth with each other."

Shelby and Sevier had known each other for years, having led many of the men who were in the field against the Indians earlier. Once out of earshot of the others, Shelby took his pipe out of his pocket and stuck it in his mouth. "Let me ask you, John, when somebody threatens to kill you and take all your possessions, what's your first reaction?"

"You know my answer. If another man calls me out like that, then we're fighting it out, the sooner the better. You came all this way to ask a dumb question like that?"

"I knew what you'd say but I still rode forty miles to get your reaction. This may take a few minutes."

When the two reached the edge of the woods, Shelby sat down on a nearby log as he described Phillips' capture at Musgrove's Mill and then the conditions of his release. After outlining Ferguson's threat a second time, Shelby added, "Seems to me that Ferguson doesn't know us very well if he thinks we'll heed a threat like that. I reckon he and Cornwallis have a mind to take control of everything east of the mountains and maybe even move further north if they can. Don't know that for sure but it seems that way to me."

Neither man spoke for a time as they gazed around at the mountains they loved, the trees near them now beginning to show signs of the coming fall—red, yellow, russet, and gold leaves from the hardwoods mixing with the shades of greens from the pines and evergreens. The taller mountains and hills to the west shielded the sun's light in places causing the valley to take on darker tones while the peaks of eastern mountains remained bathed in brilliant sunlight, the contrast a marvelous scene these two enjoyed many afternoons.

After blowing some smoke out from his pipe, Shelby looked around. "Been thinking a lot as I rode over here about living in these mountains. Yeah, we got the Indians to deal with but other than them, this land is ours to live and prosper as we wish. Folks that live here came mostly 'cause they were tired of others telling 'em what to do and how to do it. And now for another man, an Englishman at that, to threaten me and those who live here, it makes my blood boil. I resent that he even thinks we'd kowtow to him. And like you, most of the other men I know will feel exactly the same way."

"Kind of figured you'd say something like that." Sevier asked, "Since you've had a few days to stew on this, what do you think we should do?"

"Let's start by me telling a select few of the men here about the message and what Sam told me about Ferguson and his men. Where they are, how they are equipped, who their leaders are, and so forth."

After an hour of talking and going back and forth about what could be done, the two men returned to the larger gathering. It was almost time for dinner of roasted pig with some freshly- picked corn, and of course, some home brew made by those skilled in that art. Discussions about horse racing or betting were now a thing of the past.

✳✳✳✳

With the evening stars now overhead and the meal consumed, seven men sat around the low burning logs, each man now quiet in his thoughts as they absorbed Ferguson's message to Shelby, the words "Desist...I will march...hang your leaders...lay your country to waste" ringing through their minds.

All were experienced fighters, veterans of numerous short, savage battles with the Indian tribes who sought to regain their territory lost to the white settlers, and some, like Shelby, also had experience fighting the Redcoats. Each man was mentally and physically toughened to withstand the rigors of frontier life, its struggles, and its hardships.

They came from three distinct militia groups. David Vance, thirty-two, was a member of the militia commanded by Charles McDowell east of the mountains. Experienced from fighting the British at Brandywine and Germantown, he had spent the winter of 1777 with George Washington at Valley Forge. After moving south he joined McDowell's unit and took part in the fight at Musgrove's Mill. He commanded McDowell's men who were now camped at Sycamore Shoals, twenty miles to the east. The second group represented was the Washington County Militia headed by John Sevier. Because this was his home turf, he invited several of his subordinate leaders to join him at the parley: his brothers, Valentine and Robert, thirty-three and thirty-one respectively, and John Tipton. Shelby commanded the third militia unit, this one based in Sullivan County. Moses Shelby sat next to his brother. Although only nineteen, Moses already had a reputation as a fierce fighter that he earned at the siege of Savannah a year ago.

The reaction from those hearing Ferguson's message for the first time was a mix of anger and rage, hatred and disgust, resentment and bitterness. Without hesitation, all agreed that the time for action was now. While each militia was independent, it was clear from the outset that these leaders were united when it came to responding to Ferguson's threat.

Shelby summarized their discussions. "While we're all in agreement that we need to act forcibly, we also agree we need more men. Ferguson may have a thousand or so from what Sam tells me. Between our three units we can muster six hundred or so at the most to ride east since we've got to leave some back here in case the Indians decide to raise a ruckus. Seems to me we need to at least double our number, maybe even more. So where do we get more good men who think like us?"

John Tipton was the first to speak up. "I think William Campbell and his Virginians might want a piece of Ferguson."

"Yeah, William is a good man. Between him and his brother-in-law, Arthur, they might have three, four hundred men. Who else?"

David Vance was next. "I'm confident McDowell is ready to march against Ferguson and I'd bet the boys from Surrey County and Wilkes County would want to ride with us, too. Benjamin Cleveland and Joseph Winston are good men in a fight and I think they'll want a piece of Ferguson, especially Cleveland. If there's one man who'd like to hang every Loyalist he sees, that's him. And I suspect some South Carolina militia, maybe Sumter and some of his boys, might like to join us but I can't be for sure about that. What about Clarke?"

Sevier spoke up. "I like the idea about the Virginians and the North Carolina militia. Gettin' the South Carolina militias to meet up with us might be difficult depending on their situation, but we should keep 'em in mind. Just have to see how it goes once we get over the mountains. I like the idea about Clarke, but he's got to watch out for his own skin first."

"Something else to consider," said Robert Sevier, "is that there's definitely some bad blood brewing on both sides of the mountains. Last summer me and a few of my men gave a Loyalist who came from the east a new coat of tar and feathers. Heard recently he and some of his Loyalist friends wanted to get back at us for that little escapade. Since he knows the way here, I'd rather fight 'em east of the mountains to keep 'em away from our families and our land. Considering what

Tarleton did at Waxhaw, we may have a few who might like to meet up with him.”

****

Shelby and Sevier talked late into the night and then again the next morning. The two men agreed that messengers would be sent to contact William Campbell and that McDowell's men would be asked to contact Cleveland and Winston. All who could would rendezvous at Sycamore Shoals in nine days on the 25th of September. Time was short. There was much to be done: men to be notified and families to be cared for, provisions to be gathered, funds to be procured to pay for the supplies, contingencies for any Indian attacks to be considered. And in the meantime, where was Ferguson? What was he up to? And what was Cornwallis doing?

PLEASANT GARDENS NORTH OF GILBERT TOWN, NORTH CAROLINA
EARLY AFTERNOON, SATURDAY, 16 SEPTEMBER 1780

“Sir, seems to me all we're gettin' is a lot of lip and meaningless drivel from these slaves and these women. None of 'em saying anything we can use. We can only brow-beat 'em so much or the whole place will turn against us. Most of the able-bodied men are somewhere else 'cept for those who side with us and they're not saying much either. Some of 'em are still pissed off at us for killing some of their beef. They don't want to hear that is was a simple mistake.”

De Peyster let Lieutenant Allaire keep talking, his frustration showing. Their march to Pleasant Gardens, a good day's journey northeast of Gilbert Town, located near the intersection of several well-traveled trails, had the makings of a good operation, as their mission to apprehend members of McDowell's militia unfolded, but they had little to show for their efforts. No one was talking about the location of

Charles McDowell, his cousin, "Quaker Meadows Joe," or his son, Joseph. While the countryside was green with the produce of corn, beans, peas, carrots, turnips, and apple trees growing throughout the lush farmlands, De Peyster sensed a smoldering resentment toward his soldiers as they moved through the fields. Pleasant Gardens was truly a handsome property, an idyllic two-story wooden-frame farmhouse with several other log homes nearby with fields filled with crops in every direction, but underneath this picture of tranquility lay seeds of bitterness and animosity. It was clear that Pleasant Gardens was not pleasant to these of the loyalist persuasion.

"Anthony, you're right. We'll give it one more day and then head back to Gilbert Town. The major won't be pleased but we can only do so much. If we laid waste to these farms, we'd have more trouble brewing than we've got now. As you said, we're still reaping the whirlwind from killing those cows owned by that Loyalist farmer."

De Peyster could picture Ferguson's face when he reported that his two-hundred-man detachment had accomplished nothing of substance. He sensed many eyes watching every move he and his men made, but since they took no overt action, it was clear that McDowell's militia did not want to fight, at least, not right now. They only wanted to observe and report, observe and report. Many years of fighting Indians had taught them it was always best to fight on their terms, choosing the time and place that best suited them. The captain knew that, unless he could somehow surprise the Rebels, they would fight only when they thought they had an advantage. No sense in stirring the pot here any longer. The Loyalists who lived in these mountains and hills were now beginning to flock toward Gilbert Town for protection. *Once these folks start feeling secure from the safety we can provide, we'll get better information about where those who oppose are located so forays like this one can be more productive.*

"Anthony, spread the word. We'll head back to Gilbert Town tomorrow. We're not accomplishing anything by staying here any longer. Gather up what supplies we can this afternoon and make sure we give these farmers a fair price for what we take from them. We'll leave at first light in the morning."

ISAAC SHELBY'S CABIN
EARLY MORNING, THURSDAY, 20 SEPTEMBER 1780

"What do you mean Campbell doesn't want to march with us? Doesn't he realize what's going on here? Moses, this is our best chance to put the British in their place."

"I know. I told him all that. He said he knew how valuable his men would be to our campaign and he agreed the British had to be opposed. But he said he'd rather fight Cornwallis when he comes closer to Virginia. Didn't make a lot of sense to me since he'd be giving up too much land before that but I didn't want to argue with him anymore."

Shelby's patience wore thin. *Why didn't Campbell understand? It was so simple. Attack the British at a time of our choosing with a superior force. Only one thing left to do.* "Moses, I'm sending him another letter and this time I'm making it stronger and I want you to carry it back to him. At the same time, I'll send a similar letter to Arthur Campbell, William's cousin and brother-in-law. Arthur is the commander of the Virginians but in name only. Hopefully, between the two letters we'll get some action out of them. We need those Virginians. They're good fighters and we need 'em. Grab whatever food and water you need. Be ready to ride in an hour."

Shelby went right to work, the two letters containing much the same information about the situation, but the letter to William emphasized two keys this campaign required. First, some men would be needed to guard against an Indian attack. Then, with the homeland secured, the rest of the men could head east to defeat Ferguson. Without Campbell's men, there simply were not enough men to accomplish both. Shelby and Sevier needed his help. The letter to Arthur was more in the form of a plea for help.

Within the hour both letters were on their way. Shelby and the other leaders did not have time to spend worrying about the response as the mountains hummed with activity. Grist mills like those owned by Baptist McNabb and Mathew Talbot worked day and night grinding fresh corn for the soldiers' bread. When it appeared that financial backing was required to insure payment was made for the supplies needed, both Shelby and Sevier pledged their personal assets to cover the expenses of the preparation.

John Sevier's new wife of only a few months, the former Catherine "Bonnie Kate" Sherrill, spent much of her time repairing the clothing for the Sevier men to wear into battle. Sevier watched her with mixed emotions as his first wife, Sarah, had succumbed to pneumonia in the early spring, leaving John alone with their ten children. To see Bonnie Kate jump into these tasks so quickly, like so many other wives who supported their husbands, greatly pleased him.

For their part, during the day the men tended to their horses, cut firewood, brought in all the crops that could be harvested, and finished critical home repairs. In the evenings, their attention turned to the upcoming battle as they sharpened and maintained their tools of war: their knives, their tomahawks and hatchets, and most importantly, their rifles.

Almost all of the men who would gather at Sycamore Shoals carried a long-barreled rifle. Some called their weapons a "Kentucky rifle," while to others, it was known as a Deckhard or Dickert rifle, named for the Pennsylvania craftsman who first made these weapons of great accuracy. In the hands of a skilled marksman, this weapon could be counted on to deliver a .50 caliber bullet within a one-foot circle at a range of close to two hundred yards. And it was a fact that most of the men who would gather at Sycamore Shoals were better than good with their weapons.

Along with this obvious advantage in a fight over a long distance, the weapon had several disadvantages. No bayonet could be fixed to the weapon, which placed their men at risk if the British made a close-in bayonet charge. Second, the rifle was relatively fragile, making it usable as a club for only one swing or two. And third, it took almost a minute even for the best-trained rifleman to reload and fire his next shot. With all these factors considered, while the Americans had the advantage in a long-range fight, the advantage shifted to the British if the fight came at close range.

Work progressed at a fever pitch. September 25th was only five days away.

LORD CORNWALLIS' ARMY, SOUTH OF CHARLOTTE, NORTH CAROLINA
EARLY MORNING, FRIDAY, 21 SEPTEMBER 1780

The acting commander of the Legion, Major George Hanger, stood steady as Cornwallis' gaze seemed to penetrate deep into his soul.

"What happened, Major? You had your men and a detachment from the 71st Regiment with you. How could you be taken by surprise by this rabble, this band of malcontent, misinformed dissident farmers? Explain that to me. How did you let this happen?"

Hanger knew bad news never got better with time. His only chance to remain in command was to tell the unvarnished truth to his commander. To lie about the event would only bring greater shame and disgrace.

"Sir, from what we could tell, the Rebels, maybe three to four hundred of them, used the night to sneak up close to our positions. At dawn, just as we were preparing to send out patrols, they attacked from three directions. One advance was made with cavalry, the other two by foot soldiers. They pushed us with such vigor we had great difficulty in stopping their momentum. And then when our men began to gain the upper hand, these insurgents took what supplies they could and vanished. Almost like ghosts, they melted into the woods. The entire action took less than an hour."

"How many of them did you kill? Capture? What were your losses?" Cornwallis asked as he glared at the man.

"Our reports to date indicate we did not capture any of those who attacked us. Around fifty of our men were wounded or killed. We lost nearly one hundred horses and over one hundred weapons to the enemy. The plantation home at the center of the battle was put to the torch before we left."

Cornwallis' silence spoke volumes. Finally he said, "It appears to me that those who attacked you are more professional in their use of military tactics than your men. They use the cover of night to get in position to attack at a time and place of their choosing. They make a complicated attack using three avenues of approach causing us a great loss of men, horses, and weapons. Then they retreat so adroitly we have nothing to show for our efforts except one burned down home. Do I have that about right?"

"Yes sir."

"Tell me, from what has just occurred, which sounds like the more professional organization—us or them?"

When the officer made no reply, Cornwallis spat out. "You are dismissed. It is only because Tarleton remains under the doctor's care and your long service to the King that I do not remove you from this command here and now."

After the discouraged officer left, Cornwallis turned to his aide. "Brown, our men are tired of marching, and of being attacked and shot at by ghosts who can fade away as quickly as they come. Our men are losing their edge. And I am tired of waiting for the sick to heal. We have moved too slowly and have given the enemy too much time to prepare. I will waste no more time. I want to be at Charlotte in three days."

REBEL FORMATION EAST OF CORNWALLIS' POSITION
NOON, FRIDAY, 21 SEPTEMBER 1780

"James, I'm truly sorry about your home. To see your beautiful plantation in flames is something I'll not soon forget. If I'd thought they might burn it down in retaliation...What will your wife and family do?"

"They'll be all right. My wife is a strong woman. We always knew it could come to something like this. Besides, we're not the first to lose something of value in this war. While we've lost property and live-stock, my family is still alive. My wife told me a few moments ago that some our neighbors will gladly provide for her and the children for as long as needed." Captain James Walkup, the plantation owner, smelled the smoke rising to the west from his burning home. "I can only pray that something good will come from all this."

Colonel William Davie looked at the short, plump man who stood before him. Walkup, one of the older men in the fight at age fifty-four, was a good man. It was his intimate knowledge of his property that allowed Davie's men to come out of the early dawn's light to totally surprise Cornwallis' eastern flank with one hundred and fifty men. A victory by anyone's definition, but at what cost? The man's home was now burning, his crops and land ravaged; his family displaced. Davie could only shake his head, loving the man all the more for his willingness to sacrifice so much for the chance at freedom. *Where do we get such men? Where do they come from? Men who are willing to give everything for the hope of freedom?*

"Yes, James, I agree. I can only say I believe we've got Cornwallis' attention. We served him notice that we North Carolinians will not knuckle under the King's rule without a fight. Some wars are won with one or two big battles; others are won by wearing down the enemy. I would classify what we did here in the latter category. A sting to be sure, but one that they won't forget. To insure that it doesn't happen to them again, I suspect they'll put more forces to guard their bas-es, taking those from men who otherwise would be out ravaging the countryside."

"Yes, I suppose that's right."

Davie studied the man once more. "One more thing, James. Your family's story of sacrifice will be heard throughout the land. Others will hear of it and be drawn to our cause because of the price you and your family were willing to pay for the hope of freedom. It may take some time for our freedom to become a reality, but I believe we will all see it one day."

The older man wiped the sweat from his brow as he said, "Thank you, William. I believe you're right. It'll make a good story for our children one day. But as for now, please excuse me. I must go and see to my family. I will join you again soon."

7. The Gathering

"LOOK AT ALL THE PEOPLE. GOT TO BE A THOUSAND OR MORE. WHO'DA thought there were so many in this part of the country ready to fight against them Redcoats? Look at 'em all: men, women, and children. If I didn't know better, it'd be hard to tell if this was a going-away party or some other big shin-dig like a church meeting or a wedding or something else."

Sam Mackie watched as more and more men filled up the large grassy field next to the south bank where the Watauga River narrowed into the shallower, fast moving waters known as Sycamore Shoals. The area was encircled by hills north and south, all of them now rich with the deep, vibrant colors of fall. A large, log fort stood some distance away from the river at the southern edge of the grassy area. With all the activity around its gates, it was clear this was the center for all these proceedings. "Sure glad Major Vance picked us out a good spot for our men; otherwise there might not be anyplace left. Nice soft spot. Lots of firewood nearby and no pesky ant hills around."

William Morrison sat back against his saddle but didn't say anything as he, too, made his observations of the comings and goings of so many people. Finally he said, "Got to tell you this ain't what I expected. No sir, when the captain told us to head here after that fight at Cane Creek, this ain't what I expected at all. I figured we'd be hiding out in the woods; not enjoying the fresh air out here in the open.

Mackie nodded, "Yeah, you're right about that. One man over by the river told me folks in these parts, both whites and Indians, have been coming here for years. Have had some big meetings here over the years. Told me that the Indians call this place 'Broken Waters.' Even heard somebody say that Daniel Boone started one of his trapping trips into the Kentucky territory from here some years back. Easy to see why folks would meet here. It's easy to find. The field is open and flat. Plenty of good clean water flowing in the river. Tucked back here in the hills like this means the weather ain't so bad. And it's central to many of the folks who live in these parts."

"Peaceful, too. Like I said, if I don't know better, I'd say this was a big fall picnic. Women and children everywhere; easy to keep the horses and cows penned up. After what we've seen lately, it's good to hear those fiddlers strumming out some good tunes and watching folks just going around greeting folks they ain't seen for awhile. Heard a man making some pretty music from some stringed wood instrument down by the river. Really nice tunes. Got a bit of a twang to it but its not overpowering if you know what I mean. Never heard anything like that before."

"I think you're probably talking 'bout something called a dulcimer. Watched a guy play it one day. He told me it was easier to play than a fiddle so I tried it for a minute or two. Wasn't easy for me, I'll tell you that."

"Something else I noticed. If you look real careful at the men, you'll see horses getting cared for, guns and ammunition being checked, and most of the men gathering in small clumps with some serious looks. And you notice something else? Normally when you have a big get-together like this, there's always a shooting contest, but there ain't none of that going on around here. Very strange."

"You know, you're right. I suspect everyone's conserving all their ammunition and gunpowder. Heard anything about when we're leaving?"

"A few of our boys said Vance told 'em we'd be leaving early tomorrow morning, but if I've learned nothing else in my militia time, best we be ready to move on short notice. That's why I ain't spreading my stuff out too much. Just like Shelby's men over there by the fort and Sevier's boys over there by the river. They're staying close to their gear in case they get the order to ride, even though their kin are moving about."

"How many men you think Sevier and Shelby got with 'em? I'm betting about two hundred men in each outfit. Most of 'em look big and tough. How many we got?"

"Maybe close to one-fifty. That includes those like us who were at Cane Creek. And when I was over at the river early this morning, I heard talk that we're waiting for more men coming from Virginia. They'll be a welcome sight if that's true. The more we got going with us, the better."

Both men sat back closing their eyes knowing that once the movement across the mountains began, rest would be at a premium. Even though the noise level of the quiet meadow was higher than normal, it did not take long for these two to begin an informal snoring contest.

Despite the slumber of these two men, preparations continued around them as some made more bullets or sharpened knives, or cleaned and re-cleaned rifles. Others rechecked their equipment, all while passing on information and gossip and rumors. The physical strength of these men was hard to miss for whether they were short or tall, thin or brawny, each man moved with a confident stride, a purposeful spring in his steps. Most were unshaven and hair cut reasonably short as long hair was hard to keep clean in this environment. Though their formal education varied, as a whole, these men had the unparalleled ability to live and thrive in the wilds that few could comprehend.

And though they wore no uniforms, all dressed in a similar fashion: long buckskins or homespun wool which hung below their knees, with some kind of belt around their waist; moccasins or big leather boots protected their feet. Combinations of coonskins, hats with broad, wide brims, and tricons made up their headgear. Each had a drinking cup, most made from a cow horn, and a leather bag or pouch which some referred to as a wallet which was stuffed with their meager provisions of food and ammunition. Most had a wool blanket for sleeping or for protection from the rain and snow that would be rolled and strapped around their backs. And each man carried his gunpowder in a powder horn, many of which had elaborate carvings.

The center pieces of each man's equipment were his weapons: combinations of knives, hatchets, tomahawks, and, most importantly, his rifle. Without it, the man would be nothing more than an observer. The rifle made each man a hunter, a protector, a defender, and an attacker all in one.

****

Inside Fort Watauga, the large two-story log structure that had been constructed in 1772 when the first settlement outside the thirteen colonies was formed, the militia leaders gathered around the low-burning fireplace. The songs of the day, *The Rebels, Yankee Doodle*, and *Volunteer Boys*, could be heard faintly through the walls as they sat quietly, waiting.

Sevier looked over at Shelby. "Any idea when Campbell and his boys will get here? I know you said he's coming, but we both know we don't want to wait past tomorrow to start."

"Last message I had was that he'd be here today," Shelby said as he fingered his pipe. "I'm just glad he's coming. Convincing him took more effort than I figured it would. Moses and a few other messengers burned up some good horses to make sure he understood how important it was for him and his men to be here."

"What do you think finally convinced him?"

Shelby stopped to light his pipe. "I think it may have been the letter I sent to Arthur. Once he understood how important it was to move against the British, I think he helped get William fired up."

Sending a puff of smoke upward, he continued. "If William says he's coming, then he's coming. We still got four or five hours of daylight. They only had about thirty miles or so to get here from Abington, so if they started before sunup, they should be getting close. As long as they get here before dark, I think we'll be ready to ride early tomorrow. For all I know, they may have even left yesterday to get here."

Glancing over at Major Vance, Shelby asked, "David, your boys ready? How many you got here with you now?"

"Little over one-fifty. That includes those who tangled with Ferguson at Cane Creek a few weeks back. And since Colonel McDowell's spreading the word about our coming, I expect we'll have a good number joining us once we get over to the east side of the mountains. Like I said before, I expect Cleveland and Winston will be there."

"Then I'd say, no matter what, we leave in the morning. If some folks are late, they can catch up." Shelby watched the smoke from his pipe ascend upward. "Lot of folks are involved in this enterprise. All the families helping their men. And thanks to Mary and John Patton, we've got some good powder. They went the extra mile to help us, that's for sure."

Sevier glanced up. "You're right about that. Those two been making good gunpowder in these parts for almost ten years now. Watched 'em do it one day. Getting just the right mix of saltpeter, sulfur, charcoal, and water is an art. Others make powder, but nobody makes it as good as Mary. Heard she learned it from her dad."

"Yeah, that's what I understand. Good thing you and I had some money to pay 'em. Five hundred pounds of good powder is worth that bundle of money I gave her. Always did like the motto on those bills—VI Concitae—'Driven by Force; Constrained by Necessity.' Kind of sounds like what this venture is all about."

Before anyone said another word, a messenger burst through the doorway. "Colonel, the Virginians are crossing the shoals now. Where you want them to bed down?"

Sevier looked at Shelby and nodded his head. "I know Isaac, don't say it. 'Oh Ye of Little Faith.' Let's go greet our comrades."

****

Colonel William Campbell, a man several inches over six feet tall, his frame strong and sturdy, cast an imposing figure as he led his men into the great pasture. After dismounting from his horse, he greeted Shelby and Sevier with a firm handshake. "Good to see you, gentlemen. I've got two hundred men and Arthur is an hour or two behind me with another two hundred. Glad it worked out that we could join you. Once he gets here, how many men will we have all together?"

Shelby winked at Sevier before he smiled at the big man in front of him. "With your four hundred and with what we've already got here, we are close to a thousand. Once we cross the mountains, we expect another three, four hundred to join us. I don't think Ferguson knew what he was getting himself into when he challenged us. I must admit, I'm looking forward to meeting that man."

FERGUSON'S HEADQUARTERS, GILBERT TOWN, NORTH CAROLINA
EARLY EVENING, MONDAY, 25 SEPTEMBER 1780

Ferguson finished off his dinner of venison and fresh vegetables with a large glass of red wine from his personal stock, the one he carried with him in his personal baggage from his time in Charles Town. Although he was unsure of the origin of the wine he now savored, the drinking of the fruit of the vine was something he enjoyed at this time each day. For him, this was his personal time, a time to reflect upon the day, a time to think. It was a habit he had enjoyed for many years. And while many of his nights had been filled with positive reflections, tonight was not one of those nights.

Was I wrong in sending that message to Shelby? Was I too hasty in thinking that the man and those like him would back down? Could my letter have the opposite effect, stirring them up to react to my challenging their manhood? It has been what, almost ten days since I sent it, and there is still no word of any activity west of the mountains. Is that a good sign or one that should concern me? My spies have no information. Nothing. Is this the calm before the storm?

After taking another healthy gulp of the refreshing nectar of the grapes, Ferguson paused. *The best thing is to keep sending scouts toward the mountains to the north and west. That's the direction they will come from—the north or the west.*

With that settled for the moment, he walked into the area of William Gilbert's house he had designated as his personal living space. It was there that the two young women who traveled with him spent the majority of their time. Besides the wine each evening, Ferguson also enjoyed the company of his two Virginias, Virginia Sal and Virginia Paul. As he opened the door to the room, he reminded himself *Rank truly has its privileges.*

SYCAMORE SHOALS
EARLY EVENING, MONDAY, 25 SEPTEMBER 1780

As dusk began to give way to evening, those encamped around Sycamore Shoals' great meadow settled down, the smells of the roasted beef, venison, and pig filling the night air, the soft melodies of the fiddles and dulcimers giving way to quiet prayers voiced by some, and to the fantastic stories told by others. While the uncertainty of the days ahead lay heavy on the hearts and minds of many, apprehension was mixed with a sense of anticipation of the challenge before them. Almost all sensed the importance of what lay ahead.

Despite having faced the Indians and the Loyalists in battle through the years, even those who had considerable combat experience still wondered, *Will I carry the family name with honor? Will I be brave? Will I face death with courage? God help me that I don't let my friends down when we face the enemy. God help me do what is right.*

One man who had ridden in with Campbell's Virginians asked himself these same questions. Although he was an experienced Indian fighter, he was also a man of deep faith. John Rhea, twenty-seven, had been taught well by his father, Joseph, a Presbyterian minister, to follow God. Even as he prayed that he would honor his family name, he knew in his heart he must honor the Almighty first. Honoring God was his first priority. Everything else was secondary. That was his call.

SYCAMORE SHOALS
DAWN, TUESDAY, 26 SEPTEMBER 1780

The multitude gathered in the meadow in large groups under their commanders: Shelby with his two hundred and forty men, Sevier with a like number, Campbell with his four hundred, Vance with one hundred and sixty of McDowell's men, and William's four hundred Virginians. A smoky haze spread a blanket of cool air over the valley. When everyone crowded in close, John Sevier introduced his friend, Reverend Samuel Doak.

"The time to march has come. All of you are loaded up. You know where we're going and you know why. Many of you know Reverend Doak. He's a good man. A God-fearing man. I asked him to say a few words to bless us before we head out. Listen to his words, his thoughts, his blessing. And as soon as the Reverend gets finished, mount up."

With no time to waste, the preacher, age thirty-one, looked over all those assembled. He noted that the wives and children huddled close to their men, whispering their farewells as the cattle and horses shuffled in the background, sensing the time to begin was near.

The reverend held up his hands to gain their attention. Doak was a large man, one who dwarfed many in his audience. Educated at two colleges in the east before he moved into these mountains two years prior, he now was pastor of Salem Church. He was known in these lands as a man who had a passion for learning and was beginning to consider how he could start a school of higher education in the area. Respected by many, he was a man who spoke with the calm assurance as one who was close to the Almighty. His words spoke to the hearts of all those before him, his voice spreading over them strong and clear.

Each in the audience caught bits and pieces of his words and phrases, but whatever they heard and remembered, it nourished them in the days ahead.

"My countrymen, you are about to set out on an expedition...It will be filled with hardships and dangers...The Mother Country has her hand upon you...Fight for our liberty...The crown of England would take from its American subjects the last vestiges of Freedom...Your brethren across the mountains are crying for...help. God forbid that you should refuse to answer their call...The enemy is marching...Brave men, you are not unacquainted with battle...You have wrested these beautiful valleys from savage hands...Go forth then in strength...aid your brethren. Defend your liberty...Protect your homes. And may the God of Justice be with you and give you victory."

Then as a hush fell over the quiet pasture, Doak paused before he began to pray.

"Almighty and gracious God...we come to Thee, our Rock and our Fortress. Thou knowest the dangers and snares that surround us both on the march and in battle...In Thine infinite mercy, save us from the cruel hand of the savage and of the tyrant...Protect the homes of these fathers and husbands and sons who are far away fighting for freedom and helping the oppressed. Thou, who promised to protect the sparrow in its flight, we ask you keep ceaseless watch, by day and night, over our loved ones...Oh, God of Battle...Avenge the slaughter of Thy people. Confound those who plot for our destruction...Smite those who exalt themselves against liberty and justice and truth...Help us as good soldiers to wield the Sword of the Lord and Gideon. Amen."

****

At the word "Amen," John Rhea, like many of those around him, sat spell-bound. The scripture came back to him over and over, "...wield the Sword of the Lord...wield the Sword of the Lord." Having listened to his father preach on these same verses, Rhea was familiar with the passage, so he was surprised when he heard one man say to his companion, "I'm not much of a church man. What was the preacher talking about? Gideon. Who was he?"

Even as he readied a response, Rhea heard the other man provide wisdom for the ages. "Sam, the preacher was talking about a passage in the Good Book where a man named Gideon led three hundred men against a large army of Midianites. In one night Gideon and his boys whipped the enemy and killed a great number. The reverend was reminding us that no matter what the odds might be, with God's help, we too can be victorious. Even if we are small in number, we can whip Ferguson and whoever else we meet along the way if we trust in God."

Moments later as Rhea mounted his horse and took his place near Colonel Campbell in the formation, he replayed that short conversation he had overheard. *Yes, some of these I'm with are God-fearing men and some are not. Could it be that God has placed me here to be a witness for those who will fight with me against the British across the mountains? Only time will tell.*

This thought remained with Rhea for the rest of the day as the men headed up Gap Creek, their goal for the night to reach Shelving Rock, twenty miles up the mountains.

CHARLOTTE, NORTH CAROLINA
EARLY AFTERNOON, TUESDAY, 26 SEPTEMBER 1780

Lord Cornwallis was frustrated and angry: frustrated because of all the sickness and disease that had spread through his army and was slowing down his movement; frustrated because several of his key leaders like Tarleton were among the bed-ridden; frustrated because of his inability to secure his lines of communications back to Camden and Charles Town because small Rebel bands were causing havoc along the uninhabited parts of the vast countryside. The people of North

Carolina were greeting his army with clenched fists and rifle shots instead of the open arms that Governor Martin had hoped for. And now he was just plain angry and embarrassed by the way his soldiers performed as they engaged the rabble to their front. This was no way for the King's Army to act. Certainly no way for men under his command to act. No way at all!

Cornwallis had watched the debacle from behind his leading units. The mission of the Legion and some of Colonel's Webster's light infantry had been quite simple. They were to lead Cornwallis' twenty-two-hundred-man force into the center of Charlotte, sweeping aside any opposition in their path. Cornwallis knew Major Hangar would not be as aggressive as Tarleton, but what he had just witnessed was totally unacceptable. *Why did sickness have to grab hold of Tarleton? He would not have let these insurgents hold him back. He would not have stopped his charge. He would have rolled over them with a vengeance. But the soldiers commanded by Hanger stopped their charge. Twice they charged and twice they were repulsed, turned back by a handful of men. Soldiers tend to mirror the personality of their commander. What does this say about Hanger?*

Cornwallis could stand it no longer. He rode into the midst of the cavalry, their heads down, sweat on their brows, blood dripping from their wounds, horses breathing heavily.

After ordering Hangar to charge once again, Cornwallis' face grew red with rage as the men were slow to move. He tried to look each Legionnaire in the eye as he vented, "Legion, you outnumber your foes fifteen to one! The enemy is three hundred yards away. Think of your victories at Charles Town, at Waxhaw, and at Camden. And now this?"

He paused for a long time before he shouted out, "Colonel Webster."

The man who had been near the rear of the formation galloped up. "Yes, sir?"

"I want your men to take the lead and show the Legion how an attack is be conducted. Legionnaires, watch as Webster's brigade shows you how to fight! Watch and remember!"

After a few short orders, Webster's men appeared at the front of the formation and began their movement toward the enemy. Cornwallis, with Captain Brown by his side, took pride in Webster's slow but steady advance, forcing the Rebels to retreat from the stone-walls near the courthouse they so vigorously defended.

With the mission now accomplished and his anger under control, he turned toward his aide. "Look around. Look at this little town. Forty houses, two streets that cross each other. A court house in the town's center. And we've been on the march for eighteen days to get here just to be halted by those few men? Am I missing something here? Have the enemy gained a new spirit or have our men just grown weary?"

Brown sat still on his horse for a moment studying Webster's men as they conquered the last obstacle, a drill he was well familiar with. "It is true it has taken us some time to get here, but you have marshaled your forces as best you could. We could not move quickly with all the sickness we have experienced. And perhaps we underestimated the enemy. Perhaps Governor Martin painted too rosy of a picture suggesting we could expect a more cordial reception."

The captain steadied his horse as a few bullets whizzed close by them. "These are proud men who live here. They are not going to give up without a fight. They have toiled long and hard and they have tasted independence from the Crown for the last five years. They know every foot of this land and it seems to me that they intend for us to pay with our blood for each step we take. It will be a fight of wills."

Cornwallis considered his aide's words. Brown is right. Everywhere our men turn, well-aimed bullets greet them. Every orchard, every farmhouse, and every barn shelters a potential ambush. While our numbers are great, these endless skirmishes over the past six days have the men on edge. This unending harassment has cost us dearly. Our morale and our confidence have been shaken. I put too much confidence in Martin's words. I should have known better. The man is a governmental appointee. He knows next to nothing about true leadership. His calculations are made only from the perspective of personal gain of power. I was a fool to listen to him.

"So you think we should retreat? Give up our plan? Recall our forces?"

Brown smiled, watching what appeared to be the last of the insurgents race away into the wilderness. "Sir, we have a good plan. Our forces to the east are getting well established in Wilmington so we have that port to supply us. Major Wemyss may struggle for a time against those to our south, but he will eventually prevail. As long as Major Ferguson keeps our left flank secure, our main body will be able to wear down whatever forces oppose us. Then when the time is right, we can move north. There will be casualties along the way, but there always are."

Cornwallis sat still. *Yes, I have a good plan. The enemy is more resolute than I anticipated, but in time, we will weather this storm.* "You are right. The key is Ferguson. Have you selected us a place for our headquarters yet?"

****

Not more than a mile away to the east, observing the last of the fight from a small hill, the twenty-four-year-old leader of the rebel forces, William Richardson Davie, smiled with grim satisfaction. His men had performed admirably these past few days, harassing the British at every turn, maintaining the initiative, moving forward when opportunities came their way, and retreating when faced with overwhelming opposition. His plan for the defense of the town had worked well as he deployed his forces in rows, causing Cornwallis' men to deploy multiple times, wearing them down in the process, because each time Davie's men fell back, they were covered by the next row to their rear. Captain Joseph Graham was charged with the last row, covering the retreat of the rest of his men.

Calling his officers to his side, Colonel Davie was joined by Major George Davidson and Captain Walkup. "Where's Graham?"

Davidson looked at the edge of the town where Cornwallis' men were now swarming. "Last I saw, the enemy was closing on him fast. Not sure he made it out. Three or four of our men are down and maybe another five or six wounded, hard to tell exactly. You see 'em, James?"

The older man shook his head. "Last thing I saw he was surrounded. No way we could have gotten to him, Colonel. I'm sorry. There was just no way."

Davie nodded. There wasn't much more to say. Graham's men were to cover their retreat and they all knew the dangers involved in their mission. He looked once again at Walkup. The man had been through a great deal these past few days; the loss of his house and fields, his family displaced, and now his friend probably dead. *Men like these are hard to find, but I can't dwell on this. The enemy is too close. I must consider what is best for all.*

"Get the word to all your men to head north and east to the place by the river we talked about a few days ago. We'll meet there and plan our next move."

After the officers gave Davie a quick salute and rode off to execute his orders, he took one last look toward the town, hoping to catch sight of Graham. For some reason, the pain in his thigh suddenly grew in intensity, the wound a result of an injury he suffered during the Battle of Stono months ago. As the pain subsided, he stared again at the battlefield. After a few minutes without seeing anything to his liking, he wheeled his horse about, heading for the rendezvous. He could only pray that somehow Graham was still alive.

****

With dusk getting closer, Susan Wilson felt safe enough to leave the small log cabin she shared with her mother. They needed water and the stream was not far away. The bullets had flown in many directions throughout the day, several smacking against the heavy wooden siding of their home. Carefully she made her way to the stream. It was there she discovered the man.

The twenty-year-old soldier had three bullet wounds in the thigh and six saber wounds in his neck and head area. Dried blood colored his clothes. Nearly delirious from the loss of blood, the man whispered to Susan, "They wanted to finish me off...but one of their officers told 'em...not to waste ammunition...After they left, I crawled here."

Knowing she could not help the man by herself, Susan rushed home to get her mother, and with considerable effort, the two women managed to drag the man to their home where they cleansed and dressed the man's wounds, beginning the recovery of Captain Joseph Graham.

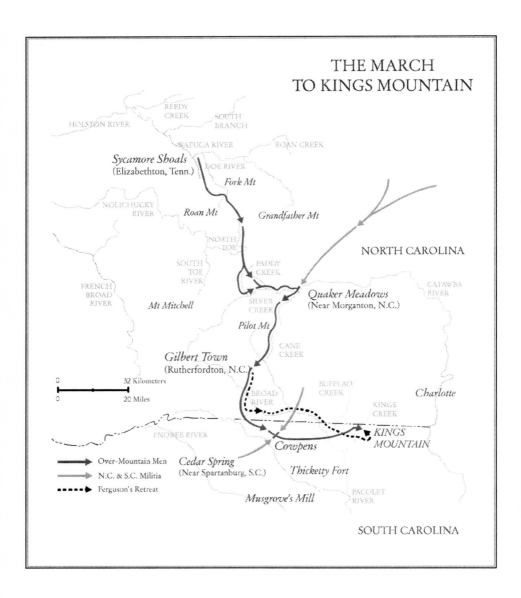

THE MARCH
TO KINGS MOUNTAIN

REEDY CREEK

SOUTH BRANCH

HOLSTON RIVER

WATUGA RIVER

ROAN CREEK

Sycamore Shoals
(Elizabethton, Tenn.)

DOE RIVER

Fork Mt

NOLICHUCKY RIVER

Roan Mt

Grandfather Mt

NORTH TOE

NORTH CAROLINA

SOUTH TOE RIVER

PADDY CREEK

FRENCH BROAD RIVER

Mt Mitchell

SILVER CREEK

Quaker Meadows
(Near Morganton, N.C.)

CATAWBA RIVER

Pilot Mt

CANE CREEK

Gilbert Town
(Rutherfordton, N.C.)

BUFFLAO CREEK

Charlotte

0   32 Kilometers

BROAD RIVER

KINGS CREEK

0   20 Miles

ENOREE RIVER

Cowpens

KINGS MOUNTAIN

Over-Mountain Men

N.C. & S.C. Militia

Ferguson's Retreat

Cedar Spring
(Near Spartanburg, S.C.)

Thicketty Fort

Musgrove's Mill

PACOLET RIVER

SOUTH CAROLINA

8. Over the Mountain

Shelving Rock, North Carolina
Late Tuesday afternoon, 26 September 1780

"LOOKS LIKE WE'RE ALMOST THERE. GLAD TO GET PAST GAP CREEK and Doe River Gorge. Climb wasn't too bad 'cept for the snow. If we have to fight much more of that stuff, me and my horse will both be worn out. No matter how many times I come through that gorge, I'm always glad to get here. Always look forward to this beautiful flat meadow. My horse is, too."

William Morrison glanced over his shoulder at his friend Sam Mackie. "I know the feeling. Now if the colonels will just figure out that all these cows we brought along to feed us are slowing us down, we'll make some good time."

Mackie smiled. "They're colonels, ain't they?" He laughed, "They're good men and I've got faith in 'em to do the right thing, but sometimes, I think they need a bigger dose of common sense. Glad we're near the front of this formation. Imagine those boys in the back are really having a rough go of it."

A few more minutes passed in silence before Morrison spoke up. "Looks like the boys ahead are splitting up to make camp. I'm ready for us to put up a little lean-to, get a fire going and get some rest."

Once the entire formation reached the flat area of Shelving Rock, the colonels made a quick decision, one that was applauded loudly by all the men, including Mackie and Morrison.

"I told you they were smart, Sam. The word is we're gonna butcher as many of these cattle as we need to feed us as we go over the mountains. What we don't butcher will be driven back to Sycamore Shoals. Least we'll have some good meat for the next few days. And since you and me are the most experienced hands at this, Major Vance told me that we're in charge of the butchering. He'll get some of the others to get the fires going."

Even though it took the two men most of the night, even with the help of several others to butcher and then cook the meat properly, Mackie and Morrison knew that their efforts would pay dividends in the end as the formation would not be burdened by the slower moving cattle.

ROAN MOUNTAIN, NORTH CAROLINA
LATE AFTERNOON, WEDNESDAY, 27 SEPTEMBER 1780

"John, we may have a problem."

"And that would be what? We got a few stragglers?"

Captain Robert Sevier, one of his older brother's subordinate commanders, sighed. "No. Wish that was the case. That would be pretty simple to solve." He paused for a moment, taking in a deep breath. "Seems two of my men, James Crawford and Samuel Chambers, have disappeared. We're not sure when they left. Could've been as early as last night once it got dark.

"You just hearing about this now?"

"Yeah, it seems that some of my men thought these two were in some other part of our formation. Once we got here, we held a roll count like you ordered so we could do some training and that's when we discovered these two were missing. I talked to my men who knew 'em best and from what I gather, it's possible, although I'd say now, more than likely, that these two got some Loyalist leanings in their blood and they took off last night after dark. Can't be one-hundred percent sure 'bout all that, but that's sure what it looks like. Since Crawford is older, he seems he might be the one who made the first move, but I can't be sure of that either."

John Sevier nodded. He knew both men and had trusted them, until now. "Did they say anything to anyone before they left? "

"Not a word. They're both fairly new to the territory and both of 'em pretty much kept to themselves. Guess that's why I've got a bad feeling about this. Based on their actions, I'm afraid they could be heading east, maybe to warn Ferguson."

John Sevier thought for a moment. *How soon could they reach Ferguson; two, three days maybe? Can't change the direction we're heading in now. Got to keep moving. Can't stop now.* "All right, Robert. I understand. I'll let Shelby and the others know. You hear anything else about this one way or the other, you let me know right away."

FERGUSON'S HEADQUARTERS IN GILBERT TOWN, NORTH CAROLINA
LATE AFTERNOON, WEDNESDAY, 27 SEPTEMBER 1780

Patrick Ferguson paced the floor of the room he was using for his office. *Where have McDowell's men gone? They couldn't have just vanished. Is it possible McDowell and his men have slipped in behind me and Cornwallis' main body? Unlikely but…? And now this message from Ninety Six is telling me Elijah Clarke may be heading north from Georgia to attack me. But there are no specifics in message? Regardless, I can't dismiss it. And there's still no word of any reaction to my letter to Shelby. Until I have some specific information, I have no idea which way I should turn.* The knock at the door brought him back to the present.

"Enter."

Abraham De Peyster closed the door behind him. "Sir, I heard you were looking for me."

"That's right. I need your perspective on a few things. First, what do you think about the message from Ninety Six?"

"While I'd like nothing better than to put a whipping on Clarke and his men because of what he did to me and my men at Musgrove's Mill, the message contains no specifics that we can go on. If Clarke is heading our way, it feels like we're sitting ducks in this town since we don't have much maneuverability here. I have the feeling something's brewing, but it's hard to tell what. I've got no facts to back that up. Call it a gut feeling."

Ferguson nodded. *I can't react to every rumor and innuendo but I must do something to regain the initiative. If nothing else, it might slow the enemy down some or cause them to expose themselves. Is De Peyster right? Is something brewing?* "I'm considering repositioning our forces to our south. When we crossed Green River coming here, I saw some good defensible ground near there. If Clarke is heading this way, that piece of ground would be a good place to counter any attack by him. We'd be far enough north to still accomplish the mission Cornwallis gave us and still be able to defend ourselves if need be. You remember the ground I'm talking about?"

"I think so. If we're thinking about the same hill, it's probably ten miles south of here. We could make that move in a day."

CATHEY'S PLANTATION, NORTH CAROLINA
EARLY EVENING, THURSDAY, 28 SEPTEMBER 1780

Although he was a strong man, James Keys felt the effects of the last two days in the saddle. The climb from Shelving Rock had traversed the sides of Roan High Knob, the steep sides of the mountain, straining both man and beast. And with the snow common this time of the year at these higher elevations ankle-deep, and in some places almost knee-deep, the going had been slow. After reaching Roaring Creek that second afternoon, the entire formation quickly made camp. And now after the third day's march, the going had been a bit easier as they traveled up the valley going both up and down some more steep slopes before reaching the plateau at this plantation near Grassy Creek.

Although he was only twenty-four, his six years of fighting Shawnee and Cherokee Indians and then British Loyalists made Keys the ideal man to be assigned as the First Sergeant of Captain David Beattie's company, part of Colonel James Campbell's formation. With a practiced eye, he was pleased with how his men were reacting to the march even though many had not ever traveled through these tall mountains before. Despite the rigors of the altitude, his men moved with a purpose, wasting little time on trivial matters.

While Beattie's company was the first of the units marching behind Colonel Campbell's command group, Keys noticed the actions of one of the men ahead of him. This man, a little older than most, was Campbell's flag bearer. Keys knew the man by reputation only, but his bearing marked him as a man Keys wanted to know more about. He took that opportunity once they halted for the night, after first seeing that his men were taking care of their bumps and bruises and had constructed some kind of shelter for the evening.

Walking over near the campfires of the colonel's entourage, he spoke to the man who was a little distance from the officers. "John Rhea, I've got to ask you, I noticed you manage to go through each day with a peaceful contented look on your face. Good weather or bad, steep climbs or treacherous descents don't seem to faze you in the least."

At that Rhea smiled. "Guess the easiest way to say it is that my father taught me well. He wanted me to know the difference between the important and the unimportant."

"Not sure I understand."

"Well that's 'cause I'm probably not explaining myself very well. You see, my father was a preacher for a time out here in the wilderness and he learned to keep his perspective in all circumstances."

"I think I heard about him. Died a few years back, didn't he?"

"Yeah, he did. In fact he died three years ago as he was getting ready to move our whole family to Virginia from Maryland. On his death bed, he made me promise that I'd fulfill his dream for the family and move 'em out here to the land he loved."

"But why to the edge of wilderness? Why lower Virginia?"

Rhea watched the last of the setting sun's rays go behind the mountains to the west before he answered. "He and another man, John Lyth, were the first two preachers to go with the Virginia regiments against the Indians five or so years back. Turns out they were the first to preach in the wilderness north and west of here. Lyth was killed by the Cherokees a few years back. Yet from what my father experienced out here, he loved the land and the people so much, he was determined that our family would become part of these lands. After he died, I honored his wish."

"Now that you say that, I seem to recall your father. Heard him preach one time. Don't remember the words he spoke that day but I know I came away thinking he was a good man."

Rhea nodded. "Yes he was. Anyway, throughout his life, he made certain we understood the difference of what he considered important from the unimportant. He'd always say, 'Things of God are important; things of men are less important.' So for me, I try and keep my mind on the things of God first and the things of man second. I'm on this venture because, like Reverend Doak said a few days ago, God is on our side and He wants us to send the Redcoats and those who think like them back across the sea. Back to where they came from."

Rhea paused as he looked once again at the tall peaks and the heavy, thick woods in the valleys below. "That's why I'm here. Doing God's bidding. Traveling up and down all these mountains is difficult, but I feel like I'm where I'm supposed to be, doing what I'm supposed to be doing. Colonel Campbell is a good man to ride beside so that's pleasing to me."

Keys stood still, trying to take in all the man had said to him. "Quite a story. Never thought much about it in that way. I mean about putting God first. Appreciate your thoughts. You've given me much to ponder. I'll have to think on that some, about what you said—the important and the unimportant. May be something to that." Keys looked around at all the small campfires springing up all around them. "Get a good night's sleep, John."

As he walked away, Keys' thought more about John Rhea. *An interesting man. He's not here seeking revenge against these Loyalists. He's not*

*here like some others who survived Tarleton's attack at Waxhaw. And he
doesn't appear to be one who is troubled by Ferguson's calling out our manhood. Seems to me, he's here to fight for God, for a higher calling. I wonder
how many are like John Rhea? Men who believe God is calling them to fight
for freedom. As long as they fight, who am I to quarrel with their reasons?
As long as they shoot straight and true when the time comes, I'm pleased.*

CATHEY'S PLANTATION
EARLY EVENING, THURSDAY, 28 SEPTEMBER 1780

Campbell asked the question. "Any more word about those deserters,
if that's what they are?"

Sevier glanced up, still embarrassed by the entire affair. "No."

Shelby sat quietly for a moment before he spoke. "Since we're not
sure where those two are or how fast they're moving, I think we should
split up just in case Ferguson has had time to plan an ambush for us.
John, how 'bout you and me along with McDowell's boys could go by
way of North Cove? It is the harder of the two routes but we've all
been that way before. That way, James, you could take your Virginia
boys the other way, past Turkey Cove. It's a little easier but since you
haven't been that way before, it'll be tough enough and we'll send
some good men with you to guide you. That way, if Ferguson has set
up an ambush, he won't get both of us. Both routes still get us to Mc-
Dowell's place at Quaker Meadows two nights from now."

After a little more discussion, the matter was settled. The formation
would split up into two groups and meet up in two days.

FERGUSON'S NEW POSITION SOUTH OF GILBERT TOWN
LATE MORNING, SATURDAY, 30 SEPTEMBER 1780

De Peyster walked up to Ferguson's tent, finding Elias Powell sitting
by the small fire in front of the closed tent flaps. "Need to see the major. I got two men here he needs to talk to right away."

Powell glanced up at the two men the captain pointed to. He noticed there were guards at each side of the men. After he gave a subtle knock on the tent pole, Ferguson's aide disappeared inside the large tent. A moment later Ferguson emerged as he buttoned on his shirt.

"And what is so important?" he asked De Peyster with an edge of irritation in his voice.

Stepping forward, the officer spoke in a whisper. "These two men claim they're deserters from John Sevier's unit, part of a large group heading our way from the western mountains, part of a group led by Isaac Shelby. If they're telling the truth, it seems your letter may have stirred the pot a bit and there are those who are looking to pay us a visit."

Ferguson nodded. *Not the reaction I hoped for but at least now maybe I can get a better grasp on the situation.* "Interesting. Get Captain Chesney. Once he gets here, I'll question these two, but I want you and Chesney to listen to what our visitors have to say."

De Peyster gave the major a questioning glance. "Why do you want Chesney here?"

"Because."

De Peyster thought about that a moment and nodded. What Ferguson is doing makes sense. Chesney knows what these men are going through when they profess to be changing loyalties. Chesney had been a Patriot at one time. He understands why a man would switch sides.

Within a few minutes, Chesney, De Peyster, and the two deserters stood before the major. The two men were dressed in well-worn buckskins, and appeared to be quite fatigued. Nevertheless, when Ferguson spoke, they both stood straighter and taller, reminding Ferguson of Sam Phillips' rugged, tough form. "I understand you two came from over the mountains west of here and that you deserted from some rebellious men who may be headed this way to do us harm. Who are you and why should I believe you?"

The older of the two spoke first. "Name is Crawford, James Crawford. This here is Samuel Chambers. We're both part of Colonel John

Sevier's command and yes sir, the colonel and a whole lot 'a men are headed this way. They figure if they can get enough men together, they can give you a whippin' or at least that's their intent."

"So why did you leave them to tell me this?"

"We've both been loyal subjects of the King for a time and the thought of fighting against him just don't make sense to us. At first, we weren't sure what was gonna' happen, but then it became obvious. The more men Shelby and Sevier and the others can gather up, the more serious they got. You pissed off a bunch o' folks who don't take kindly to being threatened with that message you sent. We left Sevier four nights ago as we were crossing the mountains heading this way. Since there was just the two of us, we figure we moved a lot faster than the rest of 'em so we're probably two, three days ahead of 'em."

"You mentioned Shelby and Sevier? Who else is with them? What are their numbers?

"Major, when we left 'em, there were maybe a thousand men and that ain't no bull. And we heard more might be joining 'em when they get to this side of the mountains. As far as who's in charge, you got Sevier and Shelby, a big group of men from Virginia under Campbell, and then some more under McDowell. Rumor has it that Cleveland and Winston will join 'em north of here. Maybe another three, four hundred, but that's just a guess. You know how rumors are."

Crawford added, "Major, we can tell you this. These men are looking for a fight. Like James said, they're mad and you're the one they're after."

Ferguson looked at the two for another minute before turning his attention to Captain Chesney. "Captain, please assign these men to one of our companies and then report back here. See that these two loyal men of the crown get all the food they can eat and give them some rest."

Glancing back at the two he said, "Thank you for coming here under such dangerous conditions. I appreciate your loyalty to our King. Be assured I'll give you every opportunity to fight for him if the likes of these men you speak about get close to us. For now, go with Captain Chesney. Get some food and some rest. Thank you for coming here."

After the three men left, Ferguson closed his eyes for a moment. *A thousand men or more headed this way, most likely two, three days away or maybe more. Maybe that letter wasn't such a good idea after all. Can't help that now.*

Glancing up at De Peytser, the major said quietly, "Get scouts out to the north and west looking for any sign of these mountain men. In the meantime, we'll keep a watch for Clarke, although I'm less concerned about him now. Let's get all of our provisions in order so we can move south southeast if we need to in the next few days. That will get us closer to Charlotte. I'll send a message to Lord Cornwallis telling him of our situation. Perhaps he could send us some reinforcements so we can rid ourselves of these Rebels once and for all."

9. Uncertainty

Quaker Meadows, forty miles north of Gilbert Town
Late afternoon, Saturday, 30 September 1780

JOHN RHEA LOOKED UP FROM THE SMALL FIRE HE WAS TENDING NEAR Colonel Campbell's headquarters as James Keys approached. "James, you look worn out. Captain Beattie got you in a twist?"

"No, nothing like that. The captain's a good man to work with. Experienced. Level-headed. Doesn't get over-excited with too much, if you know what I mean. I'm just glad we all got here in one piece before Ferguson and his boys got in our way. Been worried for three days about those deserters. I didn't like us getting split up to get through the mountains, but it worked out all right."

Rhea nodded. Word had traveled fast throughout the formation about the two deserters and the reason for taking the two routes through the mountains. For both groups, the possibility of an ambush made for a slower march as each turn of the trail required a thorough examination of possible ambush sites. Despite the slower pace, the two forces reunited earlier this morning before reaching this vast grazing land owned by the McDowells. With the mountains behind them, both men knew everyone could now concentrate on the object of their travels—Ferguson.

With darkness only a few hours away, Keys' eyes swept over Quaker Meadows. It seemed to be a quiet, peaceful land of rolling hills, with green pastures nestled between the larger mountains to the west and the smaller ones to the east. A slow meandering stream that provided nourishment to the animals and the land added to the tranquility.

Rhea stood up and took a long look around. "Heard the Indians who lived around here long ago named this place Quaker Meadows 'cause there was a Moravian bishop who spent most of his time trying to convert 'em to his religion. After the man and the Indians moved on, the McDowells acquired the land and the name stuck. From what I can see, it'd be hard to improve on that name, Quaker Meadows."

Keys nodded but had nothing to add, his gaze directed more toward a large black man who was going from one group of soldiers to the next, passing on a few words to each knot of men before moving on. Appearing older than Keys, the heavily muscled man approached the First Sergeant with a confident gait.

Speaking with an educated tongue the large man spoke first. "Sergeant, my master said you and your men can take whatever you need. We got some cattle ready for slaughter that we hid from them Redcoats. The major said for you to eat your fill. He also said you can use whatever wood you need, even the fence posts. Anything else you need, just ask for me. Name's Moses."

"Thank you kindly, Moses. I'll pass the word. But where do we find you if we need something?"

Moses pointed toward the large, white two-story house a half mile or so north that sat on the high ground overlooking the entire landscape. "That's the Major's house. Just ask anyone in there and they'll get word to me. I manage the farm for the McDowell's so I'm always around. You have a good day. You be sure to get those Redcoats for us, all right?"

****

As he moved among his men to check on them and to pass on Moses' words, Keys saw two men he had known for many years heading in his direction, Thomas McCulloch, a man in his mid-forties, and John, his son. Their home lay only a few miles from Keys'. Because of the respect he had earned over the years for his uncompromising integrity as a prominent land owner, Thomas had recently been elected to command one of Campbell's companies for this campaign. Keys felt that without a doubt, John, the more seasoned fighter of the two, had then joined up for this campaign specifically to protect his father. *Good thing for you, Thomas. Young John has a reputation for being steady in battle and for being a crack shot.*

"Thomas, you and your men getting settled in for the night?"

"Yeah, we've found us a good spot over near the creek to the east." Thomas paused to wipe some sweat from his brow with his sleeve. "Since you young guys look tired, imagine what an old man like me must feel like. From what the Colonel and Major Edmondson just told us, we should be here for the night and then probably head south in the morning. Seems Ferguson is supposed to be thirty, forty miles south of here near Gilbert Town. David Beattie telling you the same thing?"

"That's the word all right. He also said that there could be another three, four hundred men joining us later today."

Thomas McCulloch scratched his salt and pepper beard, "Yeah. Benjamin Cleveland is coming with men from Wilkes County along with Joseph Winston's men from Surrey County. Be glad to have 'em both with us. Supposed to be here tonight. The more men we got, the better I like it." McCulloch looked around. "Heard there's some good beef around here. Where do we get it?"

"Up at the big house on the hill. John, how about you taking care of that while your pa and I sit a spell?"

Without a word, the younger McCulloch nodded as he walked across the meadow toward the mansion on the hill, Keys watching the young man's long, steady stride. "You got a good son there. Smart and tough. Listens good. Men like him will make this country great one day."

"Yeah, I believe you're right 'bout that, but for now, we've got to take care of business. Indians are bad enough, but these men with Ferguson are something else. Arrogant. Always seem to have their noses in the air. It'll be good to put this Ferguson fellow in his place."

Thomas McCulloch sat down, leaning back on his elbows, his mind suddenly filled with thoughts of his family. *This upcoming fight is for my children: Robert, Rachel, Sarah, and Mary. John's big enough to take care of himself but those other four are too young right now. These Loyalists, Redcoats, Tories—whatever name you call 'em—need to be stopped. It's time to show our mettle, our courage. I've had enough of their looting and burning and killing. Got to stop this now...Oh, Lord, help me get through this. Let me hug my children one more time.*

****

As darkness made its presence known, sentries guarding the road to the northeast halted the vanguard of a large group of men approaching Quaker Meadows.

Before the guards could utter a word, a large corpulent man who dwarfed his horse grunted, "Lookin' for Isaac Shelby or John Sevier. You boys know where they are?" The gruff voice of an older man filled the air.

The guards, not ones to be cowed by any man, even one who exhibited such bluster, asked, "And who would you be?"

"Colonel Benjamin Cleveland and Major Joseph Winston. Now show us the way, boys. We've been traveling for four days and we got Redcoats to kill."

****

After Shelby apprised the two newcomers of the details of Ferguson's message and what little they knew of the Loyalists' location, Cleveland smiled. "Ah, we'll find him. If you get me close enough, I'll even smell 'em for you. We just appreciate your thinking about us and letting us have a chance to pay our respects to Major Ferguson. Between Joseph and me, we've got three hundred and forty men so that gives us a total of what, around fourteen hundred?"

116

"That's about right."

Winston, a more reserved man than his friend, asked, "So given these deserters and all, what's your best guess about where Ferguson is now?"

"Last thing we heard was that he was at Gilbert Town. But that was a few days ago. Right now we've got scouts out looking in that direction. Nor do we know what his intentions might be. Seems he's got three choices. He could attack us. He could defend where he is. Or he could move south or east, either in the direction of Ninety-Six or toward Charlotte. For all we know, he might be asking for reinforcements from Cornwallis. But as far as I'm concerned, it doesn't really matter. We just need to find him first. Then we'll fight him."

Soon general agreement was reached. At first light the formation would head south toward Gilbert Town. To do anything else was unthinkable.

BETWEEN QUAKER MEADOWS AND GILBERT TOWN
EARLY MORNING, SUNDAY, 1 OCTOBER 1780

Keys marched at the rear of his company's formation, the pace steady as they headed south toward Gilbert Town. By mid-morning, brisk winds from the west brought in some fast-moving thick gray clouds, foretelling of a powerful storm heading in their direction. Shortly after noon, a heavy, pelting downpour turned the dirt road into a quagmire. *Can't move. Too much slipping and sliding. Got to be careful or our powder will get wet. If it was up to me, I'd stop now and get the boys under whatever shelter we can till this rain stops.*

At the front of the formation, Shelby and Sevier held a quick counsel with Shelby voicing the words Keys was thinking. "John, we can't see much. Don't want to do it, but I think we ought to stop and let the boys settle down a little. Let's get the others together and figure out the best place to holdup."

And with that, the two men consulted with Major McDowell who agreed. "We're almost to Bedford's Hill. My boys know this ground real well. Some of 'em fought against Ferguson and his men 'bout a month ago near here. I'll have my men guide your boys to where they can dry out some."

Staring at Shelby, McDowell added, "I know you don't want to stop Isaac, but we've closed the gap between us and Ferguson by a good seventeen, eighteen miles or so today."

AT THE BROAD RIVER, SOUTH OF GILBERT TOWN
LATE AFTERNOON, SUNDAY, 1 OCTOBER 1780

With the wide Broad River now between him and where he thought the Rebels might be, Ferguson called a halt and gave orders to establish his camp. Turning to his second-in-command, he stroked his chin. "Abraham, this is good ground. If we need to, we could fight them right here. Pass the word. Get our units placed in a semicircle around this hill overlooking the ford. While you get everything arranged, I will be in my tent at the top of this hill."

De Peyster surveyed the ground. "The rain's been beating down on us long enough so I'm sure the men will appreciate a chance to dry out. I'll get some scouts out right away. Anything else?"

"As I've been riding up and down the column today, I've heard some rumors; men asking why we are retracing our steps. Can't blame them for asking. Once you get everyone settled in, I want a short counsel with all our commanders. Then I want to talk to all our men. Want to inspire them a bit. We'll do that right after I meet with our commanders."

"I think that's a good idea. There is some grumbling. It's almost like these mountains can talk 'cause our men know we got men looking for us. Like we've talked about before, these men are not like regular soldiers who just obey and don't ask questions. These are part-timers, and while we don't need to question their loyalty to the cause, they want to know why they're being asked to do something. If it makes sense to 'em, they'll do much better."

The officer gave a quick salute. "I'll put the word out for the commanders to meet with you in about an hour."

****

As soon as Ferguson's commanders assembled at a small clearing below his tent, Elias Powell stuck his head into Ferguson's tent, but not before announcing his intent to do so. He had learned from past experiences that an announcement was best, as the two women, Virginia Sal and Virginia Paul, were always about.

Ferguson stepped out of the tent and walked down a slight incline toward his subordinate leaders. Senior in age was Colonel Ambrose Mills, leader of the Tryon Loyalists. Next to him stood Major Patrick Cunningham of the Little River Regiment, Major Zachariah Gibbs of the Spartan Regiment from the upper Ninety-Six area, and Colonel David Plummer, the leader of the Fair Forest Regiment from the lower Ninety-Six area. In addition there were other element leaders from the Dutch Fork Regiment, the Stevens Creek Regiment's element, and the Long Cane Regiment. Joining them were Captain De Peyster, Captain Samuel Ryerson of the New Jersey (Provincial) Volunteers, a very experienced unit, and Lieutenant Abraham Chesney. Back a little from these men were several others: Elias Powell, Doctor Uzal Johnson, the only physician in Ferguson's formation, and Lieutenant Allaire. Altogether, these officers represented a combined force of eleven hundred men.

"Gentlemen, as you know, there appears to be some attempt on the part of those living in the western mountains to disrupt our support of Lord Cornwallis' drive into North Carolina. Because we have little specific information about them, yesterday I sent Cornwallis a message requesting any reinforcements he could spare so we could teach these rebels a lesson once and for all. Since some of our men have questions and perhaps even a bit of doubt about our movements, I want to speak to all our soldiers. Assemble them in the clearing down below in the next few minutes. Later tonight I will meet with all of you here to discuss our specific strategy."

****

With the bulk of the eleven hundred now gathered around Ferguson, they made an interesting picture. The American Volunteers of one hundred and twenty men wore the traditional British redcoats as their outer garment, their military bearing and their discipline setting them apart. The militia units, on the other hand, wore a mixture of clothing. While some wore the British red, most wore woodland garb similar to the rebels who were pursuing them, with buckskins and shirts of varying colors and materials, moccasins, and hats made from coonskins or felt and hides of various animals. Regardless of their outer appearance, Ferguson noted the steel in the men's eyes as he stared at them.

With few exceptions, all of Ferguson's men were armed with the British rifle, the "Brown Bess." While many in the ranks would have preferred the long rifle carried by the men with Shelby and Sevier, the British leadership equipped these men with the Brown Bess because this weapon gave their men several advantages.

While the Brown Bess' effective range was only seventy-five to one hundred yards, it could be reloaded quickly as a trained marksman could fire a .75 caliber round three to four times per minute. Because the long rifle the rebel marksmen carried took nearly one minute to reload after each shot, British officers concluded it was far better to be able to fire three times the rounds per minute. But the primary advantage to the British was that theses rifles had a seventeen-inch bayonet made of cold steel that could be mounted on the front of the muzzle. In a close-in fight, a skilled soldier armed with bayonet was a foe to be feared.

When Patrick Ferguson stepped up onto a large rock to address the men arrayed before him, the rain had stopped. Patches of blue sky could be seen breaking through the clouds to the west. As he looked over the throng, the men murmured in low undertones until Ferguson blew his ever-present silver whistle, his personal signaling device that was always close at hand. When the men quieted down, the major, without preamble, launched into his short speech. As with Reverend Doak's talk to the men at Sycamore Shoals, not all the soldiers heard every word.

"Gentlemen, as you perhaps know, those who wish to do us harm may be coming...Unless you wish to be eaten up by these barbarians... men who have murdered your sons...showing their cowardice...if you want to see your wives and daughters abused by these dregs of mankind...it is now time to grasp your weapons."

He stopped for a moment to let his words sink in, his eyes trying to hold as many in his grasp as he could. "...The Back Water Men have crossed the mountains...moving this way...If you choose to be pissed on by these mongrels, say it now...your women will turn their backs on you...now is the time to be real men and protect them....Now is the time to show those who pursue us what we're made of.

"We are close to victory...We will meet these dogs soon...Send them home with their tails between their legs like the dogs that they are...Get ready, men. Get ready...Our day will come soon, very soon."

****

As the soldiers walked back to their lean-tos to continue to dry out, John Goforth walked beside his two younger brothers. All three were lean and wiry; John was the oldest by almost ten years, his two brothers not yet twenty. He did all the talking while the other two listened.

"You both know Preston'll be one of 'em we may face. Don't know which Rebel commander he'll be with, but he'll be there for sure. My gut tells me we'll be seeing him real soon. Even though our brother is over forty, the man is a good shot, almost as good as me. So be careful. Even though he's kin, I know he thinks we're wrong just like we think he's wrong. I got a bad feeling 'bout all this, but it's too late to change any of that now. I just hope our momma will be okay when this is over."

The other two young men nodded as they kept their heads down, their thoughts lingering on Ferguson's challenge. They cooked their meal of small bits of beef and some corn that night with another Tory they hadn't seen before. He was a skinny man. They did not know his name.

But as the time wore on, the skinny fellow began to mutter to himself. "I can feel it in my bones. They're out for revenge...For what we've done to them and to their children, to their families and for Waxhaw. Yeah, they've taken an eye for an eye many times, but so have we. It's 'bout revenge. That's what it is about. Revenge."

****

At another part of the camp young Josiah Brandon listened as his father, Thomas, carried on a conversation with Captain Aaron Bickerstaff, one of the company commanders of the North Carolina Militia. "Thomas, I'm telling ya, I'm ready for a fight with these Backwater boys. They've been talking big for a long time. Time we show 'em we can stand up to 'em like Ferguson said. Shelby and Sevier are tough men, Indian fighters and all, but our men are like 'em in so many ways."

"I'm with you there. They talk about us beating people up and killing some, burning barns and houses, yet they do the same to our kinfolk and our friends when they get the chance. And that man Cleveland. He's hung more Loyalists than his share. I'm ready to stand toe-to-toe with 'em to see who comes out on top. Me and my boy, we're ready to fight."

Josiah kept his head down as he sat staring into the fire. He was a tall lad, like so many others, a good shot. He knew he could fight, but was his heart in it? *I'm only here to protect my father. There's been so much killing and hanging and looting, that at times it's almost like a sport for both sides. When does it end? Yes, I'll fight, not for a cause, but because I love my father. It's the right thing to do.*

"Josiah, you haven't said much. What are you thinking?"

Josiah took his time before he spoke, his head down. "I hear what you and the Captain are saying and I agree with some of it. There's been plenty of killing on both sides, but nothing's really come of it. There are some good men coming our way. I fought with some of 'em when I enlisted on their side a few years ago—men like Captain Davidson and Captain Boykin, and Roebuck and McDowell. I only hope that in whatever is to come, I don't have to draw a bead on one of 'em."

The lad kicked at the dirt in front of him. "That's what I was thinking. Some men here have hard feelings against those men I mentioned. And some of us are here because our relatives chose this path and we want to protect 'em and be loyal to 'em, like I am with you, Pa. I just hope I do what's right when the time comes. I just ain't sure what's right. You asked what I was thinking and there it is. I can see drawing a bead on one of 'em to protect you, but it'll be tough to shoot someone I've fought with. In case you're wondering, there are others here besides me who think this way."

Bickerstaff stared at Josiah, knowing there was truth in what he said. *Some are with us because we give 'em the best chance for survival. But when the circumstances change, they might change sides, like those two from Sevier. Will they change back again when death stares them in the face? What are others like Josiah thinking? What will they do when Shelby's, or McDowell's, or Cleveland's men point rifles in their direction? How long will they fight for the British crown that they didn't feel truly beholden to?*

The two older men pondered these questions for a while longer as they stared into the burning embers of their fire. They found no answers to their questions except to know that the real answers would come when the two sides met in the next few days.

BETWEEN GILBERT TOWN AND CHARLOTTE
DUSK, SUNDAY, I OCTOBER 1780

"They still back there?"

"Can't tell for sure, but I don't like it. You see the way they looked at us when we told them we had to get a move on? They didn't believe us for a minute. They fed us all right, but things turned bad when they started asking questions."

"Rather than heading straight for Charlotte like the Major wanted us to, I say we move north first and see if we can lose whoever is trailing us. If the men behind are rebels and they find out we're carrying a message from Ferguson to Cornwallis, they'll kill us for sure. We ain't gonna be any good to Ferguson if we get killed before we deliver his message. I say our best bet of getting' to Charlotte is north, though it'll take us a day or two longer than we wanted."

Abram Collins stopped for a moment to think and to look back down the trail. He and Peter Quinn knew the area well, which was why Major Ferguson entrusted his message to them, but now things had turned sour. *It was good we stopped to eat, but we picked the wrong house. Once the man and his son started asking some questions, it was clear they didn't like some of our answers. Good we got out of there when we did.* "I think you're right. This wet ground will help cover our tracks. Better we get there in one piece than not get there at all. So what if a two-day walk takes a few more days."

Suddenly both men looked up as they heard a faint noise two hundred yards behind them. No time for any more discussion. It was time to move and move fast. Quinn led the way as the two men ran north. Collins was right on his heels.

LORD CORNWALLIS' HEADQUARTERS AT CHARLOTTE
EARLY EVENING, SUNDAY, 1 OCTOBER 1780

"Where are the reports from Camden and Charles Town? I have seen no reports in a week."

"Sir, we have received very few messages. It seems as though the rebels south of here are determined to stop any small parties of messengers. The only messages that have come through are those carried by our larger formations."

Cornwallis knew Brown was right although it didn't help his disposition to hear it again.

"You should also know that we continue to lose a man or two, sentries mostly, from sporadic rifle fire, but the situation is better since you ordered those pits to be dug to give the men some protection. Those units camped near the center of the town are a little better off than those camped in the outskirts like near Polk's Mill.

Cornwallis took a sip of his wine, his eyes staring at the wood burning brightly in the fireplace of the prominent house he occupied as his headquarters. "It is my understanding we are also beginning to feel a pinch on all manner of food supplies."

"Yes sir. And because of that, Lord Rawdon is planning to send out a large foraging party in two days to McIntyre's Farm, a place several miles north of here. Major Doyle will command the party. Our spies tell us that area holds quite an abundance of supplies we can put to good use. Rawdon plans to discuss his plan with you tomorrow morning."

"Good. At least he and Webster have not come down with whatever ails Tarleton. With that man still bedridden, I cannot depend upon the Legion to accomplish anything. Do you have any indication of when he will be up and about?"

"It's my understanding that it may be another week or so before he's healthy enough to resume his duties. While he knew you wouldn't like what I'm about to tell you, the doctor told me yesterday that the best remedy for Tarleton is rest."

Cornwallis stormed. "Rest? How am I to settle all this turmoil while my most audacious commander rests? Such rubbish. Rest!" After walking around the room several times, the man asked, "And am I to assume that all this difficulty with messengers also keeps me from knowing the whereabouts and activities of Major Ferguson?"

"Yes, sir. We've heard nothing from him since his last message that said he was expanding our influence in the Gilbert Town area."

"Do we know anything about what is happening near the mountains?"

"Nothing of substance. We've heard some wild rumors that tell of some Rebel movement north and west of here but nothing we can be sure of. As you know, with the general sentiment so much against us in this area, getting reliable information about enemy formations or intentions is difficult. Too much pent up anger amongst the townspeople. It's a wonder we get any information about anything. If I may speak frankly, sir, I'll be glad when Tarleton is able to lead his men once again. He's the one leader who can use the swiftness of his horses to stay ahead of those who oppose us. The rest of the command is generally bound to the pace of a man marching. And since the Rebels have many horses at their disposal, they seem to be a step ahead of us. I don't mean to be pessimistic, only realistic. Once Tarleton returns to duty, I think things will change quickly to our side once again."

Cornwallis looked at his aide thoughtfully. *Is Brown right or are his words pleasing because they are the words I want to hear? While I want to be optimistic, the Rebels have the initiative. And because of that, there are too many questions unanswered. What are their intentions? Their locations? Does Ferguson have control of the mountains? If he does, then once Tarleton is back on his feet, we can regain control of the countryside around here. Like it or not, everything revolves around Ferguson. Can he accomplish his mission? What is the man up to?*

"You may be right, William. You may be right."

10. Command Decision

THE RAIN STOPPED LATE IN THE DAY. IT WAS NONE TOO SOON AS WITH all this forced idleness, the men were restless, anxious to get moving. Keys sensed it as he moved from one small campfire to another.

"Glad to see you, James," John Rhea said as he sat near Colonel Campbell's fire. "Been quite a day. The boys are on edge. Had to get in the middle of two fights and a third one that was about to turn into quite a melee. Nothing serious, but the men are just keyed up and ready to fight somebody, anybody."

"Yeah, I've heard 'bout a few of 'em. What were they fighting about? Who was the better shot? Women?"

"All those things and more. Who killed the most Loyalists? Anything and everything. As I said, these are active men and they don't like sittin' around. They're ready to fight and since Ferguson isn't here, they're just blowing off some steam and energy. Had a few bloody noses but nothing of consequence that will be remembered after tonight. Things should settle down once we get moving again. The word is tomorrow."

Keys looked up at the sky. "Yeah, that's what I hear. The way the wind is blowing, tomorrow should be all right. All I know is the colonels are having some big powwow tonight. Once they finish, I'm sure we'll be hearing something. Least I hope so. Like everyone else, I'm ready to get this business taken care of."

Keys considered Rhea's thoughts. *Those who have never been in battle would not understand the tension building in these men. We've been search-ing for the enemy, looking under every rock, around every corner now for a week, and it will only get worse until we finally fight Ferguson. War can have longs periods of quiet and anticipation when nothing happens. Then suddenly, shots can zip by you, and you can find yourself in the fight of your life, coming perhaps from a direction in which you never expected. All this tension can wear on a man. That's why they are so tight. They're like a cocked rifle that is ready to fire. The sooner we find Ferguson, the better. Let's pray we find him before he finds us.*

FERGUSON'S CAMPSITE, FOUR MILES SOUTHEAST OF THE BROAD RIVER EARLY EVENING, MONDAY, 2 OCTOBER 1780

Ferguson assembled all his commanders. "Gentlemen, we've halted here because the weather is just too miserable to keep going. Besides, with all this rain, it'll be harder for them to track us."

The commander of the Fair Forest Regiment, Colonel Plummer, piped up, "I agree. I got some scouts out and they ain't picked up any trails behind us yet."

"Good, but just in case they spotted our camp at Denard's, our move here should throw them off a bit. Keep guards out and the fires low. Have the men keep their weapons handy. Remind them to keep their powder dry. For now, get as much rest as you can. Tomorrow we'll be moving before first light. It'll be a long day."

****

The two lieutenants sat near a fire within earshot of Ferguson's discus-sion with his senior leaders. The younger of the two was first to speak. "Since we got what, thirteen, fourteen hundred men, I for one, would like to stop on some good ground and let those chasing us come to us.

Then we could fill 'em with lead and steel. I'm tired of running from 'em."

The older of the two, Lieutenant Chesney, played with the fire using a long stick before he spoke. "While I agree with you, I'm thinking the major's got something up his sleeve. First of all, we both know he sent a message to Cornwallis asking for some reinforcements and so the closer we get to Charlotte, the sooner we can expect some help. And for another thing, the man's got enough fightin' sense that I think he might have a place in mind where we'll do exactly what you're talking about. Just got to find the right spot to let the Backwater boys wear themselves out as they attack us coming uphill."

"You seem to be pretty sure about what they might do," said Anthony Allaire.

"Yeah, I am. Remember I spent time fightin' on the other side with men like Roebuck and Brandon a few years ago, so I got a feel for how they think." He stopped for a moment and pointed toward one of the men closest to Ferguson. "And since I'm now serving as Colonel Plummer's adjutant with the Fair Forest boys, I suspect Plummer's been whispering in Ferguson's ear about a good place to have this battle you're thinking about. Can't be sure 'bout that, but I wouldn't be surprised at all."

"All right. Suppose you're right. Since you know this country so well, if you were to put a wager down on where we might make a stand, where do you think it might be?"

Chesney sat still as he watched the militia leaders slowly walk back to their units to relay the orders for the night. "Can't say for sure because the man hasn't shared any particulars with me, but based on how we're crabbing along toward the south and now east a bit, there are some good hills in that direction closer to Charlotte. Couple of places near Crowder Mountain maybe. Another might be Kings Mountain. Crowder is the taller and steeper, but it would be hard to get our wagons up top. Both places got some spots that are real steep. Woods ain't so thick you can't see through 'em. And both got some big rocks to hide behind. If they ask me, I'd say either one sounds pretty good to me." He shrugged. "But nobody's asking for my opinion."

REBEL CAMP NORTH OF GILBERT TOWN
EARLY EVENING, MONDAY, 2 OCTOBER 1780

The large fire burned brightly as the senior officers gathered around it. The rain of the past two days had finally subsided and each man knew it was time for action. But before that could occur, a decision of some consequence needed to be made.

Charles McDowell began the meeting. "Gentlemen, you know the purpose of our gathering. It is to defeat this scoundrel, Ferguson, and those with him. But the question of the day is, what is the best way to assure we have unity for what lies before us? Should we have one man in charge or should we rule by committee? While we are equals in many respects, we all know from our experiences, we need some type of overall command structure we all can agree on to see our task through successfully."

While each man in the circle was a good leader in his own right, blending their individual units together into a cohesive fighting force was not something any of these men had any experience with. Their trust in their own abilities and in their individual units had served them well to this point, but each man knew that to defeat Ferguson, a different command structure was needed, a more formal arrangement to maximize the strength of all those they had so effectively joined together. Charles McDowell was the senior man present, but was he the right man for this complex role?

McDowell looked about, surveying those around the fire. They were an interesting blend of men. The colonel gave thoughtful consideration to each man as he laid his eyes upon them, one after the other. *Yes, I am a good organizer and I would be honored to lead these men, but do I have the energy, the vitality, the experience to lead so many on such an important venture? Could I lead from the front? Could I command their respect during a fight against Ferguson?*

Shelby is a fighter at heart, but he is the youngest man here. Sevier is another man with an excellent reputation as a fighter, but he has no more experience than any of the others. Cleveland is certainly a zealot when it comes to bringing Loyalists to justice, but...? Campbell, the big Virginian, can dominate most gatherings because of his physical presence, but like the others, he hasn't the experience. And Winston, perhaps the toughest fighter in the bunch and the most educated, lets his actions speak louder than his words. If we could blend the best characteristics of each of us, the issue would be settled, but that's not possible. Perhaps the best solution is to find another man from outside this group who has the requisite abilities we require. Yes, maybe that's the answer.

"Gentlemen, I have a proposal. I recommend the best way to solve our dilemma is to request that General Gates at Hillsborough appoint someone to lead us, maybe Daniel Morgan or William Davidson. Both have experience in leading larger groups of men." He let the suggestion hang in the air momentarily before asking, "What say you in this regard? Your thoughts?"

There were a few moments of uncomfortable silence before Isaac Shelby seized the floor. "I must say I don't like that idea. While the two you mentioned are good men, we have Ferguson almost in our grasp. Perhaps only twenty miles away? While we don't know exactly where he is or what his intentions may be, we know he is close. For someone to travel several days to Hillsborough, discuss all of what we know with Gates or someone else who is not familiar with our situation, then get a decision from him, and then return here with his appointed man, will take far too much time. A week or two at best; likely much longer."

He stood up and stepped closer to the fire, staring at its glowing embers. "Any delay in forcing the issue with Ferguson brings too much uncertainty. If we wait for any length of time, he'll either be long gone or reinforced. All our men, regardless of which command they belong to, left their families behind to fight and fight now. If we don't continue our vigorous pursuit of this scoundrel, many of our men will disappear out of boredom or because of the tug of family obligations and I can't say I'd blame 'em. I say we can't wait for Gates. We must find a way to solve our problem here and now and stay on Ferguson's tail."

After Cleveland and Winston voiced similar concerns, McDowell asked, "So what do we do?"

Another one of the leaders made a different proposal. "Since we're all equals, perhaps we could have a meeting, a war counsel, each evening to decide a course of action, and then rotate the leadership role among ourselves each day. That man for that day would lead us on the agreed upon course of action."

But after another gave tepid support to this idea, Shelby stood up again arguing, "I don't think that would work. We need someone who is a firm leader for the entire time we're together. Changing commanders each day could be confusing to all of us. And besides, what would happen if we were in the middle of a battle or close to it, and it was time to have a war counsel to discuss plans? Totally impractical. No, I believe we need one man in charge, one man we can look to for overall leadership, not a plan which leads to confusion of responsibility."

Joseph Winston was the first to nod his agreement. "I agree with Isaac. You all know I've spent half my life fighting somebody—Indians, the British, and the Indians again. I've seen many commanders. Some good, some not so good. Like Isaac, I believe we're better off having one man in charge; one man to lead us. I, for one, don't think we can wait for Gates to help us. He's just too far away. Besides, I must say my confidence in the man is not too high based on what happened at Camden. I say one of us must take charge and the rest of us follow."

While heads all bobbed in agreement, no one else spoke. Each was lost in his own thoughts, wondering if he should shoulder this responsibility or whom he should nominate for such a task.

Finally it was Shelby who once again broke the silence. "The way I see it, we're all North Carolinians except William Campbell. I've known him for a number of years. He's a man of good sense and warmly attached to the cause to which we are engaged. He also commands the largest body of men here right now. I for one think he should be our leader. If some of you still feel we need to communicate with Gates, at least this way we will have one man in charge until Gates can provide us with a more experienced man."

As the others considered Shelby's proposal among themselves, McDowell called for order. "All right. We have several proposals. I suggest we take a few minutes to consider them. Let's resume this discussion in fifteen minutes."

****

"Isaac, what're you doing? We both know you're the one who should head this up, not me. You're more experienced. You're respected by all of us. You were the one challenged by Ferguson. The job to lead us should be yours, my friend, not mine."

Shelby looked into the eyes of William Campbell. "William, you are a good man, one fitting of this command. I meant what I said. Because you're not from the Carolinas and you have the largest regiment, you can be perceived as unbiased. All of us will give you our full support. If we went strictly by who has the longest time as a colonel, Charles McDowell would be our leader. Good man that he is, he is not the right man to lead this group of men. We need someone who will lead from the front, in both voice and action. We need someone with strength and a willingness to take a chance if Ferguson offers us an opportunity."

He stared at Campbell. "I thank you for your compliments, but I meant what I said in front of the others. You are the one who can pull it off. I know you can. You'll be our commander and I'll help keep the others focused."

William Campbell drew himself up to his full height and gazed at the younger man. "Isaac, you and the others will have my decision when we reconvene in a few minutes. In the meantime, I wish to be alone." With that, the Virginian walked away to collect his thoughts.

****

When the decision was made, to his credit, Charles McDowell quietly nodded his head. *Yes, this is the right decision. While it is disappointing for me personally, these men are right. I'm not the right man for this task.* Nevertheless, this rejection was not easy for him to swallow.

"Gentlemen, your desire to have William Campbell lead us is clear. I think I can best serve our cause by doing two things. First, I will carry a message to General Gates concerning the actions we are taking to deal with Ferguson and to seek other guidance he may have. Secondly, in my absence, I relinquish command of all my soldiers to my brother, Joseph McDowell of Quaker Meadows. As you all know, he is an experienced leader and will lead our men in a most fitting manner. Thank you for allowing me to have a part in forming this venture against the enemy. I look with great fondness on what the eventual outcome will be. I will be off to see Gates at first light."

A sincere ovation immediately erupted when McDowell finished speaking. The others knew he had relented for the good of their cause without consideration of personal gain. It was a patriotic and generous decision on his part that all the others recognized. It was viewed by many as Charles McDowell's finest moment.

Now with the command issue settled, it was time to move against Ferguson. Campbell looked at the others now around him. "Prepare your men for an early departure in the morning. If our information is correct, Ferguson may be very close. Tomorrow may be our day!"

CORNWALLIS' HEADQUARTERS AT CHARLOTTE
EARLY EVENING, MONDAY, 2 OCTOBER 1780

"Brown, what is this concoction the doctor has prepared for me? I told the man I was feeling badly. I did not ask for something that might kill me. What is this?"

"Sir, I did not ask the doctor for the official name of the medicine, but I know he understands the urgency for you to feel your best. He is just trying to contain your illness so you will not be bedridden like Colonel Tarleton."

"All right, all right. Go find the man. I want to talk to him. But before you take leave, is there anything new from Ferguson?"

"No sir, not a word. No change from yesterday. On a different subject, as you ordered earlier in the day, preparations are complete to send out a large foraging party tomorrow so we should anticipate some additions to our supplies when they return. Is there anything else, sir?"

"No. That will be all. I think I will rest now." Lord Cornwallis sought a comfortable position but he knew it was not the illness that bothered him so much. It was Ferguson. *Where is he? Blast him! Is my flank secure or not? With all the trouble we are having here in Charlotte, I do not need any difficulties to my flank. I should have given Webster that mission, but then if I had done that, I would have deprived myself of his services here. But at least he would have kept me informed of his situation.* Cornwallis turned all night long. Sleep never came to him in bursts longer than thirty minutes.

11. The Pursuit

Cornwallis' Headquarters at Charlotte
Early morning, Wednesday, 4 October 1780

"SIR, MAJOR DOYLE REPORTING AS ORDERED. I APOLOGIZE FOR NOT seeing you last night, but I was told you were quite ill and needed some rest."

"Yes, that is true, Major, but I am feeling much better this morning. Tell me about yesterday's mission. I assume it went well."

"Yes sir. May I spread this map of the area on this table?"

"By all means."

Doyle, who was in his mid-twenties, then began his briefing as he pointed to the various locations on the map. "We followed this road right here, Beatties Ford Road, one of the better backwoods roads in the area, departing here yesterday just after noon heading northwest. My command consisted of four hundred and fifty infantrymen and one hundred and fifty cavalry that I deemed adequate to provide protection for the sixty wagons we took with us. Our mission as given to me by Lord Rawdon was to fill our wagons with all the supplies we could carry from the plantations on Long Creek in the area around McIntyre's Farm, about five miles north of here. We arrived at the farm early afternoon without any difficulty to speak of, no ambushes or shots coming at us from the woods we passed. Frankly, given all the activity we've experienced of late, I expected some resistance along the way, but none came."

Cornwallis coughed several times as he reached for the hot tea on the table next to where he stood. "No shots fired at you. Interesting.

Do you think it might have been the size of your force that caused the Rebels to show some reluctance to engage you? Could this be a key for us? While it would be costly to increase the size of each patrol, if this would keep the enemy at bay, would that not be worth the cost?

Doyle nodded. "It could very well be, sir. It is certainly something to consider."

Cornwallis grunted. "Yes, perhaps. Go on."

"When we approached McIntyre's, which is the largest farm in the area by far, I spread our men and wagons out to the smaller farms nearby. We then began to plunder the area, the barns, and the livestock pens. In short order our wagons were stuffed full of vegetables, mostly corn and turnips, and we had fifty to sixty livestock in our control, mostly beef. Everything was proceeding according to plan when several of the men accidently knocked over several large beehives, which created quite a stir."

"Yes. I can imagine it might."

"As some of our men enjoyed the predicament of their fellow soldiers, the Rebels chose that time to open fire from the wood line nearest all the commotion. Captain Payne was killed with their first shot. Within a few moments I had a number of men down. With no real feel for the strength of the opposition and knowing that our wagons were bursting with the needed supplies, I gave the order to retreat as we set fire to several of their most prominent buildings."

Cornwallis stared at the man for a moment. "How many men did you lose in this fracas?"

"Twenty dead and a like number wounded."

"And the enemy? How many did you kill or capture?"

"One, sir. A simple country lad not more than fifteen. Cocky at first, he eventually gave us two names: Captain James Thompson who was the Rebel leader. The second name he gave us was Francis Bradley. I've not heard of Thompson before, but Bradley is a name I am familiar with. Some say he's the strongest man in the territory. A good shot. My men catch a glimpse of him every now and then. A very big man."

"So are you telling me your men are afraid of this Bradley fellow? That he is too big, too strong for us to defeat? That he is some kind of superman?"

"No sir, I didn't say that. I only bring his name up because we now know where to look for him."

Cornwallis eyeballed Doyle once again. "So how many men were you facing that caused this hasty retreat? Fifty? One hundred? Two hundred? How many did the lad say?"

John Doyle looked down to avoid his leader's stare, a man whom he greatly admired. "The lad indicated that their force was only ten to fifteen men, although from the volume of fire we received, I believed we faced at least fifty men. No matter how many there were, they're all excellent shots. Most of my men who were killed were taken down with one shot to the head."

Cornwallis stared at Doyle for a long time. Doyle is a capable officer, one of Rawdon's best. This man has served with distinction at Harlem Heights, Brandywine, and at Germantown where he was severely wounded in his right leg, which accounts for his permanent limp. Because he is a man of considerable experience and courage, his account of this fight cannot be taken lightly. Yet what could have caused him to yield to an inferior force so quickly? Are even my best men being worn down by this unconventional style of those who oppose us, who pounce on us only when it is advantageous to them?

Cornwallis went over to the nearest window, staring out into space for a long time. Without turning back to Doyle, he asked, "Do you have anything else to report?"

"Only that the supplies and the livestock we brought in have been given to the commissary officer for further distribution to our units."

"Yes, I am sure that pleased him. Have the doctors look at your leg. I noticed you are limping more than I have noticed before."

After Doyle left the room, Cornwallis continued to stare out the window. *Six hundred of my men wearing the red coats of my country are chased away from valuable food supplies by bees or hornets and a handful of traitors to the King. Unbelievable! How can this be? If word gets out about this debacle, I will be the laughingstock to all those sycophants in London who have never seen or heard a shot fired in anger. I can almost hear Clinton now. 'Charles, what happened? When I left Charles Town, the Southern Colonies were secure. What have you done?'*

MCINTYRE'S FARM NORTHWEST OF CHARLOTTE
LATE MORNING, WEDNESDAY, 4 OCTOBER 1780

"I'm truly sorry about them burning down your barn," Captain Thompson said to the man next to him, the farmer one of the older men from the McIntyre clan, as they stood looking at the smoke rising from the still smoldering fire.

"Captain, we can always build another barn. It'll be harder to replace the cows and the other livestock, but if that's the price we have to pay to send them Redcoats back to where they belong, it's a good trade. How many do you think we killed? I counted ten but I saw more going down. Just couldn't tell how bad they were hit. What I do know is that you nailed that one officer right away and that threw them into some confusion, that and the bees."

"One of my better shots. For now let's keep a good eye on 'em, in case they want to come this way again, and if they do, we'll send 'em back with their tails between their legs a second time. For now, at least, our strategy to keep 'em off balance seems to be working."

Thompson took one more glance at the ground where the barn once stood, marveling once again at the sacrifices of men who believed in this fight for freedom. *What marvelous men we have on our side. What unselfish, honorable men!*

REBEL CAMPSITE AT GILBERT TOWN
EVENING, WEDNESDAY, 4 OCTOBER 1780

"I'm gettin' tired of this. Two days of doing nothing. All this marching, first over Merlin's Knob and now here, and still no sign of a Loyalist yet, at least any that will admit it. I thought for sure by now we would have met up with Ferguson. I'm looking forward to gettin' that man in my sights so then we can go home."

The second man, William Bailey looked at his friend, Andrew Hannah. "You're not alone there. I think we'd all like to take that shot. The word I got from Lieutenant Binkley a few minutes ago was that they think Ferguson and his boys headed south maybe two, three, four days ahead of us. While we've been sneaking around trying to find him, the rascal's been moving away from us. I trust Major Winston and the others know what they're doing, but right now all we're doing is getting wet and tired and we got nothing to show for it."

Hannah, born in Paxton Township in Lancaster County, Pennsylvania, came with his family to Surrey County when he was twelve. Both he and Bailey had been recruited by their Company Commander, Captain Minor Smith, only a few months earlier. Both men waited for the third man in their group to speak. He was a man of few words, but when he spoke, he shared thoughts of wisdom honed through vast amounts of experience.

"Don't get impatient, boys. Plenty of time for shooting in the days ahead. The trick is to stay ready. You never know when it's coming. Guess I've learned over time that in war there's a lot of sittin' around getting bored 'till suddenly all hell's breaking loose. You just don't know when it's coming. That's why you always got to stay ready. Seen it too many times before." Absalom Baker leaned back against the nearest tree and lit his pipe, the fragrance of the stale tobacco drifting upward.

Bailey looked over at Baker. "Absalom, heard you were at Waxhaw. Is that true?"

Baker sat quietly, watching more of his smoke drift away. "Yeah, I was there. I was one of the lucky ones. When we do catch up with Ferguson, I got a score or two to settle with those Redcoats. Been in a lot o' fights: Stono, Monck's Corner, Charles Town, Camden, but Waxhaw was the worst."

"Didn't know you were at all those places."

"Yeah. It was at Camden where I took one in the ankle. That's why I hobble around some, though it seems to be getting a little better."

Hannah thought about all this man had seen, his experiences, his willingness to remain and fight for the hope of freedom. "So when do you think we'll have Ferguson in our sights?"

Baker kept his eyes closed as he savored his tobacco. "Can't say for sure, but once we cross the Broad River in the morning, the colonels seem to think they may be able to hear more about Ferguson. Hope they're right. I'm ready to fight this guy and get it over with. And I heard that some of Elijah Clarke's men have joined us. Not Clarke himself, but one of his best officers, Major Candler. He brought thirty with him. Tough looking bunch. From what I saw, I'm glad those Georgia boys are on our side."

"Got to ask, Absalom, where did you hear all this? You've just been sitting around with us since we got here," Bailey asked.

"That's true, but when you're old like me, you learn to talk less and listen more. That way you get real good at learning what's happening around you." He winked at his friends before he closed his eyes once more, his snoring starting in less than five minutes.

The two younger men sat quietly as they nibbled their meager rations of corn and apples. After making sure Baker was asleep, Hannah broke their self-imposed silence. "I don't know about you, but my ears are still ringing from the speeches Cleveland and Shelby gave last night."

"You're right about that. Can't remember all the words with such a big crowd around us but I did hear Cleveland say something about we have a priceless opportunity to be of service to our country. Then there was something about leaving a 'rich heritage for your children.'"

"Yeah, I remember him saying something like that. What got me the most is when Shelby challenged every man there, saying if any man wanted to quit and head back to his home he should take three steps back. After Shelby said that, I looked around, and as far as I could tell, not a single man budged. Made me proud to see that."

Bailey sat up a little straighter as he recalled some more of Shelby's words that followed that challenge. "I remember him then saying something like he was glad to see each of us was resolved to fight for our country. Then he said something about when we get close to the enemy, we shouldn't wait for orders, but that we're to take advantage of every chance that may come our way. Yes, Sir, after listening to that man I was ready to face any man wearing red."

"Yeah, me too. Speaking about being ready to go, how you fixed for food? You got enough for the next few days?"

"Yeah, I'm doing all right. Guess I'm like just about everyone else. Got a few strips of beef I've saved up, a few turnips and some parched corn to nibble on as we move along. Last night, I found some honey, so I'm taking a swallow or two every now and then. Should be all right for the next few days if we just divide up what we've got. If you want some of this honey, just say the word."

****

While Bailey, Hannah, Baker and the other soldiers around them settled down for the night, the colonels carried on a heated discussion. Shelby's voice spoke for several others. "The way I see it, he could only be heading in one of two directions. Either he is going toward Ninety Six or he's heading for Charlotte to link up with Cornwallis. If he was gonna attack us, he'd a done it by now. Based on his leaving Gilbert Town when he did, he's got to know we're on his trail. I say we keep the pressure on and finish him as fast as we can. Otherwise either Cornwallis or the men from Ninety Six will reinforce him."

Sevier glanced over at his friend before he spoke. "I think Isaac's right. We gotta keep the pressure on him and hope we can pin 'em down in the next few days while we got the manpower. The real question is can we catch him?"

Cleveland and the others made similar comments before Colonel Campbell held up his hand. "All right. Here it is. Tomorrow we head south. We'll cross the Broad and maybe the Green Rivers and see what information we can pick up. For now, get some sleep. Again, Major Candler, glad you and your men joined us. We'll see if we can make your trip worthwhile. For the rest of you, if you haven't yet met the Major, please introduce yourselves to him. He's one of Elijah Clarke's men. Don't let his gray hair fool you. I have it on good authority he's one of the best men to have with you in a fight."

MAJOR FERGUSON'S CAMPSITE AT TATE'S PLANTATION
EARLY EVENING, WEDNESDAY, 4 OCTOBER 1780

"I'm glad we'll be resting here for a few days. How far did we march yesterday? Twenty miles?"

"Yeah, about that," said Sam Chambers. "Heard he's waiting for our wagons with the supplies in 'em to show up. Hope they ain't too far back."

The other deserter, James Crawford, spat out some of the tobacco he had been chewing on all day. "Wagons and the supplies they're carrying is a good thing, reinforcements is another. I'd like to hear more about 'em, but nobody knows nothing. Wonder if they're really coming."

"I'm like you. I'll feel a lot more comfortable when we've got some more of Cornwallis' boys with us. We both know Sevier and his boys. As lightly as they're packed, they can travel fast. Could be on us in no time. I don't mind telling you, James, I've got some concerns."

"Come on, Sam. We talked about this before. We did the right thing, deserting like we did. We both knew when we left Sevier, the Loyalists had the upper hand. It was time to choose a side and stick with it. We made our bed and now we're stuck in it."

Samuel Chambers took a big drag on his pipe. "I know you're right, but you can't blame a man for having some doubts. And right now, we've got some good men around us. Some of the finest I've ever seen. Take the doc, Doctor Johnson. He's young but he cares about people, like the way he took care of that infection you had on your foot with that plant oil he used. And now with Cornwallis sending us some help, I know we'll be fine. I'm kind a' hoping Tarleton's the man they send our way 'cause right now, we seem to be kinda hanging out here by ourselves."

Soon both men waited for sleep to grab them yet they both wondered, *Where is Sevier? Where is Shelby? What will happen to us if they capture us? They hang traitors, don't they?*

12. Intentions Clarified

Rebel formation south of Gilbert Town
Early afternoon, Thursday, 5 October 1780

COLONEL CAMPBELL NOW KNEW WHY SHELBY AND THE OTHERS WERE so pleased that he had accepted the mantle of leadership of this expedition. *Life was much simpler when all I had to worry about were my Virginians. Now I've got to think about all the others as well, the challenge of where units should be dispersed, sorting out information about Ferguson. Everything seems to reach my ears sooner or later. But these are good men, all joined for a noble purpose. For that I am thankful. I must not let them down.*

The formation had made reasonable progress moving south despite the mix of men, some riding horseback and some on foot as their mounts were becoming worn down because of the efforts of the past several weeks. Additionally, the shortage of food was beginning to take its toll on both men and beasts as all were starting to feel the effects of malnourishment.

They had left Gilbert Town early in the morning, fording the Broad River without difficulty. As they were preparing to cross that river, Joseph Winston rode up to Campbell's side. "William, the Lord is smiling on us today. I've just been informed that Major William Chronicle and his militia unit would like to join us. I can personally vouch for the man. While they're only twenty in number, these men have lived and hunted in these parts for years. Once we get a fix on Ferguson, I suspect William will be able to tell us everything we might need to know about the area. I'll introduce him to you at our next rest halt."

William Campbell smiled, once again thankful to be among such good men.

FERGUSON'S CAMP, FIFTEEN MILES FROM KINGS MOUNTAIN
LATE AFTERNOON, THURSDAY, 5 OCTOBER 1780

The two men sat across from each other around the small table Elias Powell had put in front of Ferguson's tent. "I can't understand why Cornwallis hasn't seen fit to send us any information about when to expect some reinforcements. It's been how many days now? Four or five days since we sent our last message?"

De Peyster nodded. "That's true, sir, but it's difficult to say what's happening in Charlotte. While we're wondering why we don't hear from him, maybe he's wondering the same thing about us. For all we know the reinforcements we requested may be an hour away. On the other hand, we don't know when, or even if any of our messengers got through. Either way I suggest we send him another message."

"Yes, yes, of course you're right. And if the reinforcements are on their way, we should meet them sooner as we move closer to Charlotte. Kings Mountain is only fifteen, sixteen miles from here. From everything I've been told, it is good defensible ground."

The captain studied the map spread out on the table. "I concur. If we left before dawn tomorrow, we'd be there well before dark. That would give us enough time to prepare a proper defense. With the wagons finally getting here late yesterday, the men have been taking advantage of the provisions they carry, but I do worry because they're always going to slow us down. I suspect the men chasing us don't have that kind of concern."

Major Ferguson paused, "Yeah, you're right. They'll move a lot faster than us."

The major glanced around his large camp, some men in various stages of catching up with their rest or cleaning their weapons, their voices low. *How I remember those days when I could just focus on my small band of soldiers. Yes, I was responsible for them, but nothing like what I have now. So much is riding on the success of our mission. I must not show any signs of fear in front of these men. I must show only confidence. I must stay focused on the present and the future. Ignore the doubts, those demons of deceit that will drive a man to destruction.*

"We'll leave here before sunrise. Issue the orders. I want the men to use the remainder of today to rest. I want to be on Kings Mountain by mid-afternoon. We've turned our backs to these heathens long enough. The battle will come in the next two or three days. Like these men before us, I, too, am ready for a fight."

"Yes sir. Me, too." De Peyster sat still for a time before he asked, "When do you want to send the next dispatch?"

"It's ready to go now." Ferguson handed the message to the captain just as the tent flap to the inner section opened and one of the young, red-haired women peered out.

"Yes?"

Virginia Paul, the younger of his two companions asked softly, "Are you ready for some more tea, sir?"

The major looked at her for a moment before replying, "Yes, I would. I'll join you shortly." Turning back to De Peyster, he asked, "Comments about this message?"

The captain took his eyes off the young woman and then read the message to himself.

"It seems to me that this is a good summary of what we know. It tells him we believe the Rebels may be receiving reinforcements; we are near Kings Mountain; the fight to come is in doubt because their numbers might be larger than ours. It tells him if he could dispatch another three to four hundred dragoons and soldiers, we would be confident in our ability to handle the situation. And, unless we hear something to the contrary we'll await the enemy on Kings Mountain. I'll see that this message is carried immediately to Lord Cornwallis."

Standing up, Ferguson smiled. "Good...Good. See to it at once. In the meantime, I think I'll have some tea."

REBEL CAMP SOUTH OF GILBERT TOWN
LATE AFTERNOON, THURSDAY, 5 OCTOBER 1780

"Well. I'll be. James Williams. It's good to see you," declared Isaac Shelby.

Turning to the man who rode next to him, he explained. "Colonel Campbell, this is Colonel James Williams, one of the men who fought alongside me and Clarke at Musgrove's Mill."

"Glad to meet you, sir," said Campbell. Looking at the dozen or so men who accompanied Williams, he asked, "You here to join us in taking down Ferguson?"

"That's the goal, all right. But for now, I'm glad I caught up with you as I want to give you some information as to where that rascal might be or at least where he might be heading."

With the purpose of Williams clearly stated, Campbell halted the formation, drawing all the leaders together to listen to what the newcomer had to say. After quickly assembling these men near a clump of pine trees away from the rest of the soldiers, Campbell introduced the South Carolinian to the others, although some were already familiar with Williams.

"Gentlemen, I've called this meeting because it seems Colonel Williams has some information about Major Ferguson." Campbell nodded at Williams. "Sir, the floor is yours."

With that introduction, Williams stepped forward and addressed the leaders. "Gentlemen, first let me say that I have some men that are ready to join you. Regarding Ferguson, I believe he's heading south toward Ninety Six. I think that is where we should head."

At that statement, Campbell and the others glanced up. Cleveland, never one to hold back his feelings, asked, "And exactly what makes you think Ferguson is going south? We have a number of scouts searching the countryside and while we lost Ferguson's trail a little ways back, none of the information we have suggests a southern movement. What exactly makes you so positive that he's heading in that direction?"

Although Williams was a large man, able to bend many to his way through his physical presence, he sensed this big bear of a man would not be easily swayed. "Sir, isn't it obvious? Where else could he be going? I'm convinced he is heading that way, and I urge this body to move in that direction as quickly as possible. Where else could he be going if not south?"

"So if I heard you right, you don't have any specific reports from spies or scouts confirming your suspicions. No hard evidence other than your feelings and intuition. Do I have that right?"

The questions seemed to put Williams off balance a bit as he haltingly commented, "That course of action just seems to make the most sense to me. If you move in that direction, I can muster many men to your cause."

A silence fell over the group, each man considering the dialogue between Williams and Cleveland. It was Colonel Campbell who spoke for all of them. "Colonel Williams, we appreciate your recommendation and we'll consider it. Right now, we need to get across the river at the ford just ahead. Once we get our camp set up on the other side, we'll be getting more scouts out in all directions. Since we'd like you and your men to join us regardless of what direction we take, where do you suggest we rendezvous?"

"Sir, I believe the best spot is along the Pacolet River at the abandoned iron works near there. I'm sure some of the men with you will know that spot." With this agreement made, Williams and those with him headed back toward Thomas Sumter's camp near Gilbert Town while Campbell's formation continued preparations to cross the Green River.

THOMAS SUMTER'S CAMP SOUTHEAST OF GILBERT TOWN
DUSK, THURSDAY, 5 OCTOBER 1780

Colonel William Hill was in a foul mood. Sumter was off parlaying with the governor; Hill's arm was swelling up again from the wound he received at the victory at Hanging Rock three months earlier; and now Colonel James Williams was standing before him. Hill was mad and getting madder by the second.

"James, I'm going to ask you again and I do not want you to dance with me anymore regarding your answers. I want the truth. It is critical that I know exactly what you said to Campbell and the others. Now tell me again exactly what you have done regarding our pursuit of Major Ferguson."

"I met with Campbell and those with him: Shelby, Sevier, Cleveland, and the others at Alexander's Ford."

"And what did you tell them?"

"We agreed that my men and I would meet them at the old iron works at the Pacolet River to reinforce them as they moved south."

Hill came out of his chair at the latest remark. "Did you happen to mention that we had a report from a spy, a very well-placed spy I might add, a man we know to be of great integrity, who came directly from Ferguson's camp at Tate's Plantation, who told us early this morning in your presence and mine that Ferguson was heading east? Did you happen to mention to Campbell or Shelby or Sevier or the others that going south toward Ninety Six would take them away from Ferguson?"

Before Williams could reply, Hill's face grew crimson with anger. "Don't bother answering that question. I can see right through you. We all can. You are a Patriot, James; a staunch fighter in everyone's judgment. But sometimes you focus too much on what is good for James Williams and your men rather than what is best for the cause we all labor for."

Hill was now fully warmed to his concerns. "We all know you tried to convince everyone that you were the hero at Musgrove's Mill regardless of the efforts of Clarke and Shelby. And while you've managed to convince Governor Rutledge of your virtues, we all know we'll follow Sumter's lead, not yours. You're lucky Sumter's in Hillsborough now or he'd probably string you up for treason. For the most part, our South Carolina militia units are operating quite well without your meddling. And now you gave Campbell and Shelby and Sevier and the others, many of whom have come hundreds of miles to help fight our enemy, false information which will send them off on a wild goose chase."

Hill stopped to catch his breath before he stormed on. "If they believed you, they'll never catch Ferguson. He'll escape and we'll all bear the brunt of your folly. Sometimes James, you disgust me. You wanted those men to move south to plunder the Loyalists near where you live so you could secure your own territory and everyone else be damned! Isn't that right?"

When Williams attempted to defend himself, his words came out without much gusto. "And what if I did? What if what you say is correct? Ferguson is North Carolina's problem. Those of us who live in South Carolina need to take care of ourselves. You should know that. Your roots are in this colony just like mine."

William Hill stared back at the man before him. James Williams was a good man, a good man to have in a fight, but he was too parochial, too short-sighted. It could not be tolerated. Softening his tone slightly, Hill brought the discussion to a close.

"James, this is not a fight of only one colony against the British and men like Cornwallis and Ferguson. If we fight for the good of all, we will win. But if we fight for only what is best for South Carolina or North Carolina or Georgia, we will lose because if we followed your way of thinking, the Redcoats would conquer each colony one by one. We win only when all the colonies fight as a united force with one common purpose in mind. Now get out of my sight while I consider how I can fix what you've done."

REBEL CAMP ON THE GREEN RIVER
MIDNIGHT, FRIDAY, 6 OCTOBER 1780

"Colonel Campbell?" The guard shook him again. "Colonel Campbell, wake up."

"What is it?"

"Sir, we have a man here who says his name is Colonel Lacey from Sumter's camp. He says he has word on Ferguson's location. We've got him blindfolded 'cause we weren't sure who he really is, coming like he did in the middle of the night and all. You want to see him?"

Campbell shook the cobwebs off before answering. "Yes, but before bringing him to see me, wake up the other leaders and have them join us. Give us about ten minutes to assemble before you bring this so-called colonel here."

Within minutes the leaders assembled. At Campbell's order, the guards brought the man forward and took the blindfold off. Without preamble Campbell asked, "Who are you, and why did you come here?"

Seeing no one he recognized in front of him, the man began, "I am Colonel Edward Lacey of Sumter's army. Colonel William Hill sent me here to give you information about Major Ferguson and also to relate to you that Colonel Williams, who met with you earlier today, gave you some incorrect information."

"Is that right? Before you tell us what you have to say, I want to know if any if you, Cleveland, McDowell, Winston, Chronicle, can vouch for this man?"

When no one stepped forward, Campbell stared at the man. "All right, Lacey, because we're fair men, we'll listen to what you have to say, but to begin with, tell me why Colonel Williams would give us false information? What purpose would it serve for him to send us in the wrong direction?"

"Because he's a South Carolinian and he wanted you and your men to head south and tear into the Loyalists who live near him. That way it would make it easier for him and his people."

"So you're saying he wanted us to fight those that are causing him trouble instead of going after Ferguson?"

"That is my understanding, sir."

"Obviously that's a different story from what he told us. Why should we believe you instead of him? And if we chose to believe you, what information do you have about Ferguson?"

Lacey looked at the men around him. With a mix of vehemence and conviction in his voice he lashed out, "Because I'm telling you the truth. Once Williams returned to our camp, he confessed to Colonel Hill what he told you. Williams knew full well a spy, a very reliable spy, came into our camp yesterday morning telling us that Ferguson is headed east in hopes reinforcements will be coming from Charlotte. We have no information about those reinforcements, but we know you're after Ferguson and we're willing to assist. That's why I've been riding half the night to find you. Don't mind telling you I got lost twice, but I wanted you to know the truth. Otherwise your entire venture would be a waste of time."

Campbell stared at the man for over a minute before he had the guards move Lacy back away from the group of leaders. "Gentlemen, I'm a Virginian. I don't know Lacey or Hill or Williams, but many of you do, at least by reputation. What are your thoughts?"

For his part Shelby remained silent, stunned at the thought that Williams would put his own gain above what would be best for all. One of the strongest supporters of Lacey was Major Winston who said, "While I've not had the privilege before tonight of meeting this man, I know he's been fighting since he was thirteen when he was with George Washington and Daniel Morgan at Braddock's defeat."

Knowing time was critical, Campbell called for a vote.

Once Lacey stood in front of them again, the tall Virginian spoke for them all. "Sir, we appreciate you coming here with this information. By the way your horse was so lathered up when you showed up here, we know you've ridden hard to find us. We have seven hundred men ready to mount our best horses in the morning. Those who are not part of that seven hundred will follow us as best they can. If, as you say, Ferguson is moving east, where do you suggest we meet you and your men so you can help us bring this affair to its rightful conclusion?"

Lacey thought for a moment. "I say we meet you at Cowpens. It's maybe twenty miles from here. The land there is owned by a Tory named Saunders. Should be plenty of beef and corn there to feed your men. In the meantime I'll return to our camp and gather up our men. If we ride hard, we should be able to meet you there by dusk tomorrow. I think I'll be able to bring about one hundred with me if that's all right with you. Kings Mountain is about thirty miles east of Cowpens."

Campbell smiled, "I never turn down offers like that. It'll be our pleasure to have you and your men ride along with us."

Turning to his men, he said, "Gentlemen, you heard the man. Cowpens it is by dusk tomorrow. As we discussed earlier, Major Herndon, you'll be in charge of all the foot soldiers and those whose horses are too beat up to ride at dawn to Cowpens. Follow along as quickly as possible. Ideally, you'll be able to meet us there some time after dark tomorrow night, God willing. Again, Colonel Lacey, we appreciate you riding here tonight with this information. We will see you in about eighteen hours."

"That is my intent, sir. If you will excuse me, I have many miles to ride."

13. On the Move

JOHN RHEA SAT ON HIS HORSE. LIKE SO MANY OTHERS NEAR HIM, HE was anxious, excited, and proud. Anxious and a bit nervous for what lay ahead; excited and proud because he was one of those chosen to be in the formation that would ride to Cowpens in hopes of catching Ferguson; glad that his horse, despite the rigors of the past days, remained strong and sturdy.

"John, you're a lucky man," said William Stewart, a younger man Rhea had known for several years. "Hopefully me and others who're marching behind you in the Foot Company will move fast enough that we won't miss the fight. Know what I mean?"

"Yeah, William, I do. We've all come a long way and I'm sorry you're not part of this first group." Rhea's eyes caught the streaks in the eastern sky, a clear sign of dawn breaking. Seeing the front of the column beginning to move, he tipped his cap to his friend. "See you tonight at Cowpens."

"You can bet on it. See you tonight, John."

And with that John Rhea and the other seven hundred riders picked up the pace. The remainder, like Stewart, followed as quickly as they could; this second group, despite their individual handicaps, was motivated by pride. All of them had given much to be at this time and place in history. None in their number wanted to miss out on the battle that loomed ahead.

****

"You doing all right, John?"

"Yes sir. No problems to speak of," Rhea replied as he answered Colonel Campbell's question. "Everything going as planned?"

"Seems to be. Figure we're about halfway there. Maybe another ten miles to go."

Neither man spoke for a few minutes as their horses ambled along next to each other. "Something eating at you, John? Anything I should know about?"

Rhea rode along for a few minutes before he spoke. "Might be, but I can't tell for sure. "I'm hearing some talk, mostly from the North Carolina boys, 'bout the fight that's coming up. Seems they think they might know some of the men who're probably marching with Ferguson. From what I can gather, there's some bad blood that's been brewing between many of 'em for some time."

Campbell stared at the man. "So you're thinking if our boys have a chance to take revenge for some earlier wrongs, some of our men might take advantage of the situation?"

"Yeah, could be. Seems that some of our boys are maybe looking to settle some old scores. Looting, pillaging, killing, beatings, harsh treatment of their womenfolk. The list goes on and on. Mind you now, I'm just listening and trying to put two and two together. All I'm saying is that it might require some watching."

"You have any specifics?"

"No. Just got a bad feeling about it. Killing your enemy in battle like the Good Book talks about is one thing, but cold-blooded murder? Well, that's another thing altogether. And to add some fuel to the fire, we got a few with us who fought at Charleston and Waxhaw and Camden, so they've got first-hand experience about how the Redcoats treat folks once the battle is over. They may be itching to repay some old debts. You know—an eye for an eye."

Campbell rode along quietly. "I've seen it before when we've tangled with the Indians over the years. Revenge can be a powerful thing. Can turn good men into animals real quick. Then later their conscience can eat at 'em for a long time."

Rhea nodded. "Yeah, I've seen that, too. Can eat a man from the inside out. Can take a long time for a man to get over something he knows he did that was wrong. Some never forget."

Campbell thought about Rhea's comments for much of the day as he continued to ride up and down the formation. *John's right. How would I feel if I had been at Waxhaw, seeing men I'd fought with being butchered by the Redcoats? Would I take my anger and my revenge out on others just because they wore the same uniform? If Rhea is right, will I be a strong enough leader that I will hold others back from committing murder?*

KINGS MOUNTAIN
LATE AFTERNOON, FRIDAY, 6 OCTOBER 1780

"Abraham, I like it. Steep sides. Some big trees down the hill might get in our way, but for the most part, it is open enough we can see anybody coming up our way for quite a distance. We've made a wise decision."

"Yes sir, I think you're right, though this isn't like any mountain I've ever seen before. Not that big. Not that tall, but as you said, it'll do. Our camp is set up as we talked about. The tents and the wagons are circled up to help keep the horses and the few heads of beef we have penned. Powell is setting up your tent now."

De Peyster paused to study the terrain in more detail. *Yes, this is a good piece of ground to defend. Maybe sixty feet up from the base, in some places almost straight up, thirty degree slope in most others. This plateau we are on is close to six hundred yards long, seventy feet wide at the southwestern end and one hundred and twenty feet wide at the northeastern end. Enough room for our formation. If they attack us on one side of the ridge, we can maneuver men from the opposite side quickly. These oaks and chestnut trees have the biggest trunks I've ever seen. If they attack, we have some good thick trees to get behind.*

"Sir, any word on the reinforcements?"

"No, but I'm sure Cornwallis would not ignore my request."

"I hope you're right." The captain smiled. "I noticed the men showed a spring in their step today. They covered those sixteen miles from Tate's with a purpose. I'm not sure if it was the two-day rest or the fact that they knew we were coming here. Or maybe it was because we're closer to Cornwallis and they feel more secure. Regardless, it was good to see."

"Yes. I detected their enthusiasm as well. Good to see."

Ferguson studied the soldiers more. "Now that we're here, there's one thing I want taken care of immediately. Because one of the strengths we have over these backcountry Rebels is our ability to fight with the bayonet, I've noticed some of our men don't carry such a weapon. For those who are not equipped with a bayonet, have them whittle down the handles of their hunting knives, so that if the situation arises, they can fit their knives into the muzzle of their rifle to act as a bayonet."

"I understand. I'll see to it at once."

Ferguson nodded. "In the meantime I'll prepare another message to send to Cornwallis giving him our location and intentions."

As De Peyster made his way around the hill to issue Ferguson's instructions, the major surveyed the hilltop once again. *Kings Mountain. A noble title for a place named for a former settler. Should have been named for a King instead of for a commoner who just happened to have that as his last name. Regardless, let these traitorous dogs attack. I'm on Kings Mountain. I'm the King of this mountain. Not even God Almighty can drive me off it."*

****

Late that afternoon, De Peyster approached his commander as he stood near the mountain's peak at the center of the plateau. "Sir, the men are well-positioned and those who needed to manufacture a bayonet are doing that now. I'll have the men start piling up logs and rocks to give us stronger defensive positions."

Ferguson looked about. "Since we have such good fields of fire and we occupy the highest points with plenty of rocks and boulders to protect us, I think we can dispense with too many logs and rocks in front of us. They may hamper our ability to shoot downhill."

De Peyster, ever the professional, nodded even though that guidance was not to his liking. "Anything else, sir?"

"Yes. Read over this message I'm sending to Cornwallis and then have it dispatched immediately. I'm telling him we've arrived at Kings Mountain and have taken up a good position which I do not think we can be forced from. But I'd still be pleased if he could send some more good soldiers to act as reserves behind our riflemen and a few dragoons as well to support the flank which would enable us to act decisively and vigorously."

After reading through the message twice, De Peyster remarked, "It sounds fine to me. I'll have this sent right away."

CORNWALLIS' HEADQUARTERS AT CHARLOTTE
LATE AFTERNOON, FRIDAY, 6 OCTOBER 1780

"Anything yet?"

William Brown knew exactly what Lord Cornwallis was asking. "No sir. We've heard nothing from Major Ferguson. Messengers are just not getting through with any regularity."

Cornwallis looked at his aide, growling, "You needn't make excuses for the man. He knows very well how important his mission is to our success. You can be sure the next time I see him, the major will not forget my feelings about not keeping me adequately informed. One-third of my Army is out there somewhere and I have no information about its whereabouts. Blast that man!"

Brown stood silently. He knew his commander well enough to know that it was best to remain quiet and let the older man vent.

Cornwallis stared out the windows facing the setting sun. *Here I sit. Hostage to Ferguson. Even if I could, I cannot move north without knowing about my flank. Perhaps he has sent messengers, but like so many others of late, these men have not gotten through to me. Yes, Ferguson is a good soldier, but thus far, his inability to keep me informed causes me to question if he should ever again be considered for advancement.*

REBEL FORCES AT COWPENS
LATE AFTERNOON, FRIDAY, 6 OCTOBER 1780

"Sergeant Keys, rumor has it that we'll be able to get some beef and fresh corn here. Assuming that's true, after the men care for their horses, see that the men get their fill. I'm sure after the last few days of minimal rations, a good meal of some cooked beef will be welcomed. Don't know how long we'll be here, so after the men eat, have 'em get some rest."

"Will do, Captain. Any idea who those men were who just rode in here? Big group. Maybe a hundred or so. Would they be Lacey's men I heard about?"

"Yeah, could be. If that's them, they had a long ride since they came from near Gilbert Town today. If they need any help, see what you can do for them. I'm gonna check in with Colonel Campbell and see what the plan is. I'll be back as soon as I can."

As he walked toward Campbell's location, Captain David Beattie looked around at the men he was responsible for. He had known many of them for years as they did battle with the Indians. He was proud to be their leader. And he was doubly proud because included in his company were his two brothers, John and William: John, one of his lieutenants; William, the youngest of the three, having just turned twenty. *Momma asked me to watch out for him. I'll do the best I can, but right now, all these men are brothers to me. But yes momma, I'll do the best I can. The best I can.*

Keys watched Captain Beattie walk over to the grove of trees designated as the colonel's headquarters. *There goes a good man...A good man.*

****

Campbell chaired the gathering of the senior commanders who comprised the inner circle of those around a large fire. Beattie stood in a larger group made up of majors and captains who formed a loose outer circle, men like himself who were listening, trying to keep up with the latest information. The sun was now low on the horizon and there was a cool nip in the air.

Beattie knew most of the men standing near him: James Dysart and William Edmondson were Virginians like himself; David Vance from McDowell's command; and Robert and Valentine Sevier along with John Pemberton from Shelby's unit. He knew the others by reputation only: Martin Gambrill and Joel Lewis of Cleveland's Wilkes County Militia; Benjamin Roebuck and James Steen from the South Carolina units; and Minor Smith from Winston's Surrey County men. These were all good men, men willing to die for their beliefs. None of them would back away from the fight.

As his chest swelled with pride, the words he had read several years before in a pamphlet entitled *The American Crisis* came to him. Thomas Paine had penned the words while Washington's army was in retreat in December 1776. As he looked around at these men all around him, he quietly mouthed Paine's words. "These are the times that try men's souls. The summer soldier and the sunshine patriot will, in this crisis, shrink from the service of his country; but he who stands now, deserves the love and thanks of man and woman. Tyranny, like hell, is not easily conquered." *Yes,* Beattie thought, *these men deserve the thanks of many.*

As he studied the senior leaders present, the captain realized that Colonel James Williams, the one who appeared in their camp yesterday, was not present. Instead, Colonels William Hill and Edward Lacey represented the South Carolina militia. Before he considered that subject too much, Colonel Campbell's intense yet level voice grabbed the spotlight.

"In summary, here's what we know. Hiram Saunders, a Loyalist to be sure, who owns this land and all the cattle and corn you see, swears Ferguson and his men have not come by here. Since we've seen no signs to contradict his statement, Saunders will be spared, but his cattle and corn-fields are ours for the taking. Make sure you and your men get their fill because when we leave here, I don't know when or where our next meal will come from."

After the leaders bobbed their heads in agreement, Campbell went on. "When Major Herndon and the Foot Company arrive, the size of our force may reach fifteen hundred men."

While the total number sounded adequate, the senior leaders sensed their enemy was not only Ferguson, but time as well. Unlike regular soldiers, each man in these militia formations was a volunteer. Each had left his family to fend for themselves. Each man's provisions, food and clothing, as well as his weapon, came from the sweat of his brow and his ingenuity. While the leaders wanted to see this pursuit of Ferguson carried through to the end, they knew the battle must come soon, very soon, lest the understandable pull of the needs of loved ones might begin to decimate their ranks.

Colonel William Hill, who had ridden with Lacey from the Gilbert Town area, turned to Campbell. "Sir, just so you know, in the numbers I have given you, I have included a small contingent under the command of James Williams, the man you spoke with yesterday afternoon. While he is in my formation, I forbade him to be a part of this council. I trust that punishment will help humble him. With your permission, I request that he be given the opportunity to regain his honor by joining us in the fight to come."

Campbell listened carefully to Hill's words. After giving the matter some thought, he pronounced, "Sir, I trust your judgment on this matter and will not speak of it again. Thank you for sharing that with us."

After looking around to assure he had everyone's attention, Campbell announced, "Just prior to this meeting, we received an unconfirmed report that requires your judgment. This information comes from Joseph Kerr, an informant who, at various times over the past few years, has provided information to our North Carolina brethren here. After Major McDowell vouched for this man's integrity, I spoke with Kerr."

After a moment of silence to build the drama, he went on. "This man says he was at Ferguson's camp around mid-day today near the home of Peter Quinn, seven or eight miles west of Kings Mountain. While there, he heard that Ferguson intends to be on Kings Mountain this evening with maybe as many as fifteen hundred men with him, although Kerr could not confirm that number. We've sent more scouts out in that direction but I'm sure we won't hear from them until first light tomorrow. Gentlemen, your thoughts please."

While everyone began to talk at once, it was Shelby's voice that rose above the others. "Seems to me we should mount up as many as we can tonight and head to Kings Mountain so we can attack him tomorrow. If we wait any longer, he'll either continue to retreat or he'll get reinforced. Either way is bad for us."

Joseph Winston followed. "I think Isaac is right. If we each pick our best men and the best horses just like we did to get here today, we could leave tonight and be on Ferguson sometime tomorrow. We got here in good shape with around seven hundred horsemen, so with Colonel Hill joining us, if they picked half of their four hundred, that gives us around nine hundred men. Like Isaac said, we could leave here tonight and the rest can follow behind us just like they're doing now."

"I like what both Isaac and Joseph said. If we can finish this affair in the next day or two, we'll have done a great service to our cause. I'm for riding later tonight." With that said, John Sevier went back to smoking his pipe.

Campbell looked about, searching the eyes of the men close to him. "Anyone else have any other ideas?"

When no one else interrupted the crackle of the fire, he nodded. "All right then, you majors and captains behind us have heard enough. Go back to your men and start spreading the word. Care for the horses. Get food in everyone's belly. Be ready to leave in two, three hours. Say around 9 o'clock. We'll do the same as today. Men with good horses will leave then. Those who marched after the horsemen today will do so again later tonight under the command of Major Herndon. While you men begin to spread the word, those of us here close to the fire will work out a few more details. Get going."

One of the men in the back row asked, "Colonel, weather looks like it's moving in. A lot of lightning to the west. You want to wait until it clears?"

"No, we've waited long enough. If we're going to get rained on tonight, let's do it as we march toward Ferguson."

****

The word spread quickly from campfire to campfire. Excitement at the possibility of the upcoming battle replaced the rest the horses and the men needed. The best riflemen would be mounted on the best horses available. From those who had come from over the mountains, William Campbell would have two hundred men in his command, Isaac Shelby and John Sevier, each with one hundred and twenty. Benjamin Cleveland would lead one hundred and ten; Joseph McDowell, ninety; and Joseph Winston, sixty. William Hill and Edward Lacey would have one hundred. James Williams, despite his earlier sin, was allowed to lead sixty men, thirty of whom were with Major Candler's Georgians. Finally, another group of late arrivals of fifty men led by Colonel William Graham and Lieutenant Colonel Hambright which included Major Chronicle's twenty men. A total of nine hundred and ten men in all.

Hill and Lacey were the last two to leave the glow of the fire. Both men were tired, but they knew their adrenaline would keep them going for many more hours.

Hill looked at his old friend. "Edward, thanks again for getting the word to these men about Ferguson's location. Without all you riding all last night, none of this would be possible."

"Had to. This is our best chance to deal a death blow to these British. Things have been going their way far too long. Time to turn the tide. I like what Campbell called this formation, a 'Flying Column.' Sounds like a good name to me. Anyway, we still got thirty miles or so to go."

KINGS MOUNTAIN
EVENING, FRIDAY, 6 OCTOBER 1780

The two officers shared a meal of venison and some fresh corn they had been given at Peter Quinn's farm earlier in the day. As they sat close to their small fire, thunderbolts and lightning flashed far to the west and the winds started to freshen, all signs that a drenching rain was coming their way.

"Any word about reinforcements?"

"No. Nor have we received any messages from Cornwallis." Abraham De Peyster bit into the meat, some of the juices running down his chin. "What worries me is that we have no idea where Shelby and the others might be. They could be heading for Ninety Six or Charlotte. For all we know, they could be sneaking up this mountain right now. We just don't know. Don't mind telling you that I'd feel more comfortable if we prepared better fighting positions for our men. I know we've got a lot of rocks to shield us, but the cautious side of me says we should prepare positions continuously."

Lieutenant Chesney kept his mouth shut. As Ferguson's aide, he tended to follow the major's lead. "I understand what you're saying, but a man of his experience would not lead us astray."

A distant rumble of thunder caught his attention. "I think for tonight, we might all look to stay under some kind of shelter lest we become soaked to the bone. Even if the reinforcements are close, they'll be hard pressed to find us tonight in this weather."

14. Moving Closer

Rebel Formation crossing the Broad River
Dawn, Saturday, 7 October 1780

"GLAD WE FINALLY GOT SOME LIGHT. NOW MAYBE THE COLONELS CAN figure out what's going on."

"You got that right. Between the rain, no moon, and these thick woods, I'm surprised we ain't all lost." Both men sat quietly in their saddles, the rain now coming down harder. After almost half an hour, they began to move east again. "Stop. Start. Stop. Start. I hate it when we do that," William Morrison said.

Sam Mackie kept his head down, letting the rain run-off the brim of his hat. No one said why they stopped. No one said why they started to move. All these two knew, like all the others around them, was that they were moving forward, slowly to be sure, but forward nevertheless. Unbeknownst to them, the colonels at the front of the formation had learned the scouts leading Colonel Campbell had gotten confused in the darkness and the rain. Valuable time was spent to find Campbell and get him on the right path.

****

Shelby smiled at his friend as he looked through the tall, thick trees above as the dark, dreary sky grew a bit lighter. "John Sevier, for an old mountain goat, you sound a bit tired and worn out."

"Nothing like that. But this rain's been annoying. A mist one minute and then a deluge the next. Don't know about you, but I'm soaked to the bone. Road ain't been too bad, but with the path so narrow and no moon or stars to help us, it ain't easy keeping everyone moving in the right direction. Don't like stopping, but we don't have much choice. We've got to get Campbell's men back in the fold. We stay here much longer, both the men and horses are gonna get cold and that's not good."

"I know, but like you said, we don't have any other options. We need Campbell. Can't go on without 'em."

Both men understood what had happened. Although the movement began on time from Cowpens, with the thunder and lightning so vicious at times, the guides with Campbell's unit became disoriented. Once Shelby realized that Campbell's men were not with them, he halted the column and sent back scouts to find the Virginians.

****

"Good to see you boys. Thanks for sending those men back to find us."

Shelby nodded, "That's all right, James. We're just glad you made it."

"So why aren't we crossing the river?" the Virginia colonel asked as he and the other leaders looked down from the hill above the Broad River.

It was Major William Chronicle who answered the question. "Just being cautious. We figured we'd cross at Tate's Crossing, but then thought better of it. Since that was the obvious place for us to cross, we thought Ferguson might have some men looking for us there. Best to cross here. Off the normal path a bit. Right now, I got my best scout, Enoch Gilmer, over there checking the area on the far side. If there're any Loyalists around, Enoch will smell 'em. Best scout I know. A combination of guile and cunning. In the meantime, we've been doing our best to keep our powder dry, some of the boys even wrapping their rifles in their shirts."

Just then, they heard a short soft whistle coming from across the river. "That's the signal for 'All clear.' Let's go." While the crossing was deep, all the men made it across without mishap. Kings Mountain and Major Ferguson were now less than fifteen miles away.

****

As the morning wore on, the grumbling and the rumors started. "When are we going to get there?" "Do these colonels really know where they're going?" "Heard Ferguson is back in Charlotte drying out." "If he's left, I'm ready to go home and see my wife and kids." "It's been two weeks since we left home and all we've done is move a lot, get wet, cold, tired and hungry, and then move some more. Ain't fired my rifle yet. If we can't find Ferguson soon, I say let's go back home. Enough of this crap." "I'm tired and hungry." "When will this be over?"

Campbell, Sevier, and Cleveland sauntered along beside each other. Sevier was the first to voice what the others had noticed. "Men are getting restless. It's been what, twelve, thirteen hours since we started this march. The horses are gonna need a rest soon."

Cleveland mumbled, "Yeah, you're right there. That little stop back there a few miles ago to grab some corn seemed to perk everyone up. Outside of that scout, Gilmer, heading off to the east, we're just plodding along hoping we're going the right way. And now with this rain coming down hard again, I say we stop for a time to give the boys a chance to rest. What do you say?"

With that proposal on the table, the three rode up next to Isaac Shelby who was at the head of the column riding along in quiet solitude. Sevier, who knew Shelby best, was their spokesman. "Isaac, the three of us have been talking. With this rain and all, we think the boys need to halt for a time. Been at it now for a long time. We think the men will do better after getting dried out a little."

Shelby seemed to ignore the three men as he continued to ride along at a steady pace, swaying back and forth in his saddle, glancing neither to the right nor to the left, his focus fixed straight ahead. When he finally spoke, his words came out crisp and strong. "I will not stop until night even if I have to follow Ferguson into Cornwallis' lines. If you want to stop, go ahead. As for me and my men, we're continuing the march."

The three colonels moved off to the side of the trail to give Shelby's men room to pass. Quietly, Campbell said to the others, "Return to your men. Tell 'em whatever you want, but let's keep going. If the report from last night was correct about Ferguson's location, we'll know soon enough."

KINGS MOUNTAIN
LATE MORNING, SATURDAY, 7 OCTOBER 1780

De Peyster had a very uncomfortable night. Between the rain pelting down and the thoughts rumbling through his head, sleep had eluded him. *Ferguson is determined to hold this place until reinforcements arrive, but when will that be? Is it pride that is keeping him from continuing on to Charlotte? And what about the Rebels? How many are out there? Enough that they can take this mountain from us? He thinks it is best to keep the bulk of our men near the peak so we can move from side to side if we're attacked. But what will happen if we're surrounded and they come up all sides at once? We'll be trapped. Having faced Shelby at Musgrove's Mills, I know he's clever. They've come too far to be turned back easily.*

And what about our Loyalists? They seem to be dependable, but will they remain strong in battle or will they wither like the wind at the first sign of trouble? Perhaps it will be best if the rebels do attack from all sides at once. That way, our men will have no place to run. The battle is coming soon. I can feel it in my bones.

The captain spent the remainder of the morning prowling around the perimeter, looking for flaws in their lines of fire, making sure the men were watchful, and that their powder was dry and their bayonets were sharp. He then sought out Lieutenant Chesney, charging him with the responsibility to continually check on the pickets spread out in the woods below. They were the first line of warning.

LORD CORNWALLIS'S HEADQUARTERS IN CHARLOTTE
LATE MORNING, SATURDAY, 7 OCTOBER 1780

"Captain Brown, did I understand you correctly? We finally have a message from Major Ferguson?"

"Yes sir. That is correct. Two men arrived five minutes ago. They're worn out but I have them standing outside whenever you're ready to see them."

"By all means, show them in at once."

Moments later two men stood in front of the British Commander. "Sir, this is Peter Quinn and Abram Collins, the messengers from Major Ferguson."

Cornwallis stared at the two frontiersmen, both of them dirty from head to foot, their faces drawn, showing all the signs of having come a great distance. Something about them stirred him deeply. While he wanted to grill them instantly, he paused to ask, "When was the last time you ate or slept?"

Quinn swallowed hard, his head down, not sure how to address the older man whose uniform was impeccable: scarlet and white, clean, all the leather shone brightly, the head of the older man covered by a thick, white-powdered wig. Everything about this man spoke of his power, his prestige. "Sir...Sir, your Lordship, it's been a day or two since we ate anything worthwhile. Can't remember when we last slept."

Cornwallis nodded. "We'll take care of your needs soon. Right now, I understand you have a message from Major Ferguson."

"Yes sir. Here it is." Handing the small parchment to Cornwallis, Quinn continued. "It ain't a long message but you can see it's signed by him. He made us memorize what's in it in case we lost it or had to get rid of it to save our necks. As you can see, it says, "The Backwater men are approaching. I would like reinforcements or an escort adequate to the occasion."

Cornwallis looked at Quinn. "When did he give you this message?"

"Bout six, seven days ago. Kind of lost track. We're coming directly here but some Rebel sympathizers got suspicious of us. We had to head north to get away from 'em. They were dogging us real good. Took three days to shake 'em. Soon as we did, we came straight here."

"What was your position when the major sent you to deliver this?"

"We were ten or twelve miles south of Gilbert Town. We had just crossed the Green River after we'd been heading south that day."

"So where is the major now?"

Quinn looked at his comrade before he answered. "Sir, we can't really say. Like I said, that was six, seven days ago when we last saw him and his men. Can't say if the Major headed south or if he stayed put or if he started in another direction. We just don't know your Lordship. Can't tell you 'cause we don't know."

****

"What do you think?" Cornwallis asked his aide.

"Sir, it seems to me, information from a week ago is of little value to us now. I suppose we could send a force to the west, but where would they be going? Their mission would be to reinforce Ferguson, but at this point, we have no idea how many are required. Until we receive more information from either Ferguson or some other source, I don't think we can do anything except have a unit prepared to march on short notice."

Cornwallis glanced at his aide and considered the man's words. *No question the man will be a good, senior officer one day. His thoughts are logical and direct. His words make sense. He is stating exactly what I am thinking. I would like to take some action, there simply is not enough information to do anything right now except to be prepared. If I send reinforcements, who should lead them? Tarleton is still ill. I can't send Rawdon or Webster because I need them here.*

KINGS MOUNTAIN
LATE MORNING, SATURDAY, 7 OCTOBER 1780

Along with the others nearest them, John and Thomas Logan continued to clean their rifles. Each man was an expert shot and both knew the importance of maintaining the rifles they held in their hands.

John, the younger of the two, periodically checked the rocks down below. "Do you think they'll be coming up this way?"

"Depends on who you mean by 'they.' You talking about the Rebels in general or 'bout our brothers?"

"Guess both. Can't help but wonder if our kin are part of the ones chasing us. Makes sense if they are."

Thomas nodded. He, too, had the same thoughts. *Yes, John and I are the younger brothers. We are loyal to the King. Why are our two older brothers so different? Why have they chosen to side against us? I can understand William. He is older. But Joseph? He's only two years older than me. Why do they see things one way and me and John see them all so differently? What will happen if we have to face each other today?*

REBEL FORMATION
LATE MORNING, SATURDAY, 7 OCTOBER 1780

"Think we'll meet 'em today?"

"Part of me wants to so we can get this over. Part of me hopes that Ferguson and his men just fade so we don't have to face John and Thomas. I ain't looking forward to that. Can't help but think that when we tangle with Ferguson, what this might mean to momma."

William Logan kept the reins loose, letting his horse keep pace with the ones in front of him. "Sooner or later this matter has to be settled. It's been going on too long. In my heart, I know we're on the right side of this. Don't think I'll ever understand why John and Thomas feel like they do. Doesn't make sense to me. Why would any man choose to be subservient to a king thousands of miles away?"

Joseph kept pace with his brother. "Whatever happens today or tomorrow or the next day, I just hope I don't have to make a choice 'bout shooting one of those two. While I think they're wrong, they're still my brothers." *I just don't want to have to make that choice.*

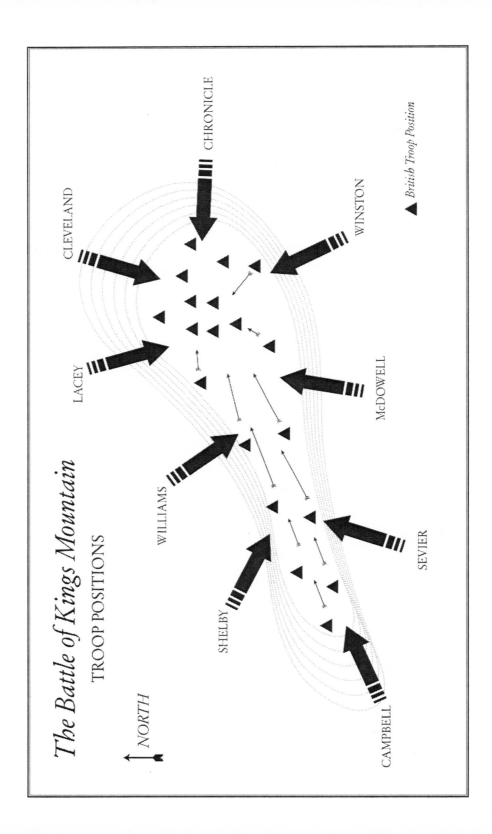

The Battle of Kings Mountain
TROOP POSITIONS

NORTH

CLEVELAND

CHRONICLE

WINSTON

LACEY

McDOWELL

WILLIAMS

SEVIER

SHELBY

CAMPBELL

▲ *British Troop Position*

15. The Noose Draws Tighter

Solomon Beason's Home, eight miles west of Kings Mountain
Late morning, Saturday, 7 October 1780

"ISAAC, WE DON'T HAVE MUCH TO DEBATE HERE. WE BOTH KNOW BEAson can't be trusted. Even if he says Ferguson is eight miles away, he's on our side half the time and on the Loyalist side the rest of the time. Comes and goes as the occasion requires. Since we know that the two men with him are Loyalists, I gave 'em two alternatives. They could either act as guides for us or they could die right here. They both chose wisely so I put one man in your column and the other in mine. I hope you don't mind."

Shelby smiled first at William Campbell and then at Benjamin Cleveland. "Benjamin, I must commend you for your powers of persuasion. Seems to me Beason is so scared right now, I believe him when he says Ferguson is close. I'll pass the word to the others."

KINGS MOUNTAIN
LATE MORNING, SATURDAY, 7 OCTOBER 1780

"Lieutenant Chesney, I want to send Cornwallis another message. I need someone who can get to Charlotte quickly."

"Sir, I believe I know just the man. Name is John Ponder. He's young, but smart. Grew up in this area. Been to Charlotte many times."

"Good. Give him this message and tell him to be on his way. Hopefully, he'll be at Cornwallis' headquarters before the sun goes down."

Within fifteen minutes John Ponder was headed down the mountain on his way to Charlotte. Because he had eaten very little the past few days, the young fourteen-year-old decided to go by way of his home three miles west of Kings Mountain to get some food before setting out for Charlotte. He knew the back roads and trails well enough to know that despite this short delay, he could easily be in Charlotte before nightfall. It was an easy ride. The young man was not worried.

SEVERAL MILES WEST OF KINGS MOUNTAIN
EARLY AFTERNOON, SATURDAY, 7 OCTOBER 1780

"Gentlemen, Enoch Gilmer has done it again."

Shelby looked at Major Chronicle. "Done what again?"

"Gotten us good information. There's a house just ahead, so Gilmer stopped there by himself, pretending to be a Loyalist. The folks in the house fell for his line, tellin' him that Ferguson's camp is on Kings Mountain, just two miles ahead. One woman said she even took some fresh chickens to him early this morning."

Shelby held up his hand to stop Chronicle from saying anything else. He pointed to several of the men close by. "Get all the colonels and majors here. Tell 'em I want them here in five minutes. Hurry!"

Within moments all the leaders gathered. Questions came rapidly, all of them asking the major what Gilmer found out.

"One of the women said Ferguson's camp was on top of the mountain on the ridge between two streams." Chronicle smiled. "Then I asked him again. 'Did you say on a ridge between two streams?' and he answered, 'Yea, that's what she said.'"

Sevier asked, "Why is that so important?"

The major looked at Campbell. "Colonel, I know that place. Me and Captain Mattocks camped in that same spot last fall when we came here deer hunting. I know exactly where their camp is. That means that Ferguson and his men are all situated near the top of the mountain. There's plenty of cover for us to surround 'em before they know we're there. Lots of trees and big rocks to make our way up in all directions.

And the wet ground will make it easier for us to move without making a lot of noise."

Campbell and the other leaders looked at the major in amazement, replaying the information in their thoughts. Ferguson is on Kings Mountain. He hadn't moved since yesterday. They knew where his camp was located. The rain might have been a blessing rather than a curse and now that the rain had stopped, they could move quicker and quieter. Through a break in the trees, they all could see the top of Kings Mountain through the haze. The men looked at each other, waiting for someone to take the lead. It was Shelby who faced Campbell.

"Sir, based on what we know, I say we surround the mountain and attack all at the same time as soon as possible. That way none of 'em will get away. We got 'em right where we want 'em. It is now our time."

Joseph Winston piped up. "That sounds simple enough, but it may be a little more complicated than that. It'll take some time for those going around the east side to get there. And we all got to be real quiet. Any sound and we'll lose surprise."

Campbell looked around at the others. "Yeah, you're right. We must leave here within a half hour to attack at, say, three o'clock. Major, how about you making us a little drawing on what this place looks like." With that, everyone gathered around Chronicle as he sketched out in the sand what they could expect on the top of the mountain. It was then that one of the guards rushed up, the man out of breath from the excitement.

"Colonel, sorry for the interruption but we just caught one of Ferguson's messengers and several of his scouts."

KINGS MOUNTAIN
EARLY AFTERNOON, SATURDAY, 7 OCTOBER 1780

De Peyster gazed at Chesney. "Make sure when you check out the men on the picket line down below, they're not getting too bored. We need 'em alert instead of just trying to dry out from all the rain."

"I'll be sure to remind them of that. Can't say as I blame 'em. With the rain stopping, it seems pretty quiet. Despite all this moving the past few days, they haven't shot a round in anger in some time." Casting a glance toward the west, the two also noted some breaks in the sky far away toward the much larger mountains, signaling that the rain might finally be coming to an end. "Looks like the weather is settling down."

"Yeah. You see the foraging party go down the mountain yet?"

"They headed down 'bout thirty minutes ago. Colonel Moore had what looked like more than one hundred men with him. He told me he expected to return before dark. I'll make sure I let the pickets know so they don't get confused thinking Moore's men are the enemy. Moore and his men headed south and east."

"It occurs to me that we may have even more potential for confusion because the foraging party could also be coming in from the same direction as any reinforcements who might be heading our way."

"You're right. I'll make sure they know that, too."

TWO MILES WEST OF KINGS MOUNTAIN TWO O'CLOCK IN THE AFTERNOON, SATURDAY, 7 OCTOBER 1780

William Campbell looked into the eyes of his subordinate leaders, all who had given so much of their time and effort these past few weeks to bring about this moment. "All right. Here's what we know.

"Ferguson's scouts and this boy, Ponder, have confirmed that Ferguson and his men are still on Kings Mountain. They're spread out all over the mountain-top. Pickets are downhill most likely on all sides. Ferguson's tent is near where the wagons are circled up on the northeastern end of the hilltop. The message the boy was carrying was asking Cornwallis for more reinforcements so we know no reinforcements have arrived from Charlotte. The boy also tells us that Ferguson is wearing a checkered coat over his red coat and he's using a whistle to signal his men. Anything else of importance I've left out?"

Someone asked, "Not about that, sir. What about Graham? Saw him riding away with another man."

"Word came to Major Graham that his wife's gravely ill. After some discussion I gave him permission to go see her. While this command should then rightly go to Colonel Hambright, he has relinquished command to Major Chronicle who knows the ground better. Hambright will ride with Chronicle. It won't be a problem."

Before any others could ask questions regarding that matter, Campbell cut them off. "We won't discuss that further. Right now, we've got Ferguson right where we want him. We've got a simple plan. If you can think of anything else, speak now."

With only a few minor suggestions coming from the others, Campbell summarized their collective wisdom. It was a plan borne out of skill and knowledge, courage and valor.

"Gentlemen, here's the plan. First, no more marching as you please. Keep everyone quiet. No talking. Approach the mountain just like you'd be sneaking up on some Indians. We'll ride in two parallel columns in column of twos. I'll be with the right column that Chronicle will lead. Cleveland will lead the left. When each of your units reaches the spot given you around the mountain, dismount and tie your horses up. Leave all your blankets and coats with your horses. Leave a few men to guard 'em. Clear so far?"

Drawing a quick sketch in the dirt, he showed everyone the positioning of each unit. "I'll be on the southwestern corner of the mountain. Next to me heading east will be Sevier, McDowell, Winston, and then Chronicle. On the north side of the mountain from west to east will be Shelby, Williams, Lacey, and then Cleveland. Cleveland and Chronicle will close the noose at the eastern end of the mountain. Shelby and I will tie in together at the western end. Questions?"

After the others shook their heads no, Campbell went on. "A few more things. Before we leave here, ask your men one more time if anyone wants to leave. If any want to, they're free to do so. I doubt any will turn tail now but...Second, have all your men fresh prime their guns and instill in them that everyone should go into this battle resolved to fight to the death. And third, lest we forget, our countersign should be easy to remember. Comes from Tarleton's massacre at Waxhaw. Our countersign is 'Buford.'"

Campbell looked around the circle of men. "I'll give you a few minutes to get this word out. We'll leave in ten minutes. I will see each of you later this afternoon on top of Kings Mountain."

16. Fight like Devils

Less than one mile from Kings Mountain
Fifteen minutes before three o'clock, Saturday afternoon,
7 October 1780

JOHN RHEA'S SENSES WERE ON HIGH ALERT AS HE RODE ALONG NOT far behind Colonel Campbell, knowing they were getting closer and closer to the enemy. No one spoke a word. Each man knew that in woods like these, every sound would be magnified; soldiers and their horses scraping tree branches, leather squeaking against leather, horses' hooves hitting the ground. Each man held his rifle tight, knowing that any metal hitting metal would travel great distances through the rain-soaked forest. After a quiet thirty minutes, Colonel Campbell gave the signal to dismount, each man handing the reins of his horse to the designated soldiers who would secure and guard the beasts of burden who had served them so well.

Rhea understood the plan, and because of his experience, he knew that in battle even the simplest order could be forgotten or misinterpreted. He knew the possibility that what could go wrong would, and always, it seemed, at the worst possible time. Because of the thickness of the tall trees nearest him, Rhea could not see all the men in Campbell's formation as they began to spread out. As he studied the men nearest him, despite the cold and hunger and tiredness all of them were experiencing, he saw determination and purpose in their eyes. As he looked closer, he also noticed that several had no shoes, their feet lacerated and bleeding. Many of the men had placed white pieces of paper in their hats so their fellow soldiers could identify them quickly. Others chose to take off their hats so they could see better.

Colonel's Campbell's last words kept ringing through him: "Fight like devils." Yet, despite the preparation, and the desire to see the task through to the end, like many others near him, Rhea's thoughts kept returning to several basic thoughts that ran deep into his core.

I must not bring dishonor to my family. I must fight to the end. I must fight for those who have been ravaged by men like these I will fight today. We must end all this nonsense now. And if this effort costs me my life, that is the price that must be paid. Remember Buford and his men. When I draw that bead on these Loyalists, I must remember Buford's men.

****

On the northern side of the mountain with Cleveland's men, Preston Goforth and William and Joseph Logan asked themselves these questions and several others. *If my brother is in my sights, will I be able to pull the trigger? And what will my brothers do? Will they shoot at me? Who will take the first shot? Why did it have to come to this? Brother against brother?*

KINGS MOUNTAIN
THREE O'CLOCK, SATURDAY AFTERNOON, 7 OCTOBER 1780

"Sir, everything appears quiet down below. The men are alert."

"Good," said De Peyster as he listened to Lieutenant Chesney's report that the pickets seemed to be watchful and prepared. "I must say I'll feel better when we see those reinforcements, but until then..." He didn't have time to finish his sentence as he heard gunfire from the western end of the perimeter.

Grabbing the reins of his horse, the captain watched Elias Powell do the same with the major's horse as he saw Ferguson burst out of his tent. "Chesney, sound the alarm. Make sure all our soldiers are ready." The two leaders then mounted their steeds and raced toward the sound of the guns as Chesney ordered the beating of the drums, calling all the Loyalists to their posts.

Unbeknownst to the two British officers, it was their men who had spotted the Rebels down below. When it was clear they had been spotted, Shelby shouted out, "They've seen us, don't wait! Press hard up the hill, boys! Press hard!" To Shelby's right, Campbell's orders were crisply given. "There they are, my brave boys! There they are," as he pointed upward. While neither man had his unit where he wished, their men had been spotted. There was only one thing to do. "Charge!"

Above them, Captain Samuel Ryerson, a tough seasoned Loyalist commander, observed the Rebels begin their dash up the hill from tree to tree. With his attention focused on his enemy, he barely noticed Ferguson and De Peyster when they joined him.

"How many are there?" Ferguson asked.

"Can't really say 'cause they're moving quick from tree to tree. Only see their faces when they're shooting. Their volume of fire hasn't built up yet 'cause it takes 'em time to reload. One thing for sure. There's plenty of 'em. From what I see, there's got to be a lot more of 'em than just these in front of me. Rest of 'em got to be close."

Ferguson quickly studied the scene below. "For now let's take care of these to your front until the others show themselves. Watch out for a trap. Are you ready to charge 'em like we talked about?"

"I am, but I want 'em to get a little closer first. That way they'll be a little more tired and we'll have the advantage. My men are ready."

The three men stood still assessing the movements of the enemy below until after one sharp volley, Ryerson sensed the time was right. At his shout, his men came to their feet. "All right men. Give it to 'em! Give it to 'em! Charge!"

And with that, Ryerson and his men raced downhill, the assault of their steel bayonets catching the Rebels by surprise.

Campbell's men who still had their rifles primed when the Loyalist assault began, fired off their one last round before those who stood to fight met those in red coats in a ferocious series of hand-to-hand, winner-take-all battles pitting the Loyalists' bayonets against the swinging rifles, tomahawks or knives of the Patriots. Some of the Patriots who should have retreated early in the contest paid dearly for their mistake.

****

"Sir, looks like our men may be going too far downhill. It may be a trap. Since we don't know where the rest of the Rebels might be, I think we should recall them now."

Ferguson's eyes remained fixed on the struggle below knowing that what De Peyster said made good sense. "I agree. Can't risk our men any more right now." And with that, he blew his whistle, signaling Ryerson to bring his men back to their original positions.

Responding to the signal, Ryerson shouted to his men, "Back up the hill, boys! Back up the hill! Stay behind the rocks and trees!" But as he feared, as he and his men made their way back up the incline, their movements were now exposed to the marksmen of Campbell and Shelby. With time now to reload, these sharpshooters began to pick off the Redcoats who did not heed their captain's warning.

Once they reached the peak, Ryerson looked about. "We've lost a few men, but we gave more than we got. They'll come again."

De Peyster studied the scene below. To no one in particular he said, "I'm sure you're right. I've heard their yells and screams before at Musgrove's Mill. They're the Backwater Men. They won't give up. They'll come again and again."

****

At the bottom of the hill Keys and Rhea caught their breath. Both had retreated slowly ahead of Ryerson's men, but now with the Redcoats returning to their earlier positions, Keys spoke out after he fired off another shot. "That was close. Don't know why they stopped only halfway down the hill. Heard a whistle from the near hilltop. Got to be

Ferguson. But now with them going back up, we got some easy shots... Got one." He paused again to reload.

"John, they got the better of us with that bayonet charge. Saw some go down. Lieutenant Edmondson and Ensign Beattie, Captain Beattie's brother. One of 'em got cut almost in half."

****

As Ryerson and his men reformed, Ferguson applauded them. "Excellent work, Captain. Excellent." But before he could encourage his men further, gunfire to the northeast interrupted him. Without another word, Ferguson and De Peyster looked at each other as they mounted their horses and sprinted in that direction. Because of their swift departure, Ferguson missed Ryerson's report that his force had been reduced by ten to fifteen percent because of the enemy fire they suffered as they returned to their initial positions.

After he watched the two senior leaders ride off, Ryerson turned back to watch the fire from his men's rifles pelt the leaves above the heads of the insurgents. Realizing their fire was ineffective, he hollered out, "Aim lower, men. We're shooting too high. Aim lower."

One of his men, a very experienced soldier, raised his head up slightly over the rocks to get a better shot. Seconds later the men nearest him heard a low thump. On closer examination, they saw the bullet hole between the soldier's unseeing eyes.

****

Like Campbell's men, Shelby's were also breathing a sigh of relief as the enemy ran back up the hill. "Now boys, reload. Get ready to give 'em more fire," Shelby hollered as he glanced up from the bottom of the hill. Looking around, he watched his friend Josiah Culbertson draw a bead on a man who appeared to be giving out orders halfway up the hill. The rifleman's unhurried aim had instant results as the

187

object of his attention fell down in a heap, never to move again. With a satisfied grunt, Shelby then watched several of his men attend to his brother, Moses, who had been wounded in the thigh during the melee.

After being assured his brother would survive, Shelby began making preparations for the next charge.

****

At the eastern end of the mountain, Major Chronicle signaled his men to begin their movement up the mountain. As each man moved quietly upward, it was still for the first few seconds. Then suddenly the hilltop above them erupted with rifle shots. Chronicle went down in the first volley, a bullet to the head. His cousin, William Rabb, standing six feet away from the major, was instantly killed as well.

But with Colonel Hambright immediately making his presence known, the soldiers pressed their attack upward. Just as they neared the crest, the Loyalists charged, driving the colonels' men back down the hill. Like on the western slopes of Kings Mountain, fighting raged in close hand-to-hand struggles.

****

After the Redcoats retreated back up the hill, one of the Rebels could be heard shouting, "Get him off me! Get him off me!"

When his friends got to the man, they feared the worst as they saw a Loyalist soldier on top of their friend who was covered in blood.

"Where you hurt?" one of them asked.

"I'm not 'cept for a few minor scrapes," the man hollered. "Blood's his. I got him with my last shot as he charged. Must be dead 'cause he ain't moved for five minutes. I wasn't so sure about myself."

****

"Lotta firing going on above us, Colonel."

Cleveland almost laughed at his men. "And what makes you think I can't hear that. Now you listen to me. Get up this little hill! I can smell them Redcoats! Get going!"

They hadn't gone too far when the cry came. "They're coming down on us, boys. They're charging. They got bayonets!" Cleveland's men, like all the others, retreated down the hill to regroup.

KINGS MOUNTAIN
FIFTEEN MINUTES AFTER THREE O'CLOCK,
SATURDAY, 7 OCTOBER 1780

The smoke from the gunfire of their first aborted dash up the mountain lay heavy over the battlefield. The ebb and flow of their first charge had taken its toll on both sides. After sorting out the wounded and the dead, the Rebels advanced once again.

Cleveland's men, like the others, now had the experience of the first bayonet charge behind them. The colonel's orders were simple. "Use all the cover you can find as you move up. Use every rock, log, and tree. Be ready for 'em to charge again!" Before giving his order to advance, Benjamin Cleveland took a moment, sensing the loss of two of his men from their first advance. Daniel Siske and Thomas Bicknell. Others like Lieutenant Samuel Johnson nursed their wounds. *Their loss is part of what this battle, this war, is all about. It is about sacrifice. A price that must be paid. Thank God for men such as these.*

Looking up, he stood tall as he wiped the salty liquid from around his eyes. His words came out strong and clear. "Charge! Let's go get 'em, men. Charge!"

Like before, the Redcoats countered this attack with another bayonet charge of their own, but this time, Cleveland's men were better prepared. After watching carefully, one of Cleveland's men saw the spot where some smoke from the powder of the Brown Bess had been fired. Keeping his aim on that one spot, he soon spotted a head and fired instantly. "Got 'em," the soldier said to himself as he searched for another opportunity.

At another part of Cleveland's sector, when the men in red charged with their bayonets flashing, Charles Gordon, one of Cleveland's young officers, waited behind a tree. As one of the Loyalists ran past him, Gordon grabbed the man by the neck. "Got you now," he screamed as the two struggled and tumbled down the hill. Seconds later, the Loyalist cried out when the wrestling match turned in his favor. "You're mine," he shouted, aiming his pistol at Gordon's head.

As Gordon dodged, the bullet ripped into his left arm, breaking it. But with his sword in his right hand, Gordon attacked, stabbing the Loyalist over and over. After catching his breath, Gordon stood over the man watching life ebb from him. No words were spoken. None were necessary.

****

McDowell's thoughts echoed those of Cleveland. *A sacrifice must be paid if we are to win. It is time.* "Boys, I think we've got 'em. They're losing some of their vigor. Their fire ain't as thick as before. Yes sir, I think we got 'em with one more charge. Be ready for their counterattack."

William and Thomas Robertson thought they recognized some of the men above them fighting for Ferguson. With his brother wounded in the first charge, Thomas launched himself forward at the command to charge again. Halfway up the hill, he heard someone call out from above, "Robertson, that you?"

When he poked his head out very carefully to see who might have called him, a bullet whistled past him, nipping the bark off the tree just inches above his head. Before the man who fired could move his head back, Thomas fired.

The tricky Loyalist, a man named Lafferty, lay dead behind his hiding place. He had been one of Thomas' neighbors.

****

One of the Loyalists who had made it back to the top of the mountain after their second charge called out to his fellow soldiers: "Lieutenant McGinnis, you here? Lieutenant?"

With this cry unanswered, the man called out more names. "Goforth? John Goforth. You here? Westerfelt. You here?"

"Yeah, but I'm hit bad. Need some help." Of the four who went down the hill only Westerfelt and his friend made it back.

****

"De Peyster, get our men ready for their next advance."

"Yes sir, I've already done that. I've also told our commanders to have their men fire lower. Looks like we're firing too high."

Ferguson wiped the sweat from his face. "I know we can hold. We must. I will not be taken by these mongrel dogs. I am the King of this mountain and I will not be taken."

17. Final Assault

Cornwallis' Headquarters in Charlotte
Afternoon, Saturday, 7 October 1780

"SIR, I UNDERSTAND YOU WISH TO SEE ME?"

"Yes, I do. I need you to prepare your unit for movement by tomorrow morning. I am considering sending either your unit or Tarleton's, if his health improves, to find and assist Major Ferguson."

Lieutenant Colonel Archibald McDonald smiled. "Sir, I would appreciate a bit of fresh air after being cooped in this village all this time and I think my men would like to take some of our frustration out on some Rebels as well."

"Yes, I suppose they would. Regardless of which unit I send, the purpose is to find out what is happening with Ferguson. He and his command are west of here somewhere. I have a message from him indicating that a Rebel force of some size is after him, but that information is a week old. Since then we have had no contact with him. I need information and I need it now. Once I make my decision as to who will carry out this mission, you will be notified."

"Sir, we will prepare and await your orders."

KINGS MOUNTAIN
THIRTY MINUTES IN TO THE BATTLE,
SATURDAY, 7 OCTOBER 1780

Despite surviving two assaults on their position, many of the Loyalists on top of the mountain were unnerved by the war-whoops of the

Rebels coming from all around the base of the mountain. "They gonna attack again?" the younger man asked his more seasoned counterpart next to him as he reloaded his rifle.

"No doubt, sonny. No doubt. And if I were you, I'd make sure you make every round count. And keep your bayonet handy. Bullets are gonna be in short supply soon and those hollering boys down below mean business." The two Loyalists and those nearest them immediately heard the blood-curdling cries increase in both volume and intensity.

Hearing the same cries, Ferguson looked around him as he assessed his men's responses. *We're surrounded. How did this happen? I'm trapped on this rock. Too late now! I must save face. We can still win. We must repel them now! We must!*

As the chants seemed to grow in zeal by the second, Ferguson saw his men near the western end of the plateau break, making the long run toward the circle of tents and wagons where the bulk of the Loyalists intended to make their last stand. Ferguson and De Peyster stood in front of their retreating men. "Stop," they cried. "Stop! Act like men. Turn to face the enemy!" While their words saved the retreat from becoming a rout, many of the Loyalists remained unnerved by the impending onslaught.

Elias Powell stood by Ferguson, holding his horse steady. "Here they come, sir. Here come those yellin' boys!"

"I see 'em, Elias. I see 'em." he shouted as he saw some Rebels crest the hill some distance away. Mounting his horse, Ferguson galloped back and forth around his men, encouraging them. "Shoot them, men. Make those miserable dogs pay!"

As he turned to face the enemy, his horse went down from a shot to its flank, but the major was unhurt as he wiggled out from under his dying horse. Grabbing the reins of a second horse from Powell, he continued to shout at his men. "Keep firing, men! Keep up the fire!" *More and more of my men are going down. We must fight to the end. My men must see me and draw strength from my presence. I must be the rock to these men. We can't give up! We can still win.*

****

After he climbed the hill with less opposition than expected, John Sevier saw the fleeing Loyalists. "Stay on 'em, boys! Stay on 'em," he cried. He looked to his left and saw William Campbell leading his men through the gaps in the trees to reach the top of the mountain. But just as he moved to the next tree, Sevier heard a grunt to his right. Turning, he saw his younger brother Robert on the ground.

"Robert, where're you hit?"

The severely wounded man could only muster a cough and an almost silent plea. "In the gut. Get Ferguson. Care for me later."

****

On the north side of the attack, James Williams' men began to make some headway, but there was danger lurking every step of the way.

"Almost got me," one man screamed as a Loyalist bullet shattered his rifle stock, rendering the weapon useless. Still, the soldier kept going upward, his knife and tomahawk in his hands.

Near him William Giles fell wounded. One of his fellow soldiers thinking Giles was dead vowed to avenge his fall, but no sooner than he mouthed the words, Giles got up to resume the fight. Holding his hand to his neck, he hollered, "They just grazed me a bit. Let's go get 'em!"

****

On the eastern side of the battle, Frederick Hambright led Major Chronicle's men up the hill. "Press 'em boys. Press 'em hard," he shouted out as they approached the crest. "Keep after 'em!" As they neared the crest, he groaned as a bullet smashed into his thigh.

The soldier closest to him hesitated as he looked at the colonel and the bodies of Captain Mattocks and John Boyd, both dead, and at another wounded man, William Gilmer, brother of the scout.

"Don't stop for now," shouted Hambright. "Take the hill."

****

"Lieutenant Taylor, take your men and charge those Rebels. Run 'em down with your horses!"

The officer, older than most, a seasoned veteran of many engagements knew the risks as he faced his twenty cavalry men with courage and honor. "You heard the major. Follow me! Let's show these dogs what we're made of."

Turning toward the charging Rebels, Taylor speared his horse toward the enemy coming over the crest of the mountain. Within a few moments, he and his twenty men lay dead, wounded, or captured.

****

While his men blazed away at the frontiersmen who continued to take advantage of every tree and rock for protection, Ferguson heard some of his men cry out. "We're running out of ammunition! We need more ammunition!" as they valiantly tried to stem the wave of attackers that seemed to grow right before their eyes.

De Peyster, who had been standing next to Ferguson, recognized the futility of the situation as the deadly crossfire swept across the hilltop. Stepping forward, he faced his commander. "Should I raise the white flag?"

An aggrieved expression came to Ferguson's face. "No! No! We can still win. I will not be beaten by these Backwater men. We must hold. Reinforcements may come at any moment!"

"Sir..."

"You heard me! Keep falling back. Use the wagons as a barricade. I will not hear any talk about surrender. I will not give up!"

The words had barely come out of his mouth, when a savage cry came from the north side of the hill as a fierce band of Rebels rushed toward the Loyalist center, this charge being led by a large man with a sword in one hand, a knife in the other. Ferguson stood mesmerized by the sight of this one man who ran faster than those he led. Then, just as this man neared the outline of Ferguson's men, this man fell, struck by multiple shots fired from Loyalist rifles. With their leader down, the combat in that area of the battlefield paused for a moment.

"What a glorious charge," Ferguson said to no one in particular. "I wonder who that man was? Shelby? Sevier? No doubt one of their leaders. A brave man to be sure."

Running up from the back of the Rebel formation, a young man could be heard crying out. "Father! Father!"

Disregarding the bullets sailing about in his direction, the older of the man's two sons knelt beside the mortally wounded colonel, the most severe wound a head injury. Holding the older man's head in his lap, the son tried to comfort his father as best he could, knowing deep in his heart, the man would succumb to his horrible wounds in a day or two at the most.

A second son, this one thirteen, soon joined his brother as the two of them watched over their father. David, the older brother, turned to Joseph. "We must remember him for all the good he did. Fighting Indians and these Loyalists and others like them. He was a true Patriot."

Ignoring the bullets that smacked the trees around them, the two sons kept watch over their father, Colonel James Williams.

****

With the circle drawing closer by the minute, the distance between the two opposing forces was now down to only thirty or forty yards. Ferguson grabbed the reins of his horse from Powell.

"Sir, what are you doing?"

"I am going to charge these heathen and break through their lines so our men can see how it's done."

"But...?"

"Enough. I don't want to hear it." Ferguson pointed to two of his unit commanders, Vessey Husbands and David Plummer, who were already mounted and ready to ride, their swords in their hands. "Are you ready?"

Without a word, the two officers nodded. It was then that Ferguson gave the command. "We ride now. Perhaps we can sting these Backwater boys enough that they'll back off."

But before beginning his charge, the major spotted some of his soldiers nearby holding up white garments and flags. Riding up to these men, Ferguson cut down these symbols of surrender, swearing, "I will not yield to such as this banditti facing us."

He then rode back to Husbands and Plummer. He gazed one last time at Elias Powell. "You're a good man, Elias Powell. A good man. Thank you for your service."

Abraham De Peyster stood next to Powell. "Sir, you don't have to do this."

Ferguson took one more look at his deputy and nodded, "Yes I do, Abraham."

Then he looked at the two men who would ride with him. "Let's go."

****

"You see what I see?"

"Yeah. Three riders coming this way fast. Look at that. One of 'em's wearing a checkered duster. Got him right in my sights."

Six, seven, maybe as many as twelve to fifteen of Shelby and Sevier's men watched as the three riders came toward them, presenting the marksmen with the opportunity many had dreamed of. When the distance closed to a range where it would be hard to miss, bullets flew at the charging horsemen from many angles. While a few missed their mark, most of the hot lead projectiles tore into the flesh and bones of men and beasts, the velocity of so many rounds knocking two of three riders to the ground. The third rider, the one whose body had been riddled the most, remained attached to his horse as his foot was caught in the stirrup, holding him fast to the dying animal.

The riflemen ran toward the man, reining in the horse, freeing the bullet-torn body from the stirrup. While many men took credit for the death of the British officer who wore a checkered duster, there was no doubt that Major Patrick Ferguson was dead.

18. Revenge

Kings Mountain
An hour into the fight, Saturday, 7 October 1780

"THE MAJOR'S DEAD. I THINK IT'S TIME."

"You sure you want to give up?" asked Powell.

"Don't have much choice. Look at 'em. They've got us surrounded and besides, we're almost out of ammunition." De Peyster could only shake his head as he thought about what might have been.

All around the top of Kings Mountain, Loyalist soldiers sensed the fight was over. While several still waged their individual battles, the majority began to quiver in their positions, some now surrendering on their own.

Yes, it is time. "Hoist the white flag," the captain shouted to a nearby soldier.

****

As the Rebel soldiers closed in around the Loyalists, the confusion of the battlefield remained. Rifle shots split the air from all directions. Smoke clouded the eyesight of many. Shouts from both sides added to the general mayhem as the two sides came in closer contact with one another. Mixed into this disorder and uncertainty were the cries of the wounded and dying.

Whether they were from Winston's group or Cleveland's or any of the others, the Rebels' blood boiled from the life and death struggles of the last hour. Their emotions of watching their friends die in the past few minutes, coupled with the pent-up anger of past times, proved to be a deadly combination. The scene quickly turned grisly as many men acted on the rule of mob mentality and raw emotion.

"Take that you scoundrel," shouted one of Cleveland's men as he crushed a Loyalist's skull with the butt of his rifle, the assault not ending until the rifle was shattered into pieces.

"This is for my sister," growled another as he shot the man before him right between the eyes, even as the Loyalist on the ground begged for mercy.

Another whose brother had died at the hands of Tarleton's men at Waxhaw shoved his knife up to its hilt into a man's chest, the man before him one he had known for several years. "This is for Buford," the soldier cried out over and over. "This is for my brother," he muttered as he finally twisted the knife out of the dead man's chest.

As the cry "Buford," was heard more and more across the battlefield, De Peyster spotted a man he assumed was one of the Rebel leaders. Running toward him, the captain cried out, "Sir, you must stop this. This is murder," even as a Rebel soldier took a swipe at him with a saber, bloodying De Peyster's hand.

William Campbell looked at De Peyster, at his bleeding hand, and at his soldiers all around him. With sweat pouring down his face and with his shirt sleeves rolled up, he stood fixed for another moment as he watched another one of his men crack a Loyalist skull with his rifle butt.

Hollering at John Rhea and his officers nearest him, Campbell shouted out, "We must stop this now. It's time to halt this madness. Cease fire! Cease fire!"

Shelby and others also recognized the makings of a massacre as they looked at the scene playing out all around them. "Cease fire! Cease Fire!"

But just as that cry began to spread across the battlefield, another group of soldiers arrived on the scene; some knew what the white flag of surrender meant but chose to ignore it. One of these was one of

John Sevier's sons. This young man flew into the mix. "These swine killed my father. I aim to shoot every one of 'em," urging those with him to do the same. But before this rampage could go too far, John Sevier rode up the hill to a tearful welcome with his son, ending the slaughter in that part of the hilltop.

****

Like his leader, William Campbell, John Rhea could stomach these atrocities no longer. This is revenge taking the place of decency. Insanity replacing morality. The Devil in these men's souls is for the moment overcoming the wisdom of God. What will we think of ourselves years from now if we don't stop this now?

"Back away," shouted Rhea as he stepped between one of his friends and a Loyalist who lay helpless on the ground. "Don't do this. It's murder if you keep at it."

The man looked up. He stopped beating the man at his feet when he recognized Rhea through his fierce anger. "But I know this man, John. I know him. I know what he did. He doesn't deserve to live. Death is what he should be given for what he's done."

"Maybe. Maybe not. For now, let God decide when he should die."

The two men stood staring at each other for what seemed a long time before Rhea's friend took a step back. "You're right, John. You're right." This same soldier then shouted to those around him. "Stop it! Stop it!" as he ran over to another of his friends, knocking the rifle from the man's hands before he could pummel the wounded Loyalist on the ground in front of him into eternity.

Finally, the butchering of the Loyalists slowly came to an end. At Campbell's direction, the prisoners were herded into a large circle, guarded by a number of still angry Rebels. With the indiscriminate killing now halted, everyone took a breath.

****

Elias Powell now had his chance. With the chaos settling down, he slowly made his way to where Ferguson's body lay. Knowing that the Rebels would scavenge all the items from the man's body and his clothing, Powell used the confusion of those around the body to his advantage as the conquerors stood around gawking at what was before them. Without asking for permission, Powell reached in to a shirt pocket and grabbed what he came for before walking quietly away. In his hand was Ferguson's whistle, the symbol of his command.

KINGS MOUNTAIN
DUSK, SATURDAY, 7 OCTOBER 1780

The leaders gathered, taking stock of the scene around them. The prisoners were now guarded by the Foot Company that arrived an hour after the battle came to a halt. The body count of the dead had begun for both sides. Wounded soldiers were being treated by the physician who had traveled with the Loyalists. Guards had been posted in a loose perimeter in case the long-awaited British reinforcements arrived. There was little food or water to be had. The adrenaline rush that enabled them to perform so well had now passed, and the inevitable tiredness and exhaustion of days past became the next enemy.

Campbell looked at the men gathered around him. "Glad the men who were trailing us got here all right. They'll be a big help in guarding the prisoners so the men who rode here can rest. Any idea how many prisoners we got?"

Joseph Winston answered first. "By a rough count, close to seven hundred. Never would have believed it, but when we started counting...some of 'em are already griping, wanting food and water. We told 'em to shut up since we don't have any for ourselves. Pissed some of our boys off about them complaining like that."

Campbell nodded. "I can understand that. How about our losses? I know we Virginians had thirteen killed. How about the rest of you?" When the totals were added up, twenty-eight Patriots lay dead and maybe three times that number wounded. Several others were not expected to survive, including James Williams, Thomas McCulloch, and Robert Sevier.

"And the Loyalists?"

Shelby answered for the others. "We're just starting to look after 'em now. Wanted to take care of our men first. Best guess now is that we killed over one hundred and fifty and they got maybe a like number that are too hurt to move. Least that's the way it looks right now."

"What do you think about where we go from here?"

Sevier spoke up first. "I'd say we leave as soon as we can and head north toward Gilbert Town. Two reasons. We got to get these prisoners to the government at Hillsborough, and second, since we're not sure 'bout any reinforcements heading this way from Charlotte, I want to put some distance between us and them."

After the others generally agreed, Campbell issued his orders. "All right then. Here is the plan. Care for our wounded as best you can. In the morning, Isaac Shelby, you lead the formation north. Move as fast you can. Use litters to carry our wounded. Make the prisoners carry all the muskets we captured after you remove the firing locks. We'll start to bury the dead at first light tomorrow. The men who are leaving with Isaac can help with that detail until they start their march north. I'll stay behind to finish the burial after you leave with my men. I plan to leave here a few hours after the rest of you. Should catch up with you late tomorrow afternoon. Right now I want to see this Loyalist doctor."

****

Although toughened by all he had seen on the frontier through the years, it was still difficult for Campbell to be around so many men suffering, their wounds ghastly to comprehend when seen in such abundance. He watched with admiration as Doctor Uzal Johnson, a man of twenty-three, labored under the poor candlelight as he went from one man to the next, giving no preference to which side the wounded man fought on in the recent battle. Johnson's care was dictated only by who needed the most care the quickest. The doctor had only enough time to acknowledge Campbell with a quick nod as he continued his task of saving as many soldiers as he could.

As Campbell walked through the confusion of stretchers and men lying about, he came upon one of his Virginians, William Moore, and saw the soldier's leg was badly damaged. "Colonel, looks like I'm gonna lose my leg. Got hit bad in the thigh," the twenty-nine-year-old, whispered, his words coming out through his gritted teeth.

"Maybe, William. Maybe. This doctor appears to know what he's doing. We'll pray for the best," was all Campbell could manage as he continued to make his way through the maze of injured men. It was not long before he heard the mournful, piercing cry of this soldier who had given his all to be here at Kings Mountain. *Such men. Oh, such men. This country will survive because of men like these. They have given their best. Their very best.*

KINGS MOUNTAIN
EARLY MORNING, SUNDAY, 8 OCTOBER 1780

"Like I said, Isaac, after we finish up here, we'll be about an hour or two behind you. Given all the prisoners and wounded you have, you won't be moving that fast."

"You're right there. You got men out looking for any reinforcements coming from Charlotte?"

"Yeah. So far nothing. Can't understand why Cornwallis hasn't reacted to this."

"Shelby shook his head. "Maybe it's just a simple matter of him not knowing where Ferguson was. If none of Ferguson's messengers got through, how would Cornwallis know about us? One thing's for sure. He'll know about us sooner or later. That's why we got to get a move on. See you tonight."

****

With the main body of his soldiers now heading north, away from Kings Mountain and Charlotte, William Campbell and his men continued the grim task of burying the dead. It was a macabre ordeal as the dead were piled into depressions in the ground and then covered up with the available logs, deadwood, and rocks.

Because there were so many to bury, and with an eye toward when Cornwallis' men might react to Ferguson's demise, the grisly task was done with haste and little attention to detail. It was also slowed by the appearance of some family members who had heard the sounds of the battle coming to claim their loved ones, searching one depression after another in hopes of finding their husband, their father, or their son underneath all the rubble. Scavenging animals and vultures now also began making their presence known.

With the sun now high in the sky, Campbell and his men could wait no longer. *Thank God we were victorious. Perhaps this victory will give our countrymen new hope.*

He took one final look as he and his men started downhill off Kings Mountain. *Things might have been different if the British reinforcements had arrived or if Ferguson had not let his pride hold him too tight to this ground. Wars have been won and lost on less crucial decisions.*

CORNWALLIS' HEADQUARTERS AT CHARLOTTE
EARLY EVENING, TUESDAY, 10 OCTOBER 1780

Cornwallis stood still as he stared into the fire burning brightly in the fireplace in the large room, knowing that all his hopes for a strategic move north, at least for now, were dashed. He turned to his aide.

"Prepare a letter for Sir Clinton. Tell him that I have just received word from Tarleton that, to quote Tarleton, Major Ferguson and his men have suffered a 'melancholy fate' on Kings Mountain. And since we believe the enemy is now in great strength, it is possible they will move toward either Ninety Six or perhaps even Camden. Tell him that we are attempting to determine this now, but that it appears for the present time, the prudent action for me to take is to postpone any further advance north. Questions thus far?"

"No sir."

"Conclude the message by telling Clinton that I will inform him in the next few days of the location of our winter quarters. As you and I discussed yesterday, I am inclined to head for Winnsboro, departing here in the next several days. I still believe that to be the best course of action. As soon as Tarleton returns, set up a meeting with all our commanders so we can reach a final conclusion."

Brown waited for more guidance, but all that came from Cornwallis was, "That is all."

After Brown left, the Southern Commander stared out the window once more. *It is time to leave this hornet's nest. It is time to reevaluate. It is time reflect. Can we still win? Can we still conquer these backwoodsmen? Are they better than my soldiers, or is it that their desire to win is greater than ours?*

19. Conscience

County Courthouse of Lawrence County, Louisa, Kentucky
Friday, 1 October 1832

THE ELDERLY GRAY-HEADED GENTLEMAN SAT ON THE OLD, SCARRED wooden bench outside the judge's office waiting to be summoned. It was his day to give his testimony to Judge Ezekiel Dunnigan. The old man knew from talking to others who had been through this process, it would take some time to tell his story and for the judge to get everything in order. The grizzled veteran anticipated the bureaucracy would move slowly, particularly because if his paperwork was in order, he would receive money from the government for his service. And he had much to tell.

Upon being called, the man stood in front of Judge Dunnigan, who smiled politely at him. In his time on the bench, the judge had heard a number of testimonies from other Revolutionary War soldiers of their remembrances of events that occurred over fifty years earlier. Their tales seldom gave detailed accounts of the battles they had been involved in, although, at times, Dunnigan wished that they would. These men had so much to tell.

Before taking the man's testimony, Dunnigan read from his script the benefits of the Congressional action passed on 7 June 1832 (4 Statute.529) that extended to more men the provisions of a law passed on 15 May 1828 (4 Statute.269). "This current Act provides that every officer or enlisted man who served at least two years in the Continental line or State troops, volunteers or militia, is eligible for a pension of full pay for life. Naval and Marine officers and enlisted men are also included. Veterans who served less than two years, but not less than six months, are eligible for pensions of less than full pay. This act does not require you to demonstrate need. And according to this law, money due from the last payment until the date of your death can be collected by your widow or your children."

After reading the paper, the judge looked up. "Sir, based on what I've just read, do you qualify for the benefits under this statute?"

"Yes, son. I believe I do."

"All right then, let's begin." After taking an oath of the truthfulness of what he was about to tell, the man took a seat at the large table facing Dunnigan.

"Sir, what we will do is start by you giving me your full name. Unless you would like to write out your testimony, I will have my clerk write out everything you say. Please give me the dates of any battles you fought in, the locations of those battles, officers you served with in those places, and any other details that you might recall that will help me and others to insure that you indeed qualify for a pension and will help us determine the correct pension due you. Depending on the information you provide me, it may be necessary for us to do some follow-up testimony if there are any questions that require clarification. Is that clear, sir?"

"It is, son, and since my writing ain't all that good, I'd like your folks to write out my words."

"Certainly. Now again, sir, your full name, please."

****

After a grueling eight hours of listening to the man's story, Judge Dunnigan stumbled out of his office, glad for the twenty-minute walk to his home on the edge of the town. He needed this respite to clear his head and to attempt to sort out the facts from fiction in what he had heard.

Since his time at Louisa paying attention to the war-time experiences of these Revolutionary War veterans, he always marveled at the memories of these men who fought so long ago, but today's interview was different. Although he was quite familiar with the battles in the northern part of the United States: Monmouth, Saratoga, Trenton and the others, it was challenging for Dunnigan to grasp the number of engagements that took place in the southern part of the country, particularly in North and South Carolina. Recently, one of his colleagues told him that more battles had been fought in South Carolina during the Revolution than any other state in the Union, and after what Dunnigan heard today, he had no reason to doubt it.

But what really spoke to his heart this day was the story about the massacre, or murder, or atrocity, or whatever the right word was for what occurred at the end of the Kings Mountain battle. He had taken testimony of others who had fought there, but with the exception of some rather broad ambiguous statements concerning some strange happenings at the battle's conclusion which Dunnigan had never felt he needed to pursue, this was the first time he sensed he was getting the complete picture of what happened on the afternoon of 7 October 1780.

Who can I share this man's story with? My wife has no background in this subject. Should I alert my supervising judge, but if I did, what could or should be the possible repercussions? Right now I have only this one man's story. Yet the way he told it, the way he stared at the wall as his words tumbled out, tells me he was reliving that day as he spoke. I believe every word he said.

Yet, he's an old man, and sometimes the recollections of old men can shift like the incoming tide, yet...I need another opinion, another man to hear this story. I need a confidant, a man whose judgment I trust. A man whose opinion I value. My Reverend told me in passing several months ago that his grandfather had fought in the Revolution. Maybe I could ask him to listen to the man's story to see if I'm hearing all this correctly.

****

The Reverend sat back in his chair, staring at Dunnigan. "Tell me again what this man said about what happened at the end of the battle."

After hearing the story for the second time, the pastor asked, "Would we be breaking a trust if I talked to this man?"

"No, I think that would be all right, particularly because he seemed so distraught as he related what happened. It was almost like he was confessing. After all these years, the man's conscience must be tearing him apart. If you could give him some peace about all this, I think we'd be doing the right thing. Let me think about this for a day or two and then I'll get back to you."

****

Two days later the pastor was given permission to speak to the old veteran. "When I speak to him, would you mind if I speak to him alone?"

"Of course not. That's the best way. I'll make arrangements for you to meet with him later this week. Thank you again. I appreciate it."

****

When the day of the meeting arrived, the man appeared at the courthouse in the same worn clothes he had on when he gave his testimony to the judge.

The pastor greeted the old soldier, and after introducing himself to the man, he smiled and ushered the veteran into a small office. "Sir, Judge Dunnigan confided in me about some of your experiences in the Revolutionary War and I was wondering if you could share with me some of the details that happened at Kings Mountain."

The man stared at the pastor for a moment. "Yes, son, I suppose that would be all right. After all these years it's good to get all this off my chest."

"I understand. Thank you. I'm particularly interested in what hap-

pened that afternoon when the Loyalists surrendered after Major Ferguson was killed."

At first the old fellow stared out the window and he said nothing.
Then he closed his eyes. "Yeah, I can do that. Even though it was a
long time ago, I relive parts of that day often."

"I understand. Take your time."

After another long pause, the story began to flow. "I was one of
Campbell's boys. The fight to get to the top was tough. Twice we went
up and twice they pushed us back down. Many men died, ours and
theirs. On the third try we made it to the top. As we were pushing
in closer to the Loyalists' lines, Ferguson tried to escape and he got
shot out of his saddle. Right after he was killed, the Loyalists, many of
them, seemed to want to surrender, to give up, calling out for mercy.
But many of the men with me wanted more blood, wanted more revenge. Many of their families had suffered for so long at the hands of
men like these. And many others were thinking of how Tarleton's men
killed Buford's men for no reason."

The warrior rose from his seat, looking out the window as the red,
gold, and orange leaves blew down from the tall hardwoods outside
the courthouse. It reminded him of that afternoon on Kings Mountain fifty-two years before.

"Shots rang out in all directions. I saw one man clubbed to death even
as he held his hands up to surrender. I looked around and thought of
what my mother and father would think. I thought of what my parson
would think. Right in front of me was a man I'd seen before. I knew from
others he was one who had taken advantage of a young girl just because
her father was a Rebel, a Patriot like me. I wanted to kill the man. But the
voices of my parson and my parents kept ringing in my brain. *Don't do it.
Don't do it.* I kept going back and forth trying to judge right from wrong."

After a long pause, the pastor asked quietly, "What happened next?"

The man turned his attention to the picture of the President of the
United States that hung on the wall of the small office. It was a picture
of Andrew Jackson.

"I threw my rifle down and cried out, 'Stop, Stop,' to all those around me. It was then I stepped in front of my best friend, knocking his rifle from his hands as he was about to kill another Loyalist even as this scoundrel before us begged for mercy. Guess I couldn't take any more of the killing. My conscience got the better of me. I just didn't want to see any more killing that day. Yeah, I hated those Loyalists, but I would've hated myself more if I'd killed any more of 'em in cold blood that day. It would have been murder."

The man took his seat again. "I wasn't the only one who was helping stop the killing. Colonel Campbell was pulling rifles out of men's hands. John Rhea, a man whose father was a parson like you, was doing the same thing. So were Colonel Shelby and some other leaders. After we started gettin' the men to think about what they were doing, the madness settled down some."

His hands held his face as the tears flowed. "Parson, you're the second man I've ever told this to. The judge was the first."

The pastor put his arms around the man's shoulders as the old man continued to cry, his tears running down the front of his shirt. After several minutes the veteran regained his composure. The pastor asked, "You mind if I ask you a few more questions?"

"No son, you go right ahead. Let's get it all out there."

"I was wondering if you know the name of the man whose life you saved?"

"Heard it once later that day as we were rounding up all the prisoners. He'd been shot in the arm so I figured he'd be all right. I heard that like a lot of 'em, he escaped a few days later. Never heard any more about him. Think his name was Micks or Nicks. Something like that."

"Sir, I appreciate you sharing all this with me. Like you, I have an interest in Kings Mountain because my grandfather fought there as well."

The man sat straight up. "Really? Was he with Shelby or Cleveland? Sevier maybe?

The pastor smiled, "No, he wasn't. After the war, like so many, he wanted to put it all behind him. As he told me some years ago, he wanted to live a quiet life."

"After what we all saw and what we went through, most of us who are still around try and do the same. Seems to be the best way. Where did your grandfather settle down?"

"After the war he moved around some. First South Carolina, then to Virginia before finally settling here in Kentucky. Had nine children. Two died in infancy. After my mother and my father married, they farmed their own land and stayed near here. They had me and six other children—four boys and three girls. All four of us boys are pastors. While I stayed around here, my three brothers have all gone west to start their churches."

"Glad to hear that, son. Sounds like you come from good stock. You made something of yourself others can learn from. Your grandfather would be proud."

"Yes, sir. I think he would. When the judge asked me if I would spend some time with you, I knew I must meet you because I wanted you to know about the good that came from what you did on Kings Mountain that day."

"Course I know that, son. We helped put our country on a path to win our freedom."

"Yes sir, you and the others certainly did that. And you saved a life on that mountain years ago instead of taking it when you could have."

The man sat still for a time. "Guess you're right about that, but like I said before, that was my conscience talking to me. I must say, after you letting me tell you what happened, I want to thank you. I can only hope that some good came out of it."

"It has, sir. It has. You see, my mother's maiden name was Nicks. Before he died, my grandfather told me his side of the battle of Kings Mountain and about a man who saved his life. You were that man, sir. Because you saved his life, I can stand in front of you today. It is I who must thank you."

The warrior stared down at his feet for the longest time before he looked into the pastor's eyes. "I can't tell you how much that means to me, son. It is though you've lifted a great weight from my shoulders. I can go to my grave with a clearer conscience. The truth of your words has set me free. I can't thank you enough."

The old man and the pastor stood up and shook hands, clasping each other's grip firmly for several minutes. Each man silently thanked the other for what he shared that day, the questions left on the battle-field so long ago now answered with truthfulness and understanding.

The two men saw each other frequently in the days that followed until the old soldier died several months later. The pastor officiated at the old soldier's funeral.

Epilogue

THE BATTLE OF KINGS MOUNTAIN DID NOT END THE REVOLUTIONARY War. It was followed by other important battles in the Carolinas at Cowpens and Guilford Courthouse before Cornwallis moved north, surrendering at Yorktown in October 1781, one year after Kings Mountain. However, over the years, the Patriot victory at Kings Mountain has been recognized as the one event that set the eventual outcome in motion. Theodore Roosevelt, our nation's twenty-sixth President, perhaps summarized it best in his book, Winning of the West: "The victory...was the first great success of the Americans in the South, and the turning point of the Southern Campaign."

Revenge at Kings Mountain is a story about something that lives deep inside of us as Americans that collectively makes us unique in the nations of the world. With the exception of Patrick Ferguson, every other man on Kings Mountain that October day, whether he was a Loyalist or a Patriot, thought of himself as an American, and because of that, the further I became immersed in writing this book, I found myself wanting to write something about every man who was on this battlefield regardless the side he fought on. Each man faced rifle fire. Each faced the bayonet or the tomahawk or the knife. Each stood for what he believed was best for our land. Hence, a meaningful biography could be written about almost all of the men who were present that day, but that is simply impractical. Instead, what follows is information about selected people who were part of our story.

ABBREVIATED BIOGRAPHIES OF SELECTED BRITISH
SOLDIERS AND OFFICIALS

After Yorktown, **Sir Henry Clinton** received his share of the blame for the loss of the colonies although he attempted through his writings to shift the blame to Cornwallis. After being re-elected to Parliament, he was promoted to full general in 1793. He died the following year at the age of sixty-five before he could assume the post of Governor of Gibraltar.

Despite his eventual defeat at Yorktown, **Charles Earl Cornwallis** was not judged harshly by those in authority in England, as he was promoted to the rank of Field Marshall in 1786 and assigned to the post of Governor General of India, a position he held until 1793. Later he served as commander of troops in Ireland. When difficulties arose in India, he returned to that country in 1805, dying there at age sixty-eight.

After Cornwallis' struggle to hold Charlotte failed, **Governor Josiah Martin**'s health declined. He eventually made his way to Long Island, New York in 1781 before sailing to England. He was forty-nine years old when he died in London in 1786.

Alexander Ross, Cornwallis' aide, rose through the ranks, becoming a general officer in 1812. He remained close to Lord Cornwallis throughout his life. Ross died in 1827 in London at age eighty-five.

The commander of the Legion, **Banastre Tarleton**, suffered a major loss in January 1781 at the Battle of Cowpens where Daniel Morgan destroyed his unit. Despite that defeat and his calling into question many of Cornwallis' actions, he remained a powerful figure in the British Army, eventually rising to full general in 1812. Tarleton died in 1833 at the age of seventy-eight at Herefordshire, England.

James Webster's distinguished career came to an end six months after Kings Mountain when he was mortally wounded at the Battle of Guilford Courthouse in March 1781. He died two weeks later at Elizabethtown, North Carolina. He was forty-one.

Anthony Allaire escaped during the march north from Kings Mountain. After the war he settled in New Brunswick, Canada. His diary of events surrounding the battle provides valuable information about the Loyalist view of what occurred. He died in 1838 at the age of eighty-three.

Having spent considerable time as a Patriot soldier before Kings Mountain, **Josiah Brandon** was granted a parole by Major Joseph McDowell after the battle. Many years later he was granted a pension from the United States government after a lengthy debate. He died in 1842 at age eighty-one in Franklin County, Tennessee.

An Irishman by birth, **Alexander Chesney** escaped from the Patriots on the march north after the battle. He fought with Tarleton at Cowpens, eventually settling in Northern Ireland at war's end.

Abraham De Peyster returned to New York after the war, later moving first to Nova Scotia and then to New Brunswick, Canada, where he became the treasurer of the province. He died in 1798 at the age of forty-five. Despite his apparent competency with money, he left little in his estate. Upon his death, his wife and children returned to New York.

After the war **Dr. Uzail Johnson** returned to his home in Newark, New Jersey, serving that community by practicing medicine there until his death in 1827 at the age of seventy.

Elias Powell helped bury Patrick Ferguson's body, wrapping it in a bear-skin blanket. As a prisoner he was taken to Hillsborough, North Carolina. He was paroled there and returned to his home in Burke County, North Carolina, where he died in 1832 at the age of seventy-seven. It is not clear how long he was able to hold on to Ferguson's silver whistle.

Samuel Ryerson, along with thirty-two of his men, was wounded at Kings Mountain. After the war this New Jersey native settled in New Brunswick, Canada.

Ferguson's two Virginias met different fates. **Virginia Sal** was killed at Kings Mountain and buried with Major Ferguson. **Virginia Paul** was held for a time by the Patriots before being released into the hands of an unnamed British officer.

Major **James Weymss,** the man sent to hunt down Francis Marion, was severely wounded in a fight against Thomas Sumter in November 1780. After his recovery he made several voyages between England and America carrying various messages. He eventually settled in the Long Island area of New York at the late 1790s. He filed for a pension from the British government in 1832. He died in 1833 at the age of eighty-five.

ABBREVIATED BIOGRAPHIES OF SELECTED PATRIOT LEADERS

Abraham Buford was found not culpable for his actions at Waxhaw, remaining in the Army until war's end. Later he settled in Kentucky, where he became prominent in establishing that state's horse racing industry. He died in Scott County, Kentucky in 1833 at age eighty-six. Three of his relatives served as General officers in the Civil War.

William Campbell was promoted to the rank of Brigadier General in the Virginia Militia after Kings Mountain. He died during the early stages of the Yorktown campaign in late August 1781 at the age of thirty-six.

A man in his early forties at Kings Mountain, **William Candler** was elected to the Georgia Legislature after the war before becoming a judge. He died in the mid-1780s in what is now Columbia County, Georgia.

After the war **Elijah Clarke** served in the Georgia State Assembly. After several ill-fated business ventures, he died in 1799 in Augusta, Georgia, nearly bankrupt at the age of fifty-seven.

Benjamin Cleveland spent many years as a judge before he died in

1806 at the age of fifty-eight while living in Oconee County, South Carolina.

After the Revolution, **William Davie** became the tenth Governor of North Carolina. He died in 1820 at the age of sixty-four, but not before becoming one of the driving forces in establishment of the University of North Carolina.

After recuperation from his wounds at Charlotte, **Joseph Graham** rejoined the fight against the British. During the War of 1812, as an iron entrepreneur, he helped supply over fifteen tons of shot, shells, and cannonballs to United States forces. He died in 1836 at the age of seventy-seven.

Edward Lacey continued to fight the British at a number of battles in South Carolina until war's end. He died in 1813 when he drowned while crossing a creek on horseback at age seventy-one in western Tennessee.

After the war **Charles McDowell** served in the North Carolina Senate from 1783 to 1788. He then spent his remaining days surrounded by the beauty of Quaker Meadows. He died in 1815 at age seventy.

When the war ended, **John Sevier** became a power in politics as he was elected to the United States Congress for several terms as well being elected the first Governor of Tennessee. He died at the age of seventy in 1815 while serving as a Presidential appointee to establish the boundary for the Creek Indian territory in Alabama and Georgia.

After the war **Isaac Shelby** moved to the Kentucky territory, where he became that state's first Governor in 1792, and was later elected again as the state's fifth Governor in 1812. After the War of 1812 he became President James Madison's Secretary of State. He died in 1826 at his estate in Lincoln County, Kentucky at the age of seventy-five.

An Irishman by birth, **Joseph Steen**, one of the most experienced Patriot fighters, continued to fight for his beliefs at Cowpens. He was stabbed to death in Rowan County, North Carolina in the summer of 1781 while attempting to arrest a Loyalist. He was forty-seven.

David Vance continued to fight for his country as a soldier through 1782. He settled in what is now Buncombe County, North Carolina. He died on his farm there in 1813 at age sixty-eight. His writings about Kings Mountain were published long after his death.

Joseph Winston played a critical role at the Battle at Guilford Courthouse in March 1781. After the war he represented the people of North Carolina at the state and federal levels for a grand total of eleven terms. He died in Germantown, North Carolina in 1815 at age sixty-nine. His body now rests at the Winston Monument near the Guilford Courthouse battlefield in Winston-Salem, North Carolina.

ABBREVIATED BIOGRAPHIES OF SELECTED PATRIOTS

After fighting under Joseph Winston at Kings Mountain, **William Bailey** fought at Cowpens and Eutaw Springs. With his wife, Elizabeth, he eventually settled in Monroe County, Kentucky where he died in 1829.

After Kings Mountain, **Absalom Baker** continued to fight for our freedom at Guilford Courthouse and Eutaw Springs. In his pension statement he gave evidence of fighting in eleven major battles during the war. He was granted his pension while living in Sangamon County, Illinois.

Like many others who fought at Kings Mountain, **Josiah Culbertson** also fought at Cowpens in January 1781 against Tarleton's Legion. He filed for his pension in 1832 while living in Daviess County, Indiana, where he died in 1839 at age ninety-seven.

Samuel Doak remained in Tennessee for the rest of his life as both a pastor and an educator, establishing several churches and an academy that became Washington College, where he was President from 1790 to 1818. He is known for his tireless work in promoting the Presbyterian faith and in education. He died at the age of eighty-one in 1830.

After recovering from a leg wound suffered at Kings Mountain, **Ebenezer Fain** married Mary Mercer at Jonesboro, Tennessee in

1781. They eventually moved to Habersham County, Georgia, raising nine children. He died at age eighty in 1842.

Andrew Hannah moved to Washington County, North Carolina (now Tennessee) after Kings Mountain in 1781 with his wife, Jane. He and Jane remained there for the rest of his days, raising their eight children. He died in 1843 at the age of eighty-three.

Robert Henry was fifteen years old when he fought with Major Chronicle at Kings Mountain. After the war he helped survey the North Carolina and Tennessee border before becoming a lawyer. His account of the battle can be found in Dunkerly's *The Battle of Kings Mountain Eyewitness Accounts*. Henry died in 1863 in Clay County, North Carolina at age ninety-eight. He is generally regarded as the longest living survivor of the 7 October 1780 battle.

After helping care for the wounded after Waxhaw, young **Andrew Jackson** served as a messenger for William Davie, surviving capture by the British in 1781. He is best known as the Commanding General at the Battle of New Orleans during the War of 1812 before being elected the seventh President of the United States.

James Keys was promoted to Ensign when he was part of a force fighting the Cherokee Indians in 1783/84. He was one of many whose statements about Kings Mountain can be found in Dunkerly's *The Battle of Kings Mountain Eyewitness Accounts*. He filed for his pension in 1833 while living in Washington County, Virginia.

After the war **Sam Mackie**, an Irishman by birth, married Mary Clark at Long Cane, South Carolina, before moving to Franklin County, Georgia where they raised their ten children. He died in 1845 at the age of eighty-four.

John McCullough was another who provided details of the battle in Dunkerly's book of eyewitness accounts. Other records indicate he filed for his pension in 1832 while living in Washington County, Virginia, where he died in 1838.

After the amputation of his leg, **William Moore** was cared for by a family near the battlefield, before being taken back to his home in

Virginia by his wife, Elizabeth, who, after learning of his injury, traveled from Virginia to the battlefield area to find her husband. His comments about the battle are told in Dunkerly's book. He was seventy-five when he died in 1826 in Washington County, Virginia.

Five months after Kings Mountain, **William Morison** was stricken with smallpox. After recovering from the illness, he fought in several other engagements against both British Loyalists and Indians. He later married Rachel Patton in 1783, eventually moving to Dickson County, Tennessee.

After Cornwallis moved his headquarters from her home in Charles Town, **Rebecca Motte** reestablished her residence at her plantation home on the Congaree River in Calhoun County, South Carolina. Several months later, when this home was occupied by the British, Rebecca gave permission to Francis Marion to burn her house down to roust out the British. She remained a staunch Patriot for the rest of her life. She died in 1815 at the age of seventy-eight.

Throughout the time of the Revolution and beyond, **Mary Patton** continued to provide quality gunpowder to her customers in the Sycamore Shoals area of Tennessee. She died there at age eighty-five in 1836.

John Rhea, an Irishman by birth, turned to politics after the Revolution, eventually representing Tennessee in the U.S. House of Representatives for a total of eighteen years. He was also one of the founding fathers of Blount College, which later became the University of Tennessee. He was seventy-nine when he died in 1832 at Sullivan County, Tennessee. He never married.

Like those in the Foot Company, men like **William Stewart** did not make it into the battle, but he and others from that company guarded the Loyalist prisoners to Salisbury. In March 1781, Stewart took part in the battle at Guilford's Courthouse. Later he married Jemima Carter, raising twelve children. He lived out his last days in Scott County, Virginia.

After recovering from his injuries at Waxhaw, **John Stokes** served in the North Carolina State Senate and was later appointed by President Washington to be the first Federal Judge in the U.S. District Court for the District of North Carolina. He died three months after this appointment in 1790 at the age of thirty-four. It is said that Stokes wore a silver knob in place of the left hand he lost at Waxhaw, banging it on tables when he wished to gain attention.

David and **Joseph Williams**, Colonel James Williams' sons, were executed by "Bloody Bill" Cunningham, an infamous Loyalist at Hayes Station, South Carolina, on 19 November 1781. David was eighteen when he was murdered; Joseph was fourteen.

Exhaustive information about all those who fought at Kings Mountain may be found in Bobby Gilmer Moss' two books mentioned earlier in the acknowledgements, *The Loyalists at Kings Mountain* and *The Patriots at Kings Mountain*.

Final comments. As the Patriots marched north with their prisoners, treatment of the British Loyalists was harsh. On the evening of 13 October at a farm near Gilbert Town, North Carolina, the Patriot leaders tried the vilest of their prisoners: murderers, rapists, and others who were true scoundrels of every description. Thirty-six were found guilty and sentenced to be hanged that night; three men at a time. After the first nine men dangled in front of the assembled formation, the Patriot leaders stopped this punishment as they decided they had seen enough blood.

In an act of remarkable forgiveness, John Sevier pardoned the two deserters, Samuel Chambers and James Crawford, who had raced ahead to warn Ferguson.

As Thomas Goforth sensed several days before the battle at Kings Mountain, 7 October 1780 was a bad day for the Goforth family: all four brothers were killed that day. The widow of Preston Goforth, the one Patriot, found her husband's body the day after the battle, and buried him in the backyard of their home.

Twenty-one Patriots who fought against Ferguson were also part of Washington's Army that defeated Cornwallis at Yorktown in October

1781. A search of various records indicates that two men who fought at Waxhaw also fought at Kings Mountain.

As Pat Alderman describes in his book, *The OverMountain Men*, after Kings Mountain was in Patriot hands, John Sevier dispatched Joseph Greer to inform Congress of the victory. Greer, who by all reports, stood well over six feet tall, braved Indians, severe terrain and difficult weather, traveling by horseback and foot, reaching Philadelphia in record time. When Greer burst into the Congressional meeting room to report news of the victory, it is said that George Washington exclaimed, "With soldiers like him, no wonder the frontiersmen won."

ED DEVOS, A HIGHLY DECORATED MILITARY OFFICER, IS AN experienced writer of thought-provoking historical fiction. *Revenge at Kings Mountain* is his third historical novel. His previous works are *The Stain* and *The Chaplain's Cross*. A Bible teacher and a military historian, he speaks in many groups throughout the Southeast. He and his wife reside in South Carolina.